SUBTLE BODIES

SUBTLE BODIES

PSYCOP 13

Jordan Castillo Price

JCPBOOKS.COM

First published in the United States in 2022 by JCP Books
www.JCPBooks.com

ISBN 978-1-944779-29-0
First Edition
Also available in audiobook

I am large, I contain multitudes.
-Walt Whitman, Song of Myself

CHAPTER 1

Aside from TV—or the occasional funeral—most people tend to go about their business without stumbling across a body.

If only I'd been so lucky.

Even if I'd never embarked on a career in Homicide, thanks to my "talent," it's pretty clear I would've ended up seeing more than my fair share of death. Might as well try to do something useful with it, I figured.

Eventually, I got used to the sight of a corpse. Not that I ever started my day hoping I'd encounter one, mind you. But see as much death as I've seen, and it almost becomes normal.

Maybe it was easier when there was a body involved. That way I wasn't the only one in danger of losing my lunch over the sight of a grisly murder that looked like nothing more than a smear of old blood to all the other cops on the scene.

But there's bodies...and then there's bodies.

And they had an alarming tendency to crop up where I least expected.

My current assignment had me scanning one of the many imposing piles of marble on Lake Michigan: The Museum of Science and Industry. I've never been big on museums, which is weird, considering I grew up among so many of them. History, art, and even the stars—no matter what your particular flavor of edification might be, Chicago's got a huge monolith with your name on it.

Maybe my lack of enthusiasm stemmed from innumerable school field trips. On these outings, we were invariably forced to team up with a "buddy" and hold hands. And, seriously, who can concentrate on a bunch of dull dioramas when you're trying to figure out whether your "buddy" has been rooting around in his nose all morning?

It's possible that as an adult, I might discover some appreciation for the culture in my very own backyard. But on our precious time off, neither Jacob nor I have ever once uttered the phrase, "Doesn't a trip to the museum sound like fun?"

And so, when I approached the museum with a baggie of salt in my pocket and my coworker Carl at my side, I found myself squinting at the place like it had sprung up in some kind of half-remembered fever dream.

"Good luck tracking down a ghost in this," I muttered. Four hundred thousand square feet of marble and plexiglass, with hundreds of folks milling around, from summer school groups to senior outings to foreign tourists with selfie sticks.

Carl simply grunted, picked a direction, and strode off.

The thing about Carl is that it's damn near impossible to tell if he's irritated with me, or if he's just hovering around his usual baseline annoyance. Since it was likely he actually knew where he was headed, though, I trotted along after him.

After a good several minutes of power-walking, we came to an exhibit called YOU, which was even more crowded than the flight simulator and the baby chick hatchery.

And no wonder. YOU was full of plasticized cadavers.

I paused at one of the many info posters—the ones that all the day camp kids were ignoring as they gawked and pointed at one of the displays. Not because they were looking at actual human remains, and not because those remains were flayed. Not even because the cadaver was posed in such a way that she looked like she might be waving down someone to help her get away from whoever'd been wielding the scalpel. But because one of her breasts was still intact. Plasticized for all posterity.

I shuddered. So much for being inured to the sight of a body. These things were just dredging up a bunch of disturbing memories I thought I'd successfully forgotten.

"I can't say I'm surprised this exhibit is pinging the Program's radar," I said. The Federal Psychic Monitoring Program keeps tabs on all things psychic, from telepathic corporate espionage to unusually accurate weather forecasts. So when photos of "ghost orbs" at the museum started cropping up on social media, our boss took notice.

According to the signage, this particular technique of preserving bodies and organs so they couldn't decompose was relatively new. Ghosts have a tendency to degrade with age, so it made sense that if there was a spirit tied to an exhibit, it would be haunting a fresh one. The signs also claimed that every body was bequeathed with the full knowledge and consent of the individual.

Still...it wouldn't be the first time a person experienced a change of heart.

Especially the torsos. I could see how they'd be pissed if they didn't sign up for spending eternity as a plasticized flayed torso.

I positioned myself in front of an exhibit of a full body (including the head) with all the various parts "exploded" out on tiny filaments so we could see how they were supposed to fit together, kind of like a diagram on those furniture assembly instructions that show where to put all those extraneous screws and bolts. I looked up into the plasticized eyeball. It was gruesome, no doubt. But it wasn't exactly scary. Sure, it was a real eyeball, connected to real blood vessels, surrounded by real bone and viscera. This thing had been a walking, talking, living person once. But without blood, it wasn't gory. Not like some of the stuff I'd seen, where even a smear of blood with a single human hair stuck to it was enough to have me skipping dinner in favor of an Auracel/Seconal nightcap.

Thankfully, I wasn't looking for a murder victim today. No, I was checking out ghost orbs. The phenomenon is as old as photography itself—and when you think about all the weird things they believed way back when, it's no wonder the random spheres of light that crop up in photos would freak people out. Not that we have technology capable of gauging that sort of thing now, either—unless you counted me as some kind of spirit Geiger counter.

Ghost orbs are the result of light refracting off dust, plain and simple. If not for the proximity to all the very public cadavers, the FPMP wouldn't bother to get involved. But where ghosts were involved, as far as Laura was concerned, better safe than sorry.

I glanced around at the architecture to get my bearings, then held my hand out to Carl and said, "Lemme see that one shot with all the orbs."

Carl pulled out his phone, poked it a few times, then fixed me with a look that was just a fraction of a second longer than it needed to be...and then tucked his phone away.

In my pocket, my phone dinged.

Seriously? Now I wasn't even allowed to touch his phone? It's not as if I'd been picking my nose.

I gave him a look that was a smidge longer than the one he'd given me, then scowled open my own damn phone and oriented myself to the ghost orbs.

A ten-foot-tall 3D heart protruded from the far wall, so it was easy enough to extrapolate where the so-called sightings occurred. My stance slid into a very subtle Warrior I—essentially just one foot in front of the other—something I found myself doing nowadays before I called down the white light, thanks to all the yoga they had me attempting back at the office. Did it help? No idea. But as habits went, I'd had worse.

I focused on my crown chakra. I stilled my mind. And I breathed.

It was a calming feeling, despite the dozens of bratty-kid voices threading through the general hubbub of the crowd. Just me and the white light, with some plasticized torsos on one side and an anatomically exploded figure on the other. Under my breath, I muttered, "If you've got anything to say, speak now, or forever hold your peace."

But the only one who piped up was a field trip chaperone who really needed to take a chill pill.

I turned away from the plasticized cadavers, then snapped back quickly, as if I might catch them shifting around once I had my back to them. But no. Nobody moving around but a few dozen shrieking summer school kids.

Satisfied that the exploded plastic man wasn't going to start clattering along after me the moment I took my eyes off him, I scanned the rest of the area. "HVAC checked out okay?" I asked. You'd be surprised how many "hauntings" are caused by random crap in the air ducts.

Carl grunted in reply. I quelled an eye-roll.

It was currently Friday afternoon. Hopefully by Monday morning he'd deign to speak to me again.

Ignoring Carl, I scanned for air vents. Though if anything, air conditioning seemed like it would filter out more dust than it generated. But hey, what do I know? With the miles of ductwork involved in circulating the air in such a massive place—a hundred times the size of the cannery, at least—no doubt something could be crumbling somewhere.

Eventually I spotted one vent, then another. Neither was close enough to be blowing dust in the spot where all the ghost orbs showed up.

I pulled down more white light. And looked some more. Nothing.

Stumped, I planted my hands on my hips and scanned the whole area again—only to notice a patch of wall behind a group of tourists lit up funny when the camera flash went off. Not in the shape of an angry cadaver ghost, thankfully, but in a ragged square.

Once the tourists moved along, I pulled out my pocket flashlight, approached the wall, and shone my beam at an angle to the surface. Yeah, I know, I can use the flashlight app on my phone, but old cop habits die hard. It took a bit of finagling, but I discovered a patch of wall that looked slightly shinier than the wall around it...and that patch of weird wall was within a few yards of the majority of the infamous ghost orbs.

Missing person interred within the museum's walls?

No, nothing quite so interesting. A couple of phone calls and a visit from the maintenance manager revealed that some school-kid roughhousing got out of hand, and one of the little darlings put his shoe through the wall. What his shoe was doing up at head level, I couldn't begin to guess. Maybe the kids these days are big on yoga.

Anyhow, the wall had been patched, creating drywall dust. And all of the ghost orb sightings occurred just after the patch was completed.

How refreshing to be part of an investigation that didn't end with me stumbling across human remains.

As soon as I had that particular thought, of course, the universe set out to prove me wrong.

A troop of senior citizens on an outing were trundling past, excruciatingly slowly. I'm not normally all that impatient, but today I was eager to escape Carl's put-upon death glare and embark on my weekend. When the stream of blue-haired old ladies showed no sign of letting up, I veered off to a side passage to swing around them...and stopped so fast in my tracks that Carl nearly ended up face-planting into my shoulder blades.

Nearly a person. That seems to be the main parameter my fight-or-flight response keys into. Anything that's the general height, stature and configuration of a human being, but is not. Mannequins. Promotional cardboard cutouts. Even your random sheet of plastic caught on a chain link fence. All of these things trigger my impulse to make one hundred percent sure that whatever I'm looking at is something other than a ghost.

And the thing that snagged my attention at the museum? Not only had it once been a person—but if anything deserved to be haunted, this thing did.

The cadavers in this section were nowhere near as fantastically arrayed as the plasticized torsos and the exploded-view body. They were sliced into half-inch slabs, then preserved and mounted perpendicular to the wall in six-foot glass frames that you could view from either side.

Whereas the newly plasticized folks were bright and colorful, like something out of an anatomy text, these poor schmucks were the color of old lunchmeat. My first reaction was that it wasn't real. Some enterprising artist had created the facsimile of a sliced and diced body based on images from an MRI. But as I drew closer to the slices, I saw that they were sandwiched between the glass panes with some kind of fluid. And then I saw the detail. The layers of bone and muscle and fat—and other stuff that must have been organs. Brains. Teeth. Even wiry hairs sprouting from what must've been the pubic area.

The plasticized cadavers had been a macabre spectacle...but this was downright haunting.

As I stared in horror, drinking white light and groping for my salt, just in case, Carl had been tapping on his phone.

In the first full sentence he'd spoken since we'd arrived, he said, "Two specimens, one male, one female."

"Specimens," I echoed, feeling vaguely barfy at the sight of two people sliced up like so much boiled ham.

"They came from a medical school in Indiana. Made sometime in the thirties. Been here since 1943."

Despite the white light I'd been mainlining ever since I got a glimpse at the not-quite-people, there were no prickling sensations at the back of my neck, no vague and unexplained chills. Had the poor schlub behind the glass left a ghost behind—one that rued the fact that he'd signed up for such an ignominious end, showcased for all posterity? If so, that ghost wasn't here. Maybe it was haunting some defunct medical facility in Indiana. But I sure as hell wasn't about to volunteer to check it out. As far as I was concerned, as a high-level medium, I had no business going around looking for trouble.

Why bother?

The ghosts always caught up with me soon enough.

CHAPTER 2

Back at the office, I typed up the narrative section of our report, two-fingered and stabby, while Carl compiled all the relevant supporting documentation to put our little ghost orb investigation to rest. Neither one of us was what you'd call chatty, even on a good day. But the silence between us was thick enough to slice into half-inch people-shaped slabs, and the sound of my own keys clacking was driving me up a wall.

I can play chicken with the best of them. And yet, knowing full well I'd be better off keeping my mouth shut, eventually I couldn't help but cave in.

"It was just a pen," I blurted out.

"From my desk," Carl snapped back.

"A pen."

Carl shook his head dismissively and focused even harder on his report.

"For crying out loud, Carl, I didn't think anyone would get so bent out of shape over a pen."

"Not just any pen." Carl swiveled in his chair and met my eyes, looking every bit as pissed off as he sounded. "That pen was presented to me by my alma mater after a speech I gave to the graduating class. Me, someone who'd had to work three jobs just to afford the part-time tuition and spent nine years getting his bachelor's—a success story. Proof that hard work and determination eventually pay off."

"Look, Carl, I know it makes you crazy when other people touch your stuff. I had no idea it was a sentimental pen. It was the end of the day, my pens had all managed to walk off, and I grabbed it without thinking."

I figured he'd be mollified, but he only crossed his arms and glared.

"What?" I said. "Are you waiting for an apology? Fine. I'm sorry."

He made a noise of disgust and turned back to his keyboard, typing extra loud. "It would be one thing if you'd just borrowed it."

I considered that as the keyboard clattered, until I finally had to admit, "I don't follow."

"You weren't writing with it when I walked in. You were scratching yourself."

Oh.

I'd picked up the unfortunate tendency to slide things up my left sleeve and itch away during eight weeks in a plaster cast. Hopefully I hadn't also picked up a habit demon—one who had a fetish for pens and was currently stuck to my forearm.

I was considering whether or not I should attempt another apology, one with a greater chance of coming off with some modicum of sincerity, when the intercom on our phone system buzzed with a summons to the Director's office.

Saved by the bell.

Laura Kim's office was in a dingy part of the building with a grand view of the nearby railroad tracks. Her predecessor,

Con Dreyfuss, had been situated in a much cushier spot on the building's top floor. But since the executive level was home to a few stubborn repeaters, Laura had set up shop somewhere a lot more utilitarian...and a lot less haunted.

Back when Laura was Con's assistant, the broad sweep of her desk had been spotless. Now, though, captaining the FPMP ship had left her spinning more plates than she was accustomed to. And she was an expert plate-spinner. Without even so much as an empty greeting, she said, "There's an assignment that's come up in Iowa that I'd like you to handle. Probably nothing—but I'd rather have you check it out. Just to be sure."

Iowa's a pretty big state. "Whereabouts in Iowa?"

"Somewhere in the middle." Gee, that narrowed it down. "Normally, I'd send Darla, but since Dr. K and Agent Garcia are driving out that way to recalibrate some equipment in South Dakota, it makes more sense logistically for them to drop you off."

Maybe. But the FPMP's got pretty deep pockets. I doubt the folks in accounting would even bat an eyelash over the cost of flying Darla out there. Maybe she'd refused the assignment—and, if so, it would behoove me to be sure "probably nothing" wasn't code for "you drew the short straw, better luck next time."

"Exactly what kind of 'nothing' are we talking?"

Laura keyed something into her computer and a large monitor on the far wall lit up with a video. It was a vertical interior shot on a shaky cell phone. The inside of a mini mart filled the screen, one of those ubiquitous places that sells everything from beef jerky to lottery tickets. A typical fixture in any town, big or small.

But the woman who'd stripped down to her bra and was tossing her T-shirt into the beer cooler? That was different.

Laura paused the video mid-toss. "Weird enough in and of itself, but she's not the only one."

Drugs would've been my first guess…but Laura wouldn't send in a medium to investigate drugs unless they involved psyactives.

"Multiple instances, same uh…strippage?"

Laura nodded. "Weird? Yes. Relevant? Not at first glance. In itself, nothing we'd need to keep an eye on. But our algorithm caught several of the police reports as stating the strippers had no memory of the event."

Ah—now I knew why I was heading for Iowa. Missing time was on the mediumship list Darla and I were working on.

Still…it was possible some of them were just blackout drunk. "I'm surprised a few weird strippings merit an in-person visit from the FPMP. Couldn't I just call them?"

"I considered that. But this is my territory. If I don't dot all my I's and cross all my T's, FPMP National might notice. I'd rather not give them any reasons to pay attention to the Midwest."

Given that National's goons had gone so far as to rough up Dreyfuss in the process of claiming his GhosTV, can't say I blamed her. "Fine. When do I leave?"

"First thing tomorrow. Dr. K should be ready to go by eight, so you and Carl can meet up with him by the elevator in the parking lot—"

"Wait," I blurted out, as I imagined Carl giving me the cold shoulder all weekend over a simple ballpoint-related misunderstanding. "If I'm gonna have to work the weekend, do I really need to be partnered with Carl, when Jacob would be just as capable of doing the job?"

Laura frowned in thought. Or maybe she was frowning over the thought of Jacob. Things just haven't been the same between them since he figured out she was the one, intentionally or not, who'd offed Roger Burke.

"Jacob's got years of experience as a Stiff under his belt," I said. "And he's already on your payroll."

Laura's frown deepened.

Fine. I'd play the just-married card. It was set to expire soon anyhow. "C'mon, Laura, I'd rather not haul my butt all the way out to Iowa without him. We're newlyweds."

Thankfully, that did the trick. If I had to spend my weekend somewhere in the "middle of" Iowa surrounded by cornfields and cow flops, at least Jacob would be suffering right along with me.

CHAPTER 3

Jacob was intrigued by the prospect of ghost-hunting together—even though I cautioned him there might be nothing more to find than a bunch of weirdos showing off on the internet. We headed out bright and early with a couple of suitcases...and an exorcism kit disguised as a toiletry bag. Just in case.

The drive to Iowa was a tedious one, and though the Lexus SUV was a lot cushier than either of our current vehicles, I wished we hadn't been told to carpool. We shared the ride with Agent Peter Garcia, a technical guy whose job involved planting bugs for the FPMP. You'd think that knowing such a guy exists would put me on edge. But Garcia credits Jacob for saving him from The Assassin, so overall, our relationship is surprisingly amicable.

Dr. Kudryasvstev is another story. It's not so much that I think he's out to get me personally. More that I don't trust psychic researchers in general. I dealt with him periodically at work, since I was literally writing the book on mediumship (or at least some really hefty papers) and he could offer guidance on the scientific method. But under those circumstances, when I'm visiting him in the lab, it's always possible for me to beat a hasty retreat to my office.

Now I was stuck in a car with the guy for a good five and a half hours.

To pass the time, we'd settled on a game of satellite radio Name That Tune. Jacob graciously let the other guys win the first few rounds—but he takes competition to the umpteenth level. Before long, he and Garcia were out for blood.

It was fascinating to watch Jacob in his zone. Eyes sharp. Nostrils flaring. Ramrod posture, as if sitting so uncomfortably would give him an edge in blurting out the titles faster than Garcia. "Okay," Dr. K said cheerfully from the driver's seat in his lilting Russian accent, "next song." He keyed in a station at random and a few notes of a stadium rock guitar solo filled the cab. I thought I might actually know that one, but before I could wrap my head around it, a bunch of junk noise announced that our satellite connection had gone kaput.

We gave it a few seconds.

Nothing.

Garcia said, "When you think about it, it's a wonder satellite radio works at all. Signals get obstructed. Frequencies contaminate each other's reception. Weather intervenes. And yet we still manage to bounce a signal off something orbiting the earth, and read it again back home. The technology really has come a long way."

"True," Dr. K said. "But there is one problem with technology. At some point, it invariably fails. And then we must spend our weekend driving out to repair it."

"Repair what?" I asked.

No one answered immediately. I figured I'd just blundered into top-secret territory when Garcia cut his eyes to Dr. K, and the doctor gave a guileless shrug. "It will make life much easier for us in the long run, Peter. You'll see."

Garcia huffed in annoyance. "Dynamic sigma fields. Nothing more than a theory—"

"So far," Dr. K put in.

"—and the damned sensor we planted fritzes out with stunning regularity."

Dr. K exhibited a distinct lack of chagrin. "If it wasn't sensitive, it wouldn't be doing its job."

Garcia grumbled, "Third time this year we've been out to recalibrate the thing."

"Couldn't you plant it a little closer to home?" I wondered.

Dr. K spread his hands in a what-can-you-do? gesture. "The site has certain characteristics that make it an ideal testing ground for the device. Think about it this way, my friend. If the technology pans out, it could mean an understanding of the way a precognitive's perceptions lie outside causal reality. A revolution in the way we see time itself. It's a modern renaissance, but instead of arts and physics, we're forging into psychic territory. You and I might be the Michelangelo and DaVinci of the age!"

Garcia sighed eloquently and fixed his eyes on the road.

"Is it possible your invention is causing the problems in Iowa?" I wondered.

Both Garcia and Dr. K had a good chuckle over that. "Sigma waves have a very limited range." Dr. K patted the radio dial. "Nothing like the waves that power radio and television. But perhaps that is for the best. At least while it is still in the development stage."

As we approached the exit marked Beauchamp, Dr. K told Jacob and me, "We'll be back first thing Monday morning. That should give you plenty of time to figure out if an FPMP surveillance presence is called for in this quaint little town."

Surveillance? And here I just thought I'd be doing medium-type stuff.

Ever since I found out the FPMP existed, I'd been horrified by the idea of some government agency getting all up in my business. How had I managed to blunder into the position of determining just which way Big Brother would be looking?

After nearly six hours on the road, it was a relief to unfold myself from the back seat of the car, stretch my legs, and bid our colleagues goodbye for the weekend. While I stood there in front of the rental car joint and watched the Lexus drive off, Jacob was watching me. I hadn't said a word about what I was thinking, but that man of mine knew me pretty darned well. Eventually, he said, "No one wants to plant any bugs—least of all, me. Now we've got the opportunity to prevent them from insinuating themselves where they're not wanted."

It was heartening to think that Jacob still thought of the FPMP as them, and not us. And as far as anyone else was concerned, we were just a couple of guys in suits asking questions—guys from an organization no one had ever heard of. The anonymity that came with the territory suited me just fine.

The rental place was minuscule by Chicago standards, and it doubled as a FedEx package drop-off. Even pulling double duty, it was devoid of customers. Behind the counter, a middle-aged woman with aggressive blonde highlights chatted on a landline with the handset cradled in the crook of her shoulder, but she scrambled to hang up just as soon as Jacob and I strode through the door.

"Did you fellas reserve the midsize sedan?"

The contrarian in me wanted to deny it, but given that it might be the only rental they'd booked all week, I didn't see the point. "That would be us. I've got a confirmation barcode here somewhere."

I pulled out my phone, but she waved it away and plucked a rental contract from the printer. "That's okay, sir, your vehicle is ready and waiting. Unless you wanted to upgrade to the SUV. We've got a Chevy Suburban on the lot fresh from the carwash and ready to go."

Jacob looked to me and quirked an eyebrow, but I decided that changing things up would just generate more fuss. The less paperwork I had to deal with, the better. Plus, the sedan would probably be a smoother ride. I shook my head. "We'll stick with what we've got."

"And were you interested in doing any sightseeing while you're here? I've got a two-for-one coupon for the Beauchamp Historical Society, though you'll need to go pretty soon if you're planning to use it, because they're only open for a few more hours and they're closed on Sunday."

"We're good," I said, already annoyed with the whole assignment.

The woman was completely oblivious to my annoyance. "Beauchamp has a lot of history. Fun fact: the town used to be called Hicksville. But after Prohibition was lifted, Roy Beauchamp started selling the bourbon he'd been aging in his basement and a whole bunch of businesses moved in. They called a referendum and re-named the town in his honor."

Can't say I blamed them. If I lived in a town called Hicksville, I'd probably be the first one to vote.

She clicked around on her computer, then spun the monitor to face us. A Wikipedia page featured a dour looking farmer with a couple of grubby boys at his side. "That's him. Too bad his son ran the distillery into the ground twenty years ago. But you can still see some of the original barrels at the Historical Society!"

"Which son?" Jacob asked.

"Marlon Beauchamp, the younger boy." She leaned across the counter as if to deliver a truly tantalizing bit of gossip. "The older one, Leland, was slow. Once Roy died, Marlon shipped him off to a home up in Ames. But people around here don't like to talk about that."

Glibly, Jacob replied, "Everyone's family has its own issues. I'm sure the people of Beauchamp have plenty to be proud of and don't need to worry about ancient history."

"Absolutely," the woman gushed. "And if you don't mind me saying, it's a real honor to have someone from the FPMP come out and deal with our current problem in person."

What the—?

I cut my eyes to Jacob to see if he might know where our so-called anonymity had gone, but he was just as surprised as me. "How did you know we were...?" I trailed off lamely.

"It's on the credit card," the woman said brightly. "Name's Ruth—Ruth Parrish. If there's anything I can do to help, you just let me know."

We shook hands—neither of us offering up our own names—and I grabbed the pen to sign on the contract's dotted line. Jacob's penmanship is notoriously legible, whereas my scrawl ended up looking more like Voter Rayon.

You don't realize how much you value your privacy until you find yourself exposed as a psych whose sole purpose is to spy on other psychs. And, in my case, to throw around the occasional handful of salt to make sure no one dead is spying on us.

Ruth looked at my signature just a moment too long, then met my eyes with disturbing intensity and said, "It's an important thing you're doing, y'know. Maybe not the easiest job in the world—but someone's gotta do it. After all, things aren't like they were when we were growing up. Someone needs to keep an eye on the situation."

I had no idea what to say. Thankfully, Jacob was there to take command of the situation before it got any more awkward. "Thank you so much for your support—it makes our job that much easier."

Ruth preened under his approval. "Happy to help. Here's my card. If you need anything while you're in town, I'm just a phone call away." She shoved a business card into Jacob's hand. "Call anytime—except between six and seven. That's when we have supper. But anytime other than that."

"Thank you," Jacob repeated graciously, while my heart hammered in my chest.

It's one thing snooping around for extrasensory reasons, but it's another when everyone knows that's exactly what you're doing. I've always preferred to fly under the radar. Back on the force, I dreaded the nasty looks and "Spook Squad" utterances just as much as I did the ghostly murder victims. Because at least the murders could be put to rest, whereas the shitty coworkers could be counted on to keep turning up like a sockful of bad pennies.

Ruth made a copy of our form and slid it back across the counter. "Fair warning—most folks around here aren't a fan of big government."

"Good to know," I said, guts twisting with the knowledge that a single word from me would have their town wired up from the cornfields to the truck stop.

She added, "But once the Federal Public Management Police take care of those damn teenagers—pardon my French—the naysayers will be singing a different tune."

Federal Public Management Police? There was a heartbeat in which my brain stumbled over way too much new information at once, but thankfully, my husband was fantastic about pretending he knew exactly what was going on. Probably because that's what he always thought. "I'm sure we've got our work cut out for us," he said smoothly, neither confirming nor denying.

"Drinking. Drugs. Partying until all hours of the night. And the Sheriff's not willing to lift a finger to take care of those obnoxious kids. Somebody has to."

"We'll look into it," Jacob said with utter sincerity, as though the federal government would send a couple of agents across state lines—on the weekend, no less—to handle a glorified noise complaint.

Ruth handed me the keys, walked us to the door and pointed out the sedan in the lot. It was white. Very white. Way too much effort to keep clean, in my opinion, but we'd only have it for the weekend, and if I got schmutz all over it, it wouldn't be my problem. Plus, with the mercury heading toward ninety, a black car would bake us like an oven, so I didn't complain.

My heart rate was almost normal again by the time we were settled in our rental car. Jacob must have sensed my discomfort. He helpfully pointed out that we each had our own temperature controls, which I waved off, having no particular opinion on the AC. Instead, I scowled open my phone and glanced through the briefing some logistics expert back the office had so helpfully compiled. "I thought we'd been made back there for sure."

Jacob considered. "Would that even matter?"

I shrugged.

"Look at it this way," Jacob suggested as we got our bearings. "It's a small town—and I know firsthand how small towns can be.

A couple of new guys in black suits can stir up a lot of curiosity. But once the rumor mill does its job, we won't have any need to explain our presence here. And asking questions will be lot easier if people think they know why we're here."

"Speaking of questions, how do you want to do these interviews? There's been a dozen striptease videos so far—twelve potential ghost encounters. But we've only got two days, and our chances of hitting all those stops in that amount of time are pretty slim. Unless you wanted to divide and conquer."

Jacob gave me an assessing look. "You're being awfully blasé about walking into a potential possession situation without a Stiff."

Frankly, it hadn't even occurred to me that I'd need one. No way would so many people in such a small town suddenly be possessed. I might be piss-poor when it comes to percentages and fractions, but even I knew we'd be unlikely to find so many possessable people in such a small population.

"Whatever is behind these random striptease attacks, I'm sure it's perfectly mundane." Drugs, most likely. I'd worked homicide long enough to know drugs played a part in plenty of cases. I scratched at the hopefully-imaginary habit demon stuck to my forearm and said, "If a ghost were responsible for all this, there'd be more history of weird happenings around here."

In fact, Beauchamp, Iowa was the epitome of dull. According to the brochure, it had even waited until after Prohibition was lifted to really start churning out the bourbon.

I added, "Given that there's no history of hauntings, possessions or other weird behaviors predating the first striptease video, it's a real stretch to think some ghost was just sitting around twiddling its etheric thumbs, and then suddenly got the urge to hop into a bunch of random bodies and whip off their tops."

Jacob considered my argument—and, naturally, countered it. "Unless it was someone who just died."

I thumbed through the recent obituaries in my briefing. All of them were elderly, with very normal-sounding lives and peaceful deaths. "More likely some kid was cooking meth in an abandoned silo and introduced a random contaminant that ended up frying its users from the inside out."

"Maybe. Or maybe a trucker dumped a prostitute's body in some undergrowth and drove off into the night."

If my years in homicide had changed the way I saw the world, the same could be said for Jacob and his career working sex crimes. He turned his laser focus on me and said, "Let's take a look at the latest footage."

CHAPTER 4

I called up the files and we bent over my phone.

The most recent incident had occurred at a small diner, where a Caucasian woman in her late thirties had stripped down to her sports bra and was giving a come-hither performance to the room at large—mostly geriatric couples looking annoyed or baffled. In the background, someone was hollering, "Danielle? Danielle! What the hell do you think you're doing?"

The phone swung around to a red-faced guy in a baseball cap and goatee, and he was clearly none too pleased.

A scuffle, and the screen went dark.

"She's toned and healthy," Jacob said. "She doesn't look like she's on meth."

And when meth heads strip down, it's usually because they think they're burning up from the inside out, not putting on a show. Plus, I couldn't deny—Danielle's abs were noticeably better than mine. "I'm not saying it's necessarily meth. Could be steroids. Some herbal concoction. Hell, maybe even a hallucinogenic fungus contaminating the well water."

"You're right. It could be any of those things." Jacob's hand dropped to my knee. "But if there's even the smallest chance we're dealing with possession, no way would I leave you to check it out alone."

You'd think after all this time together I'd be used to having someone looking out for me. Funny how accustomed I was to looking out for myself.

According to the paperwork, Danielle the provocative diner dancer was a thirty-six-year-old mother of two who made her living teaching fitness classes, from chair yoga at the senior center to spin classes at the local gym. This made her phenomenally easy to track down, as notice of all her scheduled classes could be readily found on social media.

The kid manning the desk seemed relieved that we were just there to see Danielle and didn't want to hear his thirteen-month-membership sales pitch. He gestured at a pile of paperwork he'd been keying into the computer and said, "If I knew how many gym tours I'd be stuck giving today, I would've totally called in sick."

Before I could ask what that was supposed to mean, Danielle's class let out, and a stream of active men and women emerged from a studio looking sweaty and self-congratulatory. Once most of them cleared out, we headed in.

A couple of thirty-something women had lingered behind to chat with their instructor, gushing over something she'd just said. "I would totally be up for a pole class," one of them was saying. "Even if I did need to pay an extra fee—it's just so worth it for a good, full-body workout."

"We'll see," Danielle said playfully. "There'd be a lot of pricy new equipment involved, so I'd really need enough signups before the class could officially be a go."

"I'll bet it would fill up right away," the other one enthused. "I'll make sure I tell my sister. She could really stand to get more exercise anyhow."

Given that Jacob and I were in suits instead of sweats, it was pretty obvious that we weren't there to jazzercise—or whatever it is they're calling it these days—and the women broke off their conversation as we approached, brimming with curiosity.

"Are you from corporate?" Danielle asked brightly.

Neither confirming nor denying it, Jacob gave her his most gracious smile and said, "Can we speak to you somewhere private?"

The exercise women looked him up and down like he was a prime cut of beef—and they were doing some serious Keto—then spared me a quick once-over and fled the room, whispering furiously to each other all the way.

Danielle closed the door behind them, then stood in front of it as if she was preventing us from leaving. "I only have ten minutes before my next class starts."

Ten minutes should be plenty. I said, "We were hoping you could shed some light on the video."

She tried her best to look hesitant to discuss the matter, but given the way her eyes lit up, it was pretty obvious the diner striptease was her new favorite topic.

"Well, I don't know that there's much to say," she demurred dramatically. I refrained from rolling my eyes. "I'd just finished my salad and my husband was at the register paying when I stood up from the booth, and something just came over me."

I said, "Talk more about that. The something."

She drew an arc across the floor with a pointed toe, flexing her well-muscled calf. "Well, it was like an urge. An impulse. A sudden need to move."

My gut might've been telling me this was all a bunch of nothing, but now that she'd described the feeling, I wasn't so sure.

The sensation of a ghost slipping under your skin and moving you around like a marionette is one you don't soon forget.

"Anything else?" I asked.

"Now that you mention it, I did feel a little stiff afterward. Nothing too alarming, just the sort of muscular pain you'd feel after tough workout."

Interesting. I supposed that could be expected if a ghost was moving your limbs for you, especially if their etheric body didn't quite line up with yours.

"Okay. Muscle pain. Anything else?" I asked one more time.

"I don't think so." She frowned, thinking hard. "Although…."

Jacob leaned in, looking utterly focused on her and stupidly handsome, and said, "Any detail you can remember might be significant. However small."

The tips of her ears went pink. "I thought there was music playing in the background. Not like a ringtone on someone's phone or a car radio out in the parking lot, but something strange. Even otherworldly." She gave a tiny laugh. "Or maybe I just imagined it."

Jacob told her where we'd be staying and asked her to give us a call if she thought of anything else. Once we were outside, he said, "What do you think—did this sound like possession to you?"

"Maybe I came into the assignment hoping there'd be some other perfectly rational explanation." I shuddered and chafed gooseflesh from my arms, despite the fact that the mercury was so high, heat lines were rising from the pavement. "But that feeling of something slipping under your skin? I'll never take it lightly."

Jacob nodded. "What about now—could she still be possessed?"

The goosebumps I'd just tried to chafe away developed

goosebumps of their own. "I freaking hope not."

We paused under the shade of an awning and considered. Jacob said, "From what we've seen, it's not easy for a spirit to stay in someone's body. Jennifer Chance was able to do it, but only when her host was weak or incapacitated."

"I hate the word host. Makes the whole thing sound like an awkward dinner party."

Jacob quirked an eyebrow. "Even then, the fit was less than ideal, and she had to expend a lot of effort to stay put. And, let's face it. Realizing that Richie'd been acting strange took a while because he's so unpredictable to begin with. We don't know Danielle. So we have no way to gauge whether or not she's acting like herself."

"True. But teaching an exercise class would be hard enough with all your faculties about you. If someone wearing Bethany's body started coaching me through yoga, I'd catch on pretty fast. Unless the town is haunted by fitness instructors, I think her students would have noticed if someone other than Danielle showed up."

So if there was a ghost and it wasn't in Danielle, the next logical place to look would be the spot where the possession took place.

The diner was on the outer fringe of Beauchamp, on the opposite side of town from the big truck stop—and still, we were there less than ten minutes later. It would've been sooner, if we hadn't been stuck behind a blue-haired old lady in a massive land barge navigating the roundabouts at approximately two miles per hour.

I'm always a fan of a good diner—and by good, I mean bad. The cheaper and greasier, the better. And in my experience, it's really hard to get a bad cheeseburger in a small-town

Midwestern dive. The Beauchamp Grill didn't disappoint. We were greeted by wood paneling, linoleum and naugahyde, and the smell of cooked-down coffee pervading the pores of the building.

Too bad I couldn't relax and enjoy it, since the place could very well be haunted.

I sucked down a gulp of white light, and we took a booth toward the back where we could snoop to our hearts' content.

"Anything?" Jacob asked, once I'd settled into my seat.

I scanned the room, pulled down even more white light, and looked again. "Nothing."

Nothing that I could see, anyhow.

A guy in a greasy apron took our order. While we waited for our meal, I focused on my breathing the way Bethany had showed me during our sessions. There may be no hard scientific evidence to support our idea, but we think a person's ability to hold white light might vary—and that breathing from the diaphragm might temporarily increase the size of my capacity. Plus it was a lot less conspicuous than assuming a Warrior pose in the middle of the diner.

Nothing lit up. Nothing moved that shouldn't be moving. Nothing looked transparent or herky-jerky or dead. I experienced the vague lightheadedness that accompanies my shift to extrasensory mode—the one that's followed by a nasty behind-the-eye headache when I push it too far—and still, nothing.

With a shrug, I told Jacob, "All clear." I turned to get a better look at the chalkboard listing the special of the day to check out my dessert options...and that's when I realized we weren't entirely free from a dead presence after all.

It was a head. Not a ghost head. Not a human head. But a rabbit head.

With antlers.

Mounted to a pole behind the register.

"What the hell is that?" I demanded.

"A French dip?"

"Not the specials board—the head." When Jacob looked blank, I said, "The horned rabbit. Tell me you see it too."

Jacob grinned. "Haven't you ever seen a jackalope before?"

I didn't dignify that with a response.

"I guess I'm showing my small-town roots. Don't worry, Vic—they're harmless."

Sure. If you like dead animals watching you eat dead animals.

Our burgers came, each one accompanied by a huge mound of fries, a tiny cup of coleslaw and a soggy pickle. But it was hard to really enjoy my food with those glassy eyes staring right through me.

Jacob, who misses nothing, said, "I doubt it's haunted."

"Killing an animal for food is one thing. But to make some kind of sick joke out of its body is just creepy."

"I'm sure it's just a way to get in some taxidermy practice. It was probably roadkill to begin with."

I supposed that made it less horrific—but just marginally. And I couldn't help but wonder what initially possessed someone to stick antlers on a dead rabbit's head and hang it up for all to see.

Maybe there'd been actual possession involved.

I was so busy keeping an eye on the dead rabbit head that a real, live person nearly got the jump on me. Ruth Parrish rounded the corner with an old-lady purse clamped under her arm and a toothy smile on her face. "Say, I'm glad I caught you fellas," she said brightly. "Didja try the French dip? The gravy here's real good. Anyways, I was just thinking you won't have too much luck finding those kids during the day, since they usually get up to their monkey business at night."

"That's definitely a possibility," Jacob non-answered. It sounded a lot better than what I would've said, which was, Where the hell did you come from?

"They'll probably set up in one of the vacant houses off the far end of Main Street. Rough part of town like that, there's always something sketchy going on."

Puzzled, I tried to imagine just how sketchy Beauchamp could possibly get. With an utterly straight face, Jacob managed to say, "Thanks for the input."

It was a gracious out, but Ruth didn't take the hint. She lowered her voice dramatically and said, "They're all on drugs."

While the irony wasn't lost on me that my first thought is usually the same thing, Ruth's hovering was tap-dancing on my very last nerve.

Jacob was feeding her some generic BS line about law enforcement taking all citizen complaints seriously when an incoming text from the F-Pimp research department dinged my phone. If I'd ever wondered how Con Dreyfuss had managed to show up at just the right time and place to drive me up a wall, I'd since discovered his secret: he had people.

And now, so did I.

Some poor schlub on weekend duty was alerting me that one of our striptease artists had just been spotted. Over at the truck stop, a long-haul trucker named Edie Banks had pulled into the weigh station five minutes ago. Given that we'd crossed her off the list already figuring she was probably halfway to Omaha, we'd definitely want to have a chat with her before she hit the road again.

"Duty calls," I told Ruth, eager to extricate us from her

overenthusiastic help. She waved brightly as we threw a few tens on the table and strode out the door.

"Thanks for not telling her off," Jacob said.

"I like to think I have at least a little bit of tact."

"It's hard enough keeping a low profile without the Neighborhood Watch joining in."

Too true. "And was she following us? What are the odds of her popping up at that diner?"

"Pretty good, I'd say, given that there are only two in the whole town—and the other one's in the truck stop."

Well, maybe so. But the sooner we wrote off the weirdness in Beauchamp, Iowa as a result of social media mass hysteria and headed back to the real world, the better.

CHAPTER 5

The Filling Station was a truck stop that spanned the main artery coming into town, almost a mini-village in itself, with a weigh station, an impressive 24-hour buffet, and the mini mart I'd seen in the video when Laura initially gave me the assignment. The town's big claim to fame was serving as a key trucking hub for the state's ethanol production.

Well, that...and now the impromptu stripteases.

I was more accustomed to the travel oases on the Illinois Toll Roads. Ample restrooms, lottery machines, and a raft of franchise restaurants that would invariably feature a McDonald's, a Starbuck's and a Panda Express. I'd hardly call the things sterile, but they were predictable.

The Filling Station, by contrast, was more like the Wild West.

There were not only restrooms, but showers. A dozen flavors of promotional Iowa keychains, fridge magnets and bumper stickers beckoned from a spinner rack by the door. And a massive selection of uppers flanked the cash registers—just caffeine in a dozen different configurations, but I'd wager that something stronger could be had if you knew who to make prolonged eye contact with. No doubt the same could be said for a quick hookup. I'm not bad at spotting someone who'd happily trade sex for drugs or money, but Jacob's radar for that kind of thing was a finely tuned machine.

But it was still mid-afternoon, and in the bright light of day, the Filling Station was wholesome enough. Pre-teens were gathered in a small arcade that housed a handful of console video games and a claw machine, and a few senior citizens in the diner were working on an early dinner. It looked like any other small-town Midwestern place you'd stop for gas.

And most importantly, it didn't appear to be haunted.

We found our trucker in the mini mart squinting to read the small print on a package of beef jerky. She was a Caucasian woman around my age, maybe ten pounds underweight, with graying brown hair in a stubby ponytail and a webwork of fine lines around her eyes. Maybe they were smile lines. Or maybe they'd come from years of squinting down the highway.

Given the look she turned our way when we approached, I'd guess the latter.

Jacob gave her a dazzling smile to try to put her at ease and said, "Edie Banks?"

Her eyes flicked toward the door, then back to us. "What of it?"

I flashed her my very official-looking F-Pimp ID—too quickly to read, especially from three yards away. "We're just looking into a few of the, er, dancing videos that've been showing up lately on social media."

"Cyber security is always a top concern," Jacob said, as if that had anything to do with anything. But one thing he'd learned in his years at the Twelfth Precinct, other than to spot a pervert, was to spout lies like they were God's honest truth. His tone was authoritative, so warm and reassuring, so filled with common sense, that I practically believed him myself.

So I was taken by surprise when Banks dropped the jerky and pushed past him with a curt, "Sorry, can't help you."

But there were two of us and one of her—and my legs are really long—so it was easy enough to head her off before she even made it to the keychain spinner.

"It's just a few quick questions," I said with a shrug to convey that they were nothing to write home about.

The woman's eyes darted from me to Jacob and back again.

"Totally routine," I added, trying to sound as bored as humanly possible.

White light had been streaming down in a steady flow, and I pulled a little harder to get a good look at Banks and make sure she was actually the one running the show, and not some shady ghost trying to escape my notice.

You can't always tell someone's possessed just by looking at them. Sometimes they're weird. Filmy eyes, jerky motions, breath coming out on a cloud of vapor. And sometimes you only notice the possession once you realize they've had a personality transplant. I don't know if the reason for the discrepancies was due to the strength of the spirit, the resistance of the host, or some other nebulous cause we have no way of measuring or quantifying.

But sometimes you can see a bit of slippage. Even with the really crafty ghosts.

The best place to spot a misalignment is the hands. Heads are where ghosts put the majority of their focus, since they're using it for important things like talking and seeing. And torsos and limbs are big enough to be pretty forgiving. All those tiny little digits on the end are a lot to keep track of, though, and that's where I've seen a host's hands be poked through like a worn pair of gloves.

The trucker lady's hands looked pretty normal to me.

Jacob's stride is nearly as long as mine—and he's in way better shape—so he headed Banks off before she slipped out the door. "I'm sure you don't want to cause a scene," he said reasonably.

The cashiers were already starting to rubberneck.

"Listen," I said, "it really is just a few questions, I promise." I cocked my head toward the diner to reassure her that no one was going to drag her off to a windowless room and waterboard the answers out of her. "You can answer them in the five minutes it would take you to wolf down a slice of pie. On us."

She gave me a long, wary look, then muttered, "The pie here sucks. Crust is soggy and meringue's like rubber."

"Good to know."

"But I suppose I'd take a peach cobbler."

Offering to keep our meeting public had done the trick—and I couldn't say I blamed Edie Banks for being hesitant to go anywhere with a couple of strange men in suits. Hell, I wouldn't do it either—and I'm carrying a sidearm. We slid into the booth across from her and ordered three cobblers all around, then got down to business.

"I have a prescription," she announced. There was a beat of silence in which Jacob and I both tried to figure out which dots she thought she was connecting, and when we didn't immediately respond, she felt compelled to go on. "Adult ADHD. So the Adderall is totally legit."

"We're not narcs," I said.

She looked pointedly from me to Jacob in our suits, and back again.

"We're not," I insisted.

"No?" She made a "gimme" gesture. "Then let's see that ID again."

Maybe she'd bought some drugs, and maybe those drugs were tainted, but we wouldn't know until we got some answers. It was a calculated risk, but I knew from personal experience that when it looks like you're about to be caught holding, it's impossible to think about anything else. I wasn't eager for her to know the possession we were investigating had nothing to do with controlled substances, but once she walked out that door, I doubted I'd ever see her again. So I slid my F-Pimp license across the table and let her make of it what she wanted to.

"We're not DEA," I said.

Her eyebrows shot up. "Hooker brigade? Why didn't you say so?" After yet another moment of nonplussed silence, she added, "Anyone on the road as long as me has heard of the Force for Prevention and Management of Prostitution."

"Of course," Jacob said, agreeing in that way he does without technically lying.

"But Beauchamp is one of the tamest cities on my route. Sure, there's always someone who'll play for pay at a truck stop, but the girls around here don't go around knocking on the cab doors like you usually see. They got their regulars, they swap texts when they're gonna meet up, and that's about it.

"Now, back when I was a kid, it was a different story. My uncle Dwayne drove a rig ever since he was tall enough to reach the clutch, and sometimes when he got to drinking with my dad, he'd tell stories. Beauchamp was lousy with prostitutes. Back in the nineties, some developer got the state to crack down on the trafficking and they all moved on."

"We'll make note of that in our report," Jacob said. "But there was actually an isolated incident we were hoping to get your take on." His phone was paused on a still from the video of Banks doing the hootchie-coo in the middle of the beef jerky aisle. "What was going on here?"

Her eyes flicked to the image and back up again. "No idea."

I said, "Tuesday night, nine-thirty or so." That prompted nothing but a blank look. And while I didn't want to color her answer, I did need some kind of response. "Maybe you recall an impulse? An unusual sensation?"

"Nope."

Okay, it's possible she was missing time. "But you do remember stopping here that night?"

"Sure. I weighed in, gassed up, took a leak, and hit the road."

Jacob waggled the phone. "And this?"

"It's not me."

I cut my eyes to the phone, where a stringy woman in a flannel shirt and a trucker cap was shoving her pants down. "It's clearly you," I said.

"Nope. It ain't."

I looked to Jacob for help, but he must've been used to dealing with liars who were a little more sophisticated. Meanwhile, Edie Banks was already halfway out the door, calling out, "Thanks for the cobbler—and good luck finding whatever it is you're looking for." By the time we'd both slid out of our side of the booth, she was halfway to her rig.

Jacob planted his hands on his hips and tried to pull her back with the tractor beam of his glare, but unfortunately, his etheric telekinesis didn't work that way. I said, "She wasn't gonna give us anything anyway." Whether or not we were DEA, she couldn't risk getting caught with whatever drugs were on her.

As Jacob's glare intensified, I slid back into the booth and said, "Are you gonna finish that cobbler?"

CHAPTER 6

I was adding a shot of caffeine to my sugar high when another love note from the office hit my inbox. Another dancer had just been positively ID'd—the video-still they forwarded showed a thirty-something Caucasian woman with prematurely graying hair—and her whereabouts had been traced to a local business. Not just any local business, mind you.

Beauchamp's one and only funeral home.

I can count the number of funerals I've been to on one hand—and that's unusual in my line of work, to say the least. But why tempt fate?

Jacob scanned the look on my face and said, "If you wanna sit this one out...."

My shoulders slumped. "No. Weirdly enough, I wouldn't expect the funeral home to be any more overrun than a hospital or a busy intersection. Besides, while I'm sure you can interview circles around me, I'm the one that's gotta keep an eye out for telltale ghost fingers."

That poet who said they contained multitudes wasn't wrong. We've all got bodies inside our bodies, stacked several layers deep like a bunch of nesting dolls. It's not just physical and etheric—body and soul. There's more. Several more. Astral, for one. But beyond that, other bodies, too. I'd seen them while I was doped up on psyactives at PsyTrain. When I'd wave my arm, an array of hands would snap open like a flamenco dancer's fan.

In fact, I'd seen things leave tracers behind as far back as my Camp Hell days. Even had I been in a helpful frame of mind at that time, I didn't have the language to explain what I'd seen. And truthfully, in those early days I hadn't been particularly obliging. That's why precious research dollars had never been allocated to the study of subtle bodies. Now, years later, here I was in the employ of the Federal Psychic Monitoring Program, poised to make use of all the research...and thanks to my own caginess, it didn't exist.

Grace Funeral Home was a modest brick building with ample parking in a quiet neighborhood. It wasn't scary and baroque like all the funeral homes you see in movies. Actually, it was plain and kind of sterile. Barely 7pm and Beauchamp was shutting down for the night—all except the 24-hour truck stop—but the funeral home still had a few lights on inside.

Lucky us.

While, intellectually, I didn't think the place was haunted—it was still a funeral home. A place where corpses came and went, bodies were prepped for viewing, and vital fluids ran down the drain.

Jacob considered the funeral home. "If there's a ghost, I should be able to feel it."

"That's a big if."

"But since I was bred for this...I should."

I quelled a sigh. "Jacob, don't get ahead of yourself. You'll drive yourself crazy looking for something that's probably not even there."

"How else do we do this, then? Because if I wait for you to point something out and ask me if I see it, what does that prove?"

"Fine. Stay on your toes, and if something seems off, let me know and we'll take it from there." I topped off my white light and the two of us made our way through the front door....

And right into a viewing.

Maybe we could have slipped off inconspicuously to one side, had we not managed to walk right into the funeral director—a stern older man with heavy tortoiseshell glasses and an overly-starched demeanor. He seemed like a take-charge kind of guy, in a quiet and unobtrusive way. But the funeral home was clearly his domain, and he exuded the confidence of the guy in charge. "I'm sorry for your loss," he said, steering Jacob firmly by the elbow toward a viewing room with a handful of people gossiping in the corner...and an open casket splayed out for everyone to see.

At least there wasn't a ghost. Not that I could see. But my proximity to a corpse prompted me to double down on the light-sucking anyhow before we headed in.

Once the funeral director was out of range, I whispered, "We stuck out like a sore thumb in our suits all day long, and now we just look like we showed up for the wake."

"Roll with it," Jacob said, and headed toward the front. "It'll give us a better chance to find the next woman on our list."

Part of me wanted nothing to do with the scenario that was unfolding. That part wanted to turn around and walk right back out the door. We weren't here to hunt ghosts, after all. Just to figure out why women were randomly stripping in public, and whether or not the FPMP needed to plant some bugs.

But Jacob had obviously decided he had something to prove. And so I crammed in a little more white light, followed him up to the casket, and plunked myself down on the kneeler.

The guy in the box was small, bony and Caucasian. As for age...eighty? Ninety? A hundred and ten? Hard to tell beneath the sickly orange pancake makeup caked on his withered cheeks. His lips were weirdly taut, and I couldn't help but stare, as if rigor mortis might force him to suddenly crack a smile. I wished I was looking at anything but the body—but where else was there to look? Especially when there might be a ghost hunkering down inside it, just waiting for a chance to pop out like a jack-in-the-box.

Beside me, Jacob was pretending to pray. Not that I know what his pray-face is...but I'd bet money that if any supplications were being offered, he'd be begging to get a handle on his talent. He resettled his shoulders and whispered, "It doesn't feel right in here."

I was feeling pretty squirrelly, myself...but that was nothing new. "Not-right, how?"

"If I had a more accurate word, I'd use it."

One thing I've learned about Jacob. Thanks to his massive ego, he takes everything in stride...until he doesn't. Let's just say frustration doesn't sit well with him.

Best determine whether it was his extrasensory ability talking or just the normal physiological reaction to being within two feet of a dead body. I did my best to scan the visually confusing jumble of flowers and drapery for ghosts without being too obvious about it. But now everyone's attention had shifted to us, and the mourners were unabashed in their scrutiny. If there'd been any doubt at all that they were checking us out, the old lady with the crappy hearing aid would've put it to rest.

"Are they from Pearline's side of the family? Those big-shots always thought they were too good for us."

"Aunt Sue," someone else hissed, and the scrutiny died down to a whispery grumble.

"Anything?" Jacob asked softly.

I triple-checked the vicinity. "Nothing but the weight of a dozen pairs of eyes on me. Can we get up now?"

Jacob nodded, and I unfolded gratefully from my proximity to the body. The cloying smell of carnations had coated the insides of my nostrils and I was eager to find our target, determine she was high on embalming fluid when she'd done her little internet dance, and get the hell out of there. But when I turned to make a run for the door, I barely avoided colliding with a portly woman in a powder blue skirt suit and ten tons of hairspray.

"Thank you so much for coming," the woman said, disguising her curiosity with politeness. "I'm sure Dad woulda been real glad to know you'd stopped by. Was it a long drive?"

"Oh, you know," I said vaguely. "About as long as you'd expect."

"I hope you weren't caught in the construction—did you come up the 80 or the 35?"

Probing to see if we'd come from Chicago or Kansas City—and the less this family knew about us, the better. Good thing the undercover trainers at F-Pimp had taught me to deflect questions without coming off like too much of an antisocial jerk. "Actually, we took the scenic route."

Movement from the corner of my eye caught my attention. Not ghostly movement, thankfully. Just a woman who paused briefly in the far doorway, scowled, and moved along.

Amy Grace—the very woman we were looking for.

"Gotta hit the can," I blurted out—much to the chagrin of

Jacob, who somehow manages to be a lot more socially adroit about these things—and high-tailed it off in the direction of the third striptease artist, leaving him to wrangle the curious family.

I peeled out into a vestibule just as a nearby Staff Only door whispered shut. I double-checked that I was alone, then slipped through it and into the hallway beyond. Things tend to pan out for me so seldom that I can't help but be pleased with myself when they do. Maybe a little too pleased. Because just as I was patting myself on the back for extricating myself from the viewing, I was caught red-handed wandering around where I shouldn't be.

Another door opened and a middle-aged white guy came out. He was sinewy and sharp, with graying hair buzzed short and one eye slightly squintier than the other. He wore a polo shirt and dress slacks, but the shirt was creased like he'd folded it funny and left it that way since laundry day, and his pants had an off-the-rack fit that wasn't doing his angular body any favors.

"Just looking for the john," I said—since that excuse will let you go pretty much anywhere. Since I doubt it's Kosher to be snooping around behind closed doors at a funeral home, I expected him to call me out on it. At the very least, I thought he'd point me in the direction of the can. But instead, he just dragged a janitor's cart out into the hall and glared at me until I stepped aside and let him pass.

Briefly, I entertained the notion that maybe he was actually the ghost of a former custodian. But given the faint smell of cigarettes and air freshener wafting off him, that seemed pretty unlikely.

Once I was alone again, I checked the door he'd come

from—a utility closet that was empty, save for the lingering smell of cigarettes. Another door—office. Also empty. Which left one more door. A door that led to a set of stairs going down.

Into the basement.

Of a funeral home.

Great.

Steeling myself, I sucked down a fresh volley of white light and headed down the stairs. By the time I hit the bottom, I was buzzing with light and the stirrings of a headache threatened.

As basements went, this one was par for the course: painted cinderblock walls and rubbery industrial flooring. But the chill in the air was pronounced, and the stink of powerful antiseptic prickled the back of my throat. There was only one door. And it was marked Embalming: Authorized Personnel Only.

The hairs on the back of my neck sprang up and a sheen of sweat rose on my upper lip. I blotted it on my cuff, made room for some more white light, pulled it down through my crown chakra, and shoved through the door before I could change my damn mind.

I'll say one thing for the embalming room...at least it was well-lit. And that was about the only non-horrifying thing about it.

A fat man lay on the slab. He was covered by a sheet—but he was also pitching a tent. Of every possible square inch in that room, why was his dead dong the first place my eyes landed? I looked away—medical contraption, fluorescent light, obscure machinery and sadistic metal tools—but the mental image of the shape poking up beneath the fabric blotted out all the other horrors.

Amy Grace had been pulling on a lab coat when I came in. She must've been expecting the funeral director, and she did a double-take when she saw it was some tall, sweaty stranger instead. "Sir?" she snapped. "You shouldn't be here."

"I'm with the FPMP." I flashed my identification, too weirded out to bother scraping together a convincing lie. "Just a few questions and I'll be out of your way."

Her eyes tracked from my ID card to my face. She stared for a moment...and then her shoulders slumped. "Fine. I told them someone from Mortician Protocols would show up for a surprise inspection one of these days. But does anyone around here ever listen to me?"

According to my handlers back at the office, the less you say, the more people allow their own preconceptions to fill in the gaps. I'd never fully appreciated the amount of mental gymnastics people would do to convince themselves your random jumble of alphabet letters were some sort of known commodity. Seemed unlikely to me. Still, best not look a gift horse in the mouth—or a corpse in the turgid penis. "Right. Well. I won't take up too much of your time. If you could just fill me in on the events of Thursday night."

"The Skidmore viewing?"

"More specifically, the incident in the parking lot. The one on the video."

Amy's face fell—like she'd been expecting me to say something about it, while simultaneously hoping I was actually there for some other reason...any other reason at all. A rolling stool was parked under a table full of grotesque instruments—picks and scalpels and hooks—and she pulled the stool out with her foot and plunked herself down. There was nowhere for me to sit. Not unless I wanted to hop up on one of the embalming tables. I backed up a pace and did my best not to loom over her.

"Okay," she said, "I realize it looked pretty bad. But I've been under a lot of stress lately."

No doubt. Frankly, I had no idea how she did it. Handling all those human remains had to take a toll.

She added, "Though to be honest, there's not much I do remember."

Of the women we'd interviewed so far, Amy was the one who tugged at my heartstrings the most. Was she popping whatever pills I suspected the other two were on? I wouldn't be surprised. But given the type of grisly stuff she had to see (and even handle), I could hardly blame her. "Don't worry, no one's here to put a ding on your permanent record." I'm not big on empathy—either the psychic variety, or the mundane. But I'd seen so much death in my years of homicide, how could I help but feel for her? "We were just hoping to get some context on what happened."

"I'm not sure you'll believe me."

"Try me."

She fiddled with the edge of her lab coat and sighed. "It probably sounds made up...in fact, I know it does. But I was sleepwalking."

A chill played across the back of my neck that was only partially due to the air conditioning. "Is this a new thing? Or has it happened before?"

Amy stiffened, as if she was hoping I'd just laugh it off, and my willingness to take her seriously was unwelcome. "This is a real medical condition, you know. You can't revoke my license because of it."

"That's not what this is about."

"Because that would be discrimination, pure and simple."

"No one's revoking anything," I snapped—because apparently it took way more than sympathy to build the type of rapport I needed to question her effectively. But whatever those build-ing blocks might be, I had approximately zero. "If you'd just take a breath, think back to the event, and tell me what you do remember—"

One minute I was botching my interview, and the next I was watching my subject's eyes roll back in her head. Luckily I'd been looking directly at her while it happened, and I was able to lunge forward and catch her as she slumped sideways and the stool shot out from under her.

I lowered her to the floor—dammit, why hadn't I wrangled the nosy family and let Jacob handle the interview?—and tried to figure out if I had a seizure on my hands or a heart attack.

Yeah, I get an annual refresher in CPR. Too bad those practice dummies are nothing like real live people you've been arguing with for the past five minutes. But I knew enough to know you don't just start whaling on someone's chest unless they've been without pulse or respiration for ten seconds.

When I pressed my fingers to her carotid, they kept right on going. For a nightmarish moment I thought either she was collapsing in on herself, or I'd just held a conversation with someone made of cream cheese. But then my perception shifted, and I saw that it wasn't my normal fingers sinking into her neck...but my nonphysical ones.

And then her spirit tumbled out.

CHAPTER 7

"Don't panic," I said. "But we may have a situation."

Amy's ghost stood up and dusted herself off. How I knew it was her ghost and not some random stowaway when it looked almost nothing like her, I can't really say. The spirit looked like she was dressed up for goth night at a trendy nightclub. Her hair was dark and blunt-cut, and her eyes were thick with eyeliner. But there was an Amy-ness to it—a rightness—that made it seem somehow more her than the body on the floor.

"I'll call 911," I said.

She cocked her head and said, "No, don't bother. This happens all the time."

"And you didn't think to say something when I was asking you about the incident in the parking lot?"

"To be fair, I had no idea you realized this sort of phenomenon exists. Why is it that you can see my ka?"

I'd heard the term before, back in my Camp Hell days, but it was nothing that came up in common conversation. Egyptian term for soul, if I remembered right. So the hair and cat-eye makeup on her spirit made a lot more sense.

"I see lots of things," I told her, and struggled to shift my focus into my physical fingertips and take her pulse.

"Don't worry about that. It's just a shell."

"A shell that allows you to function in the physical plane."

"True," she said. "And my ka doesn't usually separate unless I'm somewhere private. Maybe it knew you were sympathetic to the cause?"

No clue. In fact, I'd been hoping she could tell me. "Is there something weird about the energy here?" I wondered.

"Obviously not, with all the work I do making sure the dead cross over safely. Otherwise they get confused. Sometimes the living can feel it—but they mistake it for grief or wishful thinking or superstition. But nothing like that is happening around here. I run a tight ship."

I'd met a handful of spiritual crossing guards before. But none of them had ever still been alive at the time. "And I'm sure you're doing a great job...it's just that my partner felt a little funny upstairs in the viewing."

"Lots of people do. It's a physical stimulus with a psychological response. We keep it cold in here—for obvious reasons." She nodded toward the tent-pole guy. "And we keep our humidity low, too. Folks feel a tingle of static, they realize they're in the proximity of a body, and suddenly their limbic system is off and running."

Fight or flight. Normally, I'd buy it. But.... "What if they're actually picking up on something?" I nodded toward her ka. "What if they can sense you?"

"The people who can perceive anything beyond what they can physically see, hear or feel are few and far between. Do you think anyone gives a damn about the state of their immortal consciousness? No—they're too busy sipping their lattes, posting pictures of their lunches, and financing the latest, greatest

SUV. Either they put their faith in a bearded white guy perched on a throne in the sky—a capricious taskmaster who will wipe clean a life of greedy mediocrity if only they beg prettily enough—or they think that this," she gestured dismissively to the world at large, "is all there is."

This lady could have one hell of a chat with a certain consignment specialist in Chicago—a conversation I'd be sure to stay as far away from as possible.

Still, if anyone could give me an inside scoop on what was happening here in Beauchamp, it was Amy. "Do you mean to say there is nothing supernatural going on here? The random stripteases, the missing time? That's all got some perfectly logical explanation behind it?"

"I hardly concern myself with such petty things. What do I care about a video when I'm helping the newly departed navigate the unfamiliar terrain of the afterlife?"

"You were one of the strippers. That doesn't concern you?"

"My body has a mind of its own," she said with a shrug. "Neurons fire. The brain stem reacts to stimulus. It's no big deal."

"But it's your body!"

I looked down at her physical form. Was it even breathing? I pressed two fingers to her pulse, focusing hard on my own physical body so as not to jostle anything else free...and it swatted my hand away, sat up, and said, "Quit it!"

I jerked back as her spirit said, "It probably would've just laid there if you hadn't kept poking at it."

"What the hell?"

"Just let it do what it wants."

"But what if it wants to wander out into traffic?"

"Don't underestimate the body's impulse for self-preservation. That sort of thing is hardwired in the brain. Even amoebas know enough to move away from anything painful."

It seemed like it should be obvious that Amy's physical form was currently lacking a soul, but honestly, there was nothing in her mannerisms or facial expression that screamed out "autopilot mode." She stood up, strode purposefully over to a counter full of embalming equipment, and began rearranging the creepy metal instruments.

"How is it self-preservation to take off your clothes in public? Maybe you should be more worried about what your body is up to."

"My physical shell is irrelevant. Frankly, the only thing it's good for is putting me in the vicinity of the newly departed." She prodded the foot of the chunky boner guy on the table, but thankfully, nothing etheric shook loose. "It's ironic. I fought tooth and nail to stay out of the family business. I wanted to go to film school. But my older brothers both joined the service to get away from here and left me stuck in the mortuary. In the end, it turned out I was exactly where I needed to be. This is my purpose. My calling. Most people go into the mortuary business to bring closure to the living. But I bring closure to the dead."

It sounded like she considered herself a one-trick pony, same as me. But instead of ruing the fact that all she was good for was talking to dead people, she embraced it. With that kind of focus, though, she only cared about crossing over ghosts, and nothing else.

Still, if anyone was poised to provide me with insight on all the stripping, it was Amy. Or her subtle body, anyhow. "So when your physical body was in the parking lot making a spectacle of itself, what was your ka doing?"

"Exploring."

"Exploring," I repeated, deadpan.

"Lately when I separate, more often than not, there's no one waiting around to be escorted to the afterlife. This ability is a gift. I'd hate to squander it. So I use the time to check out the area and learn more about my surroundings."

"Okay. What have you learned?"

"It's hard to put into words...but there's so much more to existence than the world we think we know. Reality has layers, kind of like a body. There's skin on the outside. Muscles, blood vessels and organs inside. A skeleton holding it all up. What our consciousness thinks of as existence is just one part of the body of our reality."

Great. Now, not only did I have to wonder which way the chakras were facing when they spun, but whether I was living in the skeleton or the skin.

Metal clanged against metal as Amy's body got to work rearranging a stack of shallow stainless steel trays, putting the top one on the bottom and the bottom on the top.

I did my best to ignore it. "With everything you've learned, everything you know, you're bound to have some idea what's going on with the stripping."

Before her spirit could answer, my phone chimed. Normally, I'd ignore that too, since talking to a ghost pretty much trumps anything else on my agenda. But it was the special ding I'd assigned to HQ...and they wouldn't be dinging me on a Saturday night unless it was important. I glanced at the message.

Incident in progress.

There was an address. I read it off to Amy and said, "Where is that?"

"Somewhere in the physical plane."

Given that I'd accidentally nudged her ka out of its shell, I could probably strangle it if I really wanted to. Lucky for her I'm a patient guy.

My phone dinged again—Jacob this time. Striptease happening right now. Evidently the office had notified him too. I'll grab the car.

If I'd been partnered up with one of my old Stiffs—with Bob Zigler, or even Maurice—I would've had them head over without me so I could try to get more from Amy. But even though Jacob was a competent investigator (maybe even over-competent, depending on who you asked) we weren't one hundred percent sure how his psychic powers worked, and I wasn't about to risk sending him off to butt heads with something nonphysical alone. And so, reluctantly, I decided to wrap up my interview with Amy's ka, and texted Jacob to meet me in back so as to avoid being tackled by the undertaker.

I bolted out the back door, where the smoke-smelling guy in the creased polo shirt was polishing the headlight of a hearse. He paused to watch me blankly, then went back to his polishing with zero interest as Jacob pulled the rental car around the corner.

Jacob peeled out of the lot before I even had a chance to buckle my seatbelt. The car came equipped with a massive built-in GPS with a touchscreen that was likely more advanced than my newish laptop. Unfortunately, I couldn't figure out how to make it do much of anything while Jacob squealed around every corner on two wheels. At least it wasn't as if we were in any danger of being T-boned as we blew through the stop signs. The streets of Beauchamp were pretty much empty for all of the four minutes it took us to get there.

The address in question was a public park, a small postage stamp of green in the middle of a nondescript business district that held a couple of bars, a used book store and a payday loan joint. There was a bronze statue in the center—presumably a couple of dead white guys—and a few unsavory-looking twenty-somethings lingering at a nearby picnic table. The live white guys were catcalling a woman maybe ten years older than them as she hurried away, straightening her T-shirt. She looked upset, and she was dragging a small, energetic dog along behind her. The dog was barking up a storm, like it wanted to make sure those punks knew it wasn't intimidated by them in the least.

"That's the subject," Jacob said, pulling over a few yards ahead so we could intercept.

She seemed startled when we hopped out of the car—but not scared. The effect of wearing a suit can really go either way. While someone like our long-haul trucker figured we were on a drug bust, your normal, upstanding citizen with nothing to hide will have a much better reaction.

"Are you okay?" Jacob asked, all concern, cementing our instant rapport with the woman as the jerks in the park melted away into the night.

She stopped, looked around, and tugged at the hem of her shirt. "I—uh, yeah. I think so."

"What just happened?" I asked.

She blinked. "I was just walking Mulligan—quiet, Mully!—and then these obnoxious guys started yelling stuff at me."

She smoothed down her shirt yet again. Jacob noticed too, but he didn't call her on it. He'd gone into his comforting authority mode, one he'd honed over a decade of questioning victims who wanted nothing more than to curl up in a ball and wish the world would go away. His body language was gentle, and his big, dark eyes were soft and soulful by the light of the nearest streetlamp. He was a bodyguard and confidante all in one. And ridiculously good looking, which doesn't hurt.

It wasn't exactly an act, this demeanor of his. But he was able to pull it on at a moment's notice like a well-worn T-shirt. "Things like these can be traumatic, so it's best to process them right away. Is there anything more specific you can remember about what just happened? Anything at all?"

"No, I'll be fine. It's really pretty safe around here. They were just yelling a bunch of stupid stuff, that's all. Besides, I've got Mulligan to protect me." She went down on one knee to lavish some praise on her guardian.

The dog skittered back a few steps.

"What's wrong, Moo-moo?"

The dog whined. His tail was low, tucked down between his legs. As she spoke to him in singsong dog nonsense, it perked up. But just a little. Eventually it wagged, albeit timidly.

Animals pick up on those layers of reality that people usually miss. Maybe because they have no reason to explain it all away so as not to call too much attention to themselves.

I'd muted my phone, but a quick vibration told me HQ wasn't done with me. While the woman was focused on her dog, I tapped the play button in my inbox. A wobbly shot of the park. And the subject peeling off her T-shirt.

I paused mid-peel and flashed the image at Jacob. He winced ever so slightly and inclined his head toward me, begging me to field this new information. While I understood it was best for at least one of us to stay on the woman's good side, I lived with so much general discomfort, I hated to be the one to inflict it on someone else.

Jacob gave me a pointedly beseeching look.

Fine. I'd play bad cop. This time.

"Why did you take off your shirt?" I asked.

The woman rocked back as if I'd slapped her. "What?"

"That's what got those guys all riled up," I said, "wasn't it?"

"I...I don't.... Wait, are you saying this is all my fault?"

"You strike me as a sensible person—just wondering why you'd do something like that."

"Don't worry," Jacob assured her. "No one's blaming you. We just want to understand what happened to make sure it doesn't happen again."

"Starting with the reason you took off your shirt," I pressed.

"I don't know! It's really humid, okay?" She gave Mulligan's leash a twitch. "So mind your own business and leave us alone."

I stood aside as the woman and her dog strode off in righteous indignation. Well, the dog more or less scampered. Its legs were pretty stubby.

"Next time, you're bad cop," I told Jacob.

He pondered the woman until she turned a corner and disappeared from our line of sight. "Could she have been possessed?"

I glanced around to see if any disembodied spirits were lingering around, but didn't see anything. "If it was just an isolated incident, I'd be more likely to think so. But possession is a pretty rare phenomenon. It's something I've only seen happen to a medium. Most people's subtle bodies are cemented in place pretty well—and what are the chances of finding such a high concentration of mediums all in the same small town? Unless they're all related to Amy Grace."

Jacob shot me a look...and I realized I had some explaining to do.

CHAPTER 8

To say Jacob was annoyed that he missed the whole extrasensory conversation with Amy was putting it mildly. I gave him the short version in the car as we made our way to our motel, a small and unassuming place with fake stucco walls and the stink of industrial air freshener hanging heavy in the hallways. We settled into our room. It was a low-ceilinged cave with way too much polyester and two full-sized beds that looked none too comfortable. Thankfully, we'd only be there a couple of nights.

Jacob paused between the beds, planted his hands on his hips, and said, "Amy projected her etheric body?"

"She called it her ka—but that's my best guess, given how she can use it to interact with the dead. Then again, subtle bodies don't exactly come with an instruction manual."

He smoothed his beard, thinking. "What if the other women are related? They could all have the same father."

"The undertaker?" I shuddered.

"Who says Mr. Grace is necessarily Amy's biological parent? Maybe thirty or forty years ago there was a psychic Lothario who knocked up half the town. Or a shady researcher swapping out the sperm at the fertility clinic."

Or maybe Dr. Kamal's eugenics program had extended into Iowa. I didn't suggest that possibility. No doubt it was the first idea that crossed Jacob's mind, anyhow.

"Weirder things have happened," I allowed. "But I'm still not convinced what's going on is possession. Ghosts have a pretty limited range—maybe a few blocks, if the size of Jackie's territory by my old apartment is anything to go by. Let's set aside the unlikelihood of a ghost possessing someone for the sake of making her strip off her clothes. These incidents happened all over the town. Even if a dozen different women in Beauchamp happened to be psychic mediums—and that's a big if—how is the ghost managing to show up in all these different locations?"

Jacob considered the question and his steel-trap mind clicked into gear. "We need to get a better look at the pattern."

Lucky for us, the motel had a so-called business center… essentially, an unused meeting space with an old desktop computer and a spotty, wheezing laser printer bigger than the mini-fridge in our room. But it was good enough for what we'd set out to do: creating a big map of Beauchamp.

We called up a street map online. To get all the granular detail we needed, we zoomed in as far as we could and printed the image across multiple sheets of paper. The night clerk wanted to be stingy with the office supplies, I could tell. But Jacob was in the zone. And when he commandeered the scotch tape and short stack of yellow sticky notes, the guy gave them up with hardly a fight.

Back in our room, we discovered that not only were our printouts faded and speckled with toner, but they were slightly warped and didn't quite line up. We matched up the streets as best we could and taped the thing together. It made our evidence board look less like police work and more like the ravings of a psycho conspiracy theorist...but I could tell Jacob wouldn't let it rest until he had some answers.

Once the map was cobbled together, we pulled up our strip-tease sightings and marked them each with a pink highlighter X. I'd been hoping a pattern would emerge.

I suppose if you call "a bunch of random X's" a pattern, then we were right on the money.

Jacob scowled at the map. "Maybe it starts at one end of town and moves toward the other. What are the dates of the incidents?"

I gave him the info, and he labeled each X with a date and time. Our map was just screaming out for some string art, but I doubted the night clerk had pins and string on hand. Heck, we'd been lucky to get a highlighter out of him. Jacob settled on connecting the X's with arrows instead.

Still, no pattern.

Jacob sounded annoyed when he said, "These are only the incidents we know about. Situations where there was someone willing to record it and post it to social media." He worked his jaw a few times, a telltale sign if ever there was one, and I took in his stance. His intensity. His overall demeanor. He wasn't just annoyed—he was royally pissed.

"Okay," I said carefully. "You want to get to the bottom of this. I do, too. So...you wanna tell me why you're suddenly taking this all so personally?"

Jacob glared hard at the wall. "If you'd kept me in the loop back at the funeral home, I could've helped you question Amy Grace."

Great. I'd somehow managed to trigger his psychic insecurity. "I thought we were in divide-and-conquer mode."

"And you could have said something in the car."

"While you were busy breaking the sound barrier on the way to the park? Look, Jacob, I'm sorry you weren't there when the weird thing happened." I'd wager that sometimes I was the one MIA when the weird thing happened, only Jacob couldn't see the weirdness carrying on all around him. Not like me. But I knew better than to float that theory. He was feeling frustrated enough as it was. "I wish you had been there. Maybe you would've picked up on something I missed. At the very least, you might've gleaned a more useful statement from Amy's spirit body, since you've got all the talking-skills that I sorely lack."

I took him by the shoulders and turned him to face me. He met my eyes, but only reluctantly.

"I know that's not exactly what you wanted to hear," I told him. "After everything you've gone through—hell, everything your whole family has gone through, with Kamal taking so much of an interest in your gene pool—I understand. It seems like there should be a big psychic trophy waiting for you when you cross the finish line. But we need to keep this between you and me. To figure it out ourselves. Because I guarantee you, mister, the trip through the research meat-grinder I endured is not something you want to experience yourself."

"That was years ago. Back in the early days of Psych, back when people like Kamal were given free rein—it was ugly. No doubt. But things are different now."

Apprehension settled in my gut like a big wad of soggy cobbler. "Don't tell me you're thinking of turning yourself in."

"Not turning myself in," he corrected me. "Asking for help. And, yeah. How could it not occur to me every time my so-called talent yields absolutely no results?"

Now it was my turn to get hot under the collar. "You'd risk

everything to hear some expert say you're not just a Stiff?"

"What would I be risking, exactly?"

"Plenty. They find out you're telekinetic—the rarest thing of them all? You'd live out the rest of your life as a glorified lab rat."

"You're thinking of Camp Hell. That's not how the FPMP operates. We both know that. We've seen it from the inside."

"Our own office, maybe. But even Laura Kim is leery of the upper echelons." I flashed back to our last encounter at the Clinic with the goons from FPMP National, one where I ended up with a broken hand for my troubles. Not that they were the ones who broke it—I'd done the honors myself. But the way guns were pointing at the time, if I hadn't, I can guarantee one of us would've ended up with a lot worse than a couple of months in a plaster cast. "Anything you say back at the office, you might as well cc our boss's boss. And you'll end up with a lot more 'help' than you bargained for."

His dark brows drew together stubbornly. I cupped his face in my hands and smoothed a thumb across his cheekbone, ignoring the itch now crawling along on my forearm from my memories of being confined in the cast. "Jacob, I know you're sick of being in psychic limbo, but you've gotta bide your time. Not for you. For me."

I kissed him, deliberate and slow. It wouldn't have surprised me if he'd tried to resist...but thankfully, he didn't. We got each other, Jacob and me. Even if we weren't any closer to cracking the code on Jacob's gifts, I could hope that the mutual understanding we shared would tide him over. At least for now.

I backed him against one of the beds and eased him down onto it. I straddled him, pressing our foreheads together, and shoved my groin into his. He made a small sound in his throat.

I kissed him again, mostly because I was worried about saying the wrong thing and breaking whatever fragile understanding we'd just forged. But though I might be preoccupied with how I'd probably manage to screw everything up somehow, that feeling of straddling his rock-hard thighs was really pretty sweet.

Jacob flexed his hips and his junk bumped mine...and it was my turn to let a tiny grunt escape me.

We paused only long enough to slip out of our suits, since we'd only brought along one apiece for the weekend. We draped them over the spare bed. Once we ditched the rest of our clothes, Jacob caught me around the waist, tipped back onto the free bed, and rolled me on top of him.

That position felt totally different naked.

The hair on his thighs tickled the smooth spots on the insides of mine. The ambient air chilled my exposed hole. And when I leaned in for yet another kiss, his thickening cock brushed the base of my belly.

"We probably shouldn't be wasting our limited time here doing something we could do to our hearts' content back home," I said, with little to no conviction.

"I have it on good authority that none of the witnesses would be willing to talk to us after midnight." Jacob gave my bare ass a two-handed squeeze. "And I can't think of a better way to wipe the slate clean and approach this problem with a fresh set of eyes."

Is that what they were calling it these days? It was such a huge relief to hear Jacob's trademark confidence return, I refrained from asking.

CHAPTER 9

The motel room atmosphere was nothing like the cannery. We're used to a certain stillness, with the outside world filtered by sturdy brick walls twice as thick as they would be in any residential building. There's no air conditioning, though we don't really miss it until the height of summer—and we make do with a fan.

Here, the thick, midwestern July air smelled like a stale AC unit, which rattled as it labored away at keeping the room clammy. That baseline racket was punctuated by a barking dog and a distant strain of music. But it felt more like camouflage than noise. An auditory smokescreen that let Jacob and me make all those sex-noises we were so intent on wringing from one another without worrying about who might be listening in.

Maybe it was just an annoying habit of mine, this niggling sense that the FPMP might be privy to what we were doing at any given moment. But I wouldn't have discussed Jacob's talent so plainly if I truly thought we were currently under the microscope. Either that or I had a big case of vigilance fatigue.

Jacob's free hand was warm against my skin as it smoothed down my back and settled on my ass. I wasn't in the position to do much fondling, as my hands were currently being used to brace myself above him. But whatever it was I did manage to do—kisses, thrusts, the occasional unfortunate sex-noise—was enough to keep him interested.

While he stroked us both off in one hand, he gripped my ass hard and walked his fingers toward the crack. That manhandling did it for me, despite the fact that if anyone else so much as hints at forcing me to do something, I'm compelled to do the exact opposite. Because I knew it was Jacob. And I trusted him completely.

I came first, pulsing in his grip. Jacob groaned when my jizz anointed his belly, and he stiffened all over beneath me. I clamped my thighs hard around his and crushed our mouths together, joining them to each other as best I could. Not to make us one. We're too different to ever merge into the same being. But to show him how tightly we fit.

Afterward, once I'd slid off to the side and Jacob swabbed himself down with a huge handful of cheap tissues, I threw an arm across him and half-dozed as I basked in the afterglow. It was late, and I'd had one hell of a long day. I was just about to drift off when Jacob said, "Amy Grace must be the key to whatever's going on. Because now that I think about it, I'm positive something felt off, back at the funeral home."

I dragged the covers over us and answered with a grunt. I didn't have the heart to tell him that according to Amy's ka, any hinky sensations we might've experienced back there could be attributed directly to the HVAC system.

Unfortunately, now that I'd finally managed to soothe Jacob's insecurities, my own worries took the opportunity to surge to the forefront. In a town where women were suddenly acting weird, there had to be a connection. Plus, the local mortician could launch her spirit body from her physical. Correlation or causation? Or just one hell of a coincidence?

I'd probably still be blaming it on drugs, if not for the fact that the dog walker we'd talked to directly after the event didn't seem at all high to me. But even though she'd cobbled together some flimsy excuse for her behavior, I wasn't so sure she even remembered taking her top off in a public park. Missing time. Prime possession behavior. And so, reluctantly, I found myself climbing back out of bed and returning to our map of pink highlighter X's.

Jacob came and joined me, fitting himself against my naked back. "I can't sleep," he murmured into my hair. "Why don't we go back to the park and give it another look?"

Might as well, I decided, scratching at my forearm. It wasn't as if I'd get much shut-eye while I was busy ruminating on whatever was happening in Beauchamp.

We threw on some street clothes and headed back to the park. If the roads were quiet before, they were utterly abandoned now in a way that never quite happens in Chicago. We pulled over in the spot where we'd questioned the woman, and I opened up my crown chakra and pulled down white light. "I'm powering up," I told Jacob. "So don't steal my light."

He took a half step back so he didn't brush against my arm and cause my mojo to jump over to him. "Even this." He gave his head a disgusted shake. "Even your white light seems like something I should be able to do. But I try, and nothing happens."

"This again?" Apparently my sexual advances were nowhere near as distracting as I'd given them credit for. "We're wired differently, Jacob, so even if I did have a trick up my sleeve to teach you, it wouldn't do you a whole hell of a lot of good. Try yoga. Try that brain wave app on my phone. Try some mugwort tea or say a prayer or light a candle. Maybe those things will work for you, maybe not. Dumb as it might sound, the thing that seems to make the most difference for me is thinking about the light and trying really hard. And if focus is the main requirement, you've already got that. In spades."

Frankly, our abilities were so different that I wasn't sure he was even capable of powering up. Maybe his only recourse was to grab the white light once my reservoir was full. But since that would leave me a sitting duck in the face of a potential possession, it wasn't something I wanted to try out anytime soon.

Then again, if there was a ghost riding around inside a borrowed body, it wasn't as if we'd find it at the park. The place was totally empty. "We'll check the perimeter," I said, and set out to scan the periphery with big, ground-eating strides. The nighttime air was cooler, but not much, and humidity settled thick against my bare arms and neck. The telltale frosty nip of ghost activity was notably absent.

I double-checked the statue in the center, just to be safe. What better place for a person-shaped apparition to hide than a person-shaped monument? But the bronze figures were quiet and still, though surprisingly modern. I read the plaque: Roy and Marlon Beauchamp. "I thought there were two sons," I said, and Jacob shrugged. Apparently the one who'd lost the family fortune got to preside over the sorry little park in posterity while everyone pretended the slow one didn't exist.

We circled around and came back to the spot where the obnoxious kids had been catcalling the dog walker. Since when had I started thinking of men in their 20s as kids? Maybe it was because that's how Ruth the car rental lady referred to the troublemakers. Or maybe the fact that they had nothing better to do than sit around and be stupid. The picnic table where they'd been loitering had a scattering of empty beer cans around it, and one of the benches had been pulled off. The wooden plank lay to one side, with fresh splinters sticking up from the screw holes.

I considered the vandalism, thinking I wouldn't mind actually being part of the Municipal Police—or whatever it was Ruth had pegged us to be—so I could saddle those dumbasses with some choice community service. Jacob, however, had his mind on matters far less mundane. "I think I feel something."

I snapped out of my tangent and scanned the area for ghosts. Nothing.

"Anywhere in particular?" I asked, hoping that my tone didn't convey that I thought it was likely a case of wishful thinking.

Jacob planted his hands on his hips and looked around. He huffed in frustration.

"You've spent your whole life thinking that psychic abilities were a bunch of hokum—and once you learned otherwise and got tested, that you had no aptitude whatsoever. Sorting out these impulses you've been squelching all this time isn't gonna happen overnight."

Taking a deep breath, Jacob closed his eyes—presumably to count to ten so he didn't bite my head off—but then his scowl of aggravation twisted into confusion.

"What?" I asked.

"It's easier with my eyes shut. Maybe because I don't have visual information competing with the tactile."

He took a tentative step forward. Then another. Then he veered off to one side...and very nearly collided with a trash can. "Stop, Jacob—if you go running around with your eyes closed, you'll just end up face-planting in a pile of dog crap."

Reluctantly, he opened his eyes. "Then what do you suggest?"

If I thought there was really a ghost in the vicinity, I wouldn't dream of doing what I was about to do. But there was clearly no one on this stretch of turdy lawn but Jacob and me. I touched his forearm, and white light zapped him like a nasty case of static. He gasped...then broke into a grin. "Take my arm," I said. "I'll lead you."

Generally, I'd be leery of strolling arm-in-arm through small-town Iowa with my husband even if we weren't on assignment. But Beauchamp had rolled up its sidewalks tight, and there was no one around to see us but the cicadas droning in the trees. And who knows if they even registered us as anything other than moving scenery.

"This way." Jacob tugged, and we veered to the right.

"Slow down," I said. "Tree roots." He let me lead him around the uneven ground, then picked up speed again. We wove through the park diagonally, from one corner to the other. Then onto the sidewalk, pausing to step down the curb and across the street.

"Curb," I said, and Jacob shuffled forward until his toe hit the concrete, and stepped up.

We went on like this, around buildings, across lawns, and up and down a few more curbs. You don't appreciate how many obstacles there are in a three-block walk until you have to point them all out to someone else. But since every time Jacob cracked his eyes open, he second-guessed himself about his impressions, that's what I had to do.

Meanwhile, I did my best not to let on that this "psychic impression" was clearly all a bunch of wishful thinking. Because if there was any ghost action in the vicinity, I'd be the first to know. How long we'd keep wandering around before Jacob called it a night, I had no idea. Hopefully he'd tire himself out eventually.

He paused in front of a dumpy, single-story house with an empty lot on one side and a multi-family building on the other. The neighborhood was old and not particularly well-kept. Maybe this was the "rough" part of town Ruth had been worrying about before. By Chicago standards, it seemed safe enough, just a little run down.

Inside the house, the living room lights were on, glowing through the mini blinds in a striped horizontal pattern, but there was no vehicle parked in the drive. Jacob tugged and we walked toward the building next door, but then changed his mind and led me back. He let go of my arm, opened his eyes, and said, "This house feels...different."

"Okay...but now what? It's past midnight."

"But the lights are on."

That didn't mean anything. Back when we were first dating, I'd only started turning off all the lights at bedtime when Jacob insisted on staying over. "I don't think you can construe lights as an invitation to knock on the door."

Jacob planted his feet at the base of the stairs and glared at the doorknob...or maybe he was trying to turn it with his mind. Unfortunately, unless it was a ghost door—and I sure as shit hoped it wasn't—he was fresh outta luck.

"We'll come back in the morning," I offered, but that suggestion went in one ear and out the other.

"If there's spirit activity we need to know about, it might be history come morning." Before I could reluctantly agree, Jacob was already trying the doorknob.

Luckily, it was locked. Otherwise we'd probably find ourselves on the wrong side of a shotgun. "Cool your jets, Jacob!

Are you trying to get us both killed?"

"There's something here," he ground out. "I can feel it. We can't just do nothing. I'm checking the back door."

"Hold on. Think for a second—we're in our civilian clothes. We'll come off as a couple of home invaders."

His scowl deepened. "We can't just walk away."

Maybe he couldn't. And just as much as he couldn't let it go, I couldn't simply leave him to wake up an irate homeowner and face the music by himself. I scanned the building's crappy façade, hoping that some etheric entity would make itself known so we could do our business and get the hell out of there. But there was nothing.

I pulled down white light to refill whatever reservoirs had spilled into Jacob while we were arm in arm, pitched my voice a little louder, and said, "If there's anyone who needs to get something off their chest here, anyone who needs to set the record straight...now's your chance."

Still nothing.

And now Jacob was looking at the door as if he was seriously considering kicking the damn thing down.

The two-flat next door felt too close for comfort, just across the driveway. Apparently one of its residents agreed. A shrill, yippy bark cut the silence, followed by an aggravated, "Shut up!" This repeated a couple of times, until the owner realized they had no hope of winning this fight and put on some music to drown out the dog.

Letting out a cautious sigh of relief, I crept up the stairs.

The porch was nothing fancy—it would fit maybe a couple of folding chairs, though it was currently empty—and it gave us access to both the front door and the living room window. There was a sticker in the lower corner of the window announcing that the premises was protected by some kind of security service. It's my experience, in shoddy properties like these, that a sticker is usually nothing more than a sticker. Still, the last thing we needed was to draw more attention to ourselves. Did we really want to risk setting off an alarm?

"Jacob." I pointed to the sticker.

He shook his head. "It's fake."

"Maybe."

He turned the full heat of his scrutiny from the sticker to me. "What's the real reason you're so reluctant to check the place out?"

"What do you mean, real reason?"

"It's because I found it, not you. If you'd been the one to sense something here, you wouldn't be so quick to write it off."

Arguing with Jacob is an exercise in futility—even if he's dead wrong, he'll find something to be right about. Like the fact that if I'd been the one who'd seen something hinky, I wouldn't just chalk it up to a false positive. I scanned the building yet again, hoping for something to let me out of the corner he'd just backed me into...and that's when I saw it. Not a ghost. But an alternative to busting through the front door like the freakin' Hulk.

The mini blinds. They were the same type I had in my old apartment—cheap, utilitarian plastic things that gathered dust like nobody's business. Like the blinds in my old apartment, they hung closed. Also like the blinds in my old apartment, a few of the slats were slightly warped. One of them at eye-level, at least for those of us who topped six foot and change.

Jacob was busy gearing up to provide more evidence to support his theory that I didn't really believe in him, but I held up a finger, nodded at the window and said, "Before we go off half-cocked, let's take a look."

I crept up to the window, feeling for creaky floorboards, but the porch only gave off a quiet squeak—definitely no louder than the two of us voicing our differences of opinion. Although the lighting inside was dim, it seemed bright since my eyes were acclimated to the dark. Initially, that brightness was painful. But only for a second. And once my pupils constricted, I made sense of what I was seeing. The living room with its thrift store furniture. Couch and recliner, empty. The television set bathing the vacant room in the flickery, bluish light of a nondescript sitcom. Not a modern TV. An old one. Really old. Not just a tube TV, but a console set. A real doozy of a console, with a hi-fi stereo and record player built in over one speaker and a place for a bar on the other.

But it wasn't just the kitsch value that snagged my attention. It was the heart-thumping, pulse-pounding realization that there'd been one GhosTV still unaccounted for in a safe house in an undisclosed location in the Midwest.

And the possibility that I was looking right at it.

CHAPTER 10

I turned to say something eloquent to Jacob—something along the lines of holy fucking shit on a stick—when instead of Jacob, what I saw was a wall. Cheesy stucco above the chair rail and crappy paneling below.

Somehow, I was in the living room.

Disorientation, like I'd just spun around a few times and suddenly stopped while my equilibrium kept right on going. Had I been possessed? My light wasn't all that high—more of an afterthought, really. Because, let's face it. I really had thought Jacob was leading me on some wild goose chase in his eagerness to take his talent for a spin. And now I was missing time. Dammit.

I backpedaled to put some distance between the TV and me, only to back right through the wall and onto the porch to catch the tail end of a conversation. Jacob saying, "If it means that much to you, we'll get a nightlight."

Who in the hell was he talking to, I wondered...and then I answered. "Forget it—those things only make more shadows. You should give sleeping with the lights on a try. You sleep past sunup all the time, no problem."

It was my voice, anyhow—but I wasn't currently talking. At least, I didn't think I was...until I turned around and saw a tall, gangly guy in my favorite T-shirt and jeans in a heated discussion with my husband, as recognition dawned. Jacob wasn't talking to me. He was talking to my body.

Not only that, but he was lit up like a beacon with thick veins of red energy. Without my physical eyes to distract me, I saw his talent plain as day.

"Jacob!" I said, but my voice came out muted and flat. Maybe he could have heard me, or at least sensed me, had my dumb body not been carrying on.

"You doze off with the bedside lamp on all the time—when you're supposedly 'reading.' It's just a matter of leaving things well enough alone if you happen to wake up."

"Do we really need to get into this right now?"

"Jacob!" I called again. No good. My body was just too distracting.

"I make all kinds of accommodations for you," it claimed. "It's only fair."

I tried to dope-slap myself and my hand passed right through. Not like my body was thin air...more like a set of sheer curtains fluttering in the wind. And for just the briefest moment, I caught the glimmer of an afterimage of my head lagging behind as my physical head nodded, like I'd knocked one of my other subtle bodies out of alignment.

At least hoped it was one of my other subtle bodies, and not a stowaway.

Then again, how would a stowaway know about the lights?

I sidestepped, hoping to line myself up with my body and snap back into the driver seat, but instead I just staggered out the other side. Damn it.

"Where is this all coming from?" Jacob asked, more confused than anything—not surprising, since I usually avoid confrontation at all cost.

"Jacob!" I called out, right in his ear. Nothing. "That's not me!" Frustrated, I tried to jostle him, expecting the same sheer-curtain effect that happened with my body. But the white light he'd stolen from me earlier jolted back to me in a sickening rush.

His red webwork of veins constricted and he swung around, rubbing his shoulder. "I definitely felt something," he said...in a tone that spoke volumes about my obvious lack of belief. "There's something strange going on in this house."

"Oh, you don't know the half of it," I said, while my body scratched vigorously at the back of my left wrist. "And quit that," I snapped at my physical shell. "You'll just make it worse."

At least I could see there wasn't a habit demon to blame. Just the firing of my itch-neurons and my own lack of self-control.

Jacob stepped around my body, careful not to touch it, and tried to peek through the blinds. His ka didn't fall through the wall like mine had—too firmly anchored in his physicality to just spill out willy-nilly. He stared for a moment, struggling like he could hardly believe his eyes...then said, "Vic...is that the...?"

And my spirit snapped back into my physical body with a sickening lurch as the GhosTV went black.

✢ ✢ ✢

All in all, I'd say Jacob took the news pretty well that my ghost fell out and he'd been holding a conversation with only my body. At least that's how I chose to interpret the stunned silence as we walked back to the rental car.

We climbed in, but instead of turning over the ignition, he just stared at the dash...and I had to wonder if maybe my talent had finally proven to be too damn weird for him after all. "Look, Jacob, if it's any consolation—I really am okay with sleeping in the dark."

He looked at me like I'd just sprouted a second head...and hopefully I hadn't, since it was a distinct possibility that one of my subtle bodies was still sticking out somewhere.

"Vic—how is the TV here?"

"We knew there was still a GhosTV floating around somewhere." I struggled to think it all through. "What I'm more worried about is...why is the thing playing?"

Master strategizer that he was, Jacob had already come up with a half dozen ways we were fucked. "Maybe Jennifer Chance had more allies than we knew about—and they're carrying on her work. Or maybe she left documentation behind, and someone discovered it—someone just as twisted as her. Or maybe she's figured out how to claw her way back through the veil...and she's using someone here in Beauchamp like she used Richie."

"Or maybe the final GhosTV just sat here gathering dust for a couple of years until someone randomly turned it on."

I could tell Jacob liked my theory the least, but he was kind enough not to say, And maybe the moon really is made of cheese. "The question is, what are we gonna do about it?"

"Well, we can't just leave it here." Clearly it was the reason for the striptease action—I wasn't sure how or why, but no way in hell were they not connected. "It's not safe. But if we commandeer it somehow, then what? Dr. K and Garcia might notice if we try to sneak it into the trunk come Monday morning."

"Hold on. You want to take it?"

I looked at him hard, sizing him up. "You don't?"

"People died for the GhosTVs. Chance came back from the dead to defend them. And neither of us can afford to be on

National's radar."

Here's the thing. Every point he made was a hundred percent true. And back when I had a GhosTV in my possession, I'd hidden the damn thing under the basement stairs and utterly ignored it when I should have been trying to figure out how it worked and what it could actually do.

I never thought I'd get another chance. But there we were.

"We can't just leave it where it is," I said. "It's making too many waves."

He grunted. I chose to take that as an agreement.

I added, "If we were to bring it home with us...F-Pimp doesn't need to know."

"Vic." Jacob said my name in that way he does when he thinks I'm being phenomenally dense. "What are you saying?"

"Only that it sounds like you wanna take it out of the equation for good—but I don't think we should be so quick to do something that can't possibly be undone. That's all."

Jacob flexed his grip on the steering wheel a few times and worked his jaw.

"Listen," I said. "Our ride won't be here until the day after tomorrow. That's a hell of a lot longer than we usually get to make a decision. Let's not squander that time."

Logical words, but I wasn't fooling anyone. I just wanted to bring Jacob around to my way of thinking.

"Fine," he said evenly. "We'll sleep on it."

And no doubt Jacob was planning the exact same thing as me.

Unfortunately, there wasn't much sleeping involved. And not for any PG-13 reasons, either. Strange room, strange bed—and yeah, I really would've been a lot more comfortable with the damn lights on. My brain kept looping on the thought that I'd wasted my opportunity with the last GhosTV and I couldn't bring myself to piss away a second chance.

Given the way Jacob kept rolling over, sighing, and rolling back, he wasn't getting much shut-eye either. But somehow we both must've slept for at least a few hours. He snorted awake when the whine of a vacuum cleaner intruded from the hall, which startled me into wakefulness right along with him.

We both climbed out of bed, silent and pensive, and I tried to blast some wakefulness into myself in the shower while Jacob paced the room like a caged panther. He cornered me, still damp in the bathroom doorway, and said, "We need to get rid of it."

"Jacob—"

"Like we did with Kamal's journal. Bust it up in a bunch of small pieces and scatter them throughout every dumpster in the city. Because otherwise it'll end up falling into the wrong hands."

I gave the back of my hand a final, damp chafe with the rough terrycloth and flung the towel over the shower rod. "If National hasn't found it by now, who's to say they're even looking? When you think about it, right now we're in an ideal position to grab the thing and stow it somewhere safe. We could drive to Chicago, dump it off somewhere, and be back before nightfall, no problem."

"Not with the rental car. They keep track of the mileage—and don't tell me Laura wouldn't notice an extra five hundred miles on the expense report."

I considered renting a second car—if the rental joint was even open on Sunday. But now that Jacob mentioned that thing about the mileage, I wasn't so sure it was a good idea. For all we knew, one of the random coworkers we glimpsed back in the

FPMP lunchroom from across the salad bar could be scrutiniz-
ing all our personal credit card purchases as a matter of course.

Thinking out loud, I said, "We could let it sit for a couple of
weeks and come back for it. Find a way to handle everything
in cash so we leave a minimal paper trail."

Jacob gave me the side-eye. "You'd be willing to just walk
away from the TV?"

"For a couple of weeks," I repeated.

He actually considered my suggestion. Probably because he
was confident that in the course of those couple of weeks, he
could wear me down and get me to change my mind.

But two could play at that game. After all, hadn't I talked
him into picking up his own damn socks? Sure, it took me
two years—and resulted in a lot of perfectly good socks being
"accidentally" thrown in the trash. But I got my way in the end.

Jacob rounded the beds and approached me, reaching for
my hand. He stopped just short of taking it. "Is it okay if I
touch you?"

Why wouldn't it be, I wondered—it's not as if I expected us to
always agree on everything. And then I realized that he didn't
want to steal my light (for once) and I wasn't even juiced up. I
grabbed his hand instead.

He squeezed my fingers earnestly. "First things first. Can we
both agree that we need to get our hands on that TV?"

I knew those big, dark doe-eyes he was giving me couldn't
be trusted, since Jacob is a master at bulldozing anyone and
anything to get what he wants. But regardless of what we ulti-
mately decided to do with the TV, it wasn't as if we could just
leave an entire town exposed to its effects. "Fine. We grab the
TV and then we'll figure out our next step."

Jacob frowned harder. "We can't just march up to the door.

Maybe Roger Burke and Jeffrey Allen Scott weren't the only ones who bought into Jennifer Chance's whole scheme. What if whoever lives there now is another one of her people?"

You'd think any "people" she might've had would scatter once she dropped off the radar. Especially with Roger's very public murder. Then again, fearing for your life is a pretty plausible reason to lie low. "If someone's backed into a corner, maybe they'd jump at a chance for amnesty."

"You think Laura would go for it?"

Laura might be a soft touch when it came to GoFundMe campaigns and endangered animal charities, but she always erred on the side of caution wherever Jennifer Chance was concerned. "Yeah...maybe not." Plus, bringing Laura into the loop would inevitably lead back to National somewhere down the line. "Still, we can't come up with a game plan until we figure out who lives there." I gestured vaguely with my phone. "Without using F-Pimp resources they can track. That should be fun."

Jacob sat on the bed and scrubbed at his face. "Even the computer downstairs in the business center isn't safe. Maybe the office isn't actively monitoring what we're doing now, but if they have any reason at all to do it retroactively, our searches will be an open book."

"We could always make up some bullshit excuse as to why we wanted that info...." But I supposed you never knew when a telepath might be privy to your interview. And while Jacob was impervious to that sort of scrutiny, I wasn't. I couldn't live with myself if I went down for some cockamamie scheme and took him down with me.

In the end, the only thing we could think of that wouldn't leave an incriminating electronic trail behind was a plain, old-fashioned stakeout. We donned our suits, then loaded up on coffee and danishes from the so-called continental break-fast. Jacob also insisted on taking a couple of oranges. Call me a purist, but a stakeout's not a stakeout unless you're eating something blatantly unhealthy. Besides, who has time to fiddle around peeling oranges?

I guess it was a rhetorical question, as Jacob was too amped up to actually eat, whereas I'd developed the skill of shoving stuff down my maw without even registering that I was eating. Though as I plowed through the danishes, I had to wonder if it was actually me chewing and swallowing, or just my physical body, driven by the brain stem and running on autopilot.

The residential street was Sunday morning small-town quiet. It was muggy and the sun was high, but since we could pay for gas with cash if it seemed like we'd burned through an inor-dinate amount, we sat with the engine running and the AC on. Still, being hyperaware of our every move was giving me worse heartburn than a dried-out danish.

We'd been sitting there for the better part of an hour when finally Jacob said, "I'm only trying to look out for you."

"How so?" I said cautiously.

He dropped his hand to mine and gave it a squeeze, hard enough that my wedding band dug into my finger bone. "I worry what National would do if they ever got serious about testing out the GhosTVs. We've both watched them make the TVs disappear. What if the next thing that goes missing is you?"

Even after tossing and turning all night and baking in the sun all morning, Jacob looked fresh-pressed and put together, sharp and formidable. His wide shoulders filled out his black suit in all right places, and his intelligent eyes didn't miss a trick.

Jacob always comes off so capable, so competent, so

unshakeable. I hardly know what to do when he tells me something's gnawing at him.

I considered how openly we could actually speak, and decided that unless National sent someone out before us to bug all the rental cars in Beauchamp, this was as good a place to talk as any. "If National wanted me, they would've grabbed me by now."

Frankly, I was more concerned about Jacob. If they knew about the red energy at his command—whatever it did—I worried they'd slap him under a microscope. The rest of his family, too.

I said, "Whatever we decide to do, I want it to be on our terms."

He gave me a dark-eyed look so scorching I'm surprised it didn't melt my boxers off. "Always."

Jacob could be distracting, no doubt—but when someone finally did amble down that empty street, I couldn't help but notice. Especially since he noticed us, too.

The middle-aged Caucasian guy had a perpetual squint despite the baseball cap shading his eyes, and his skin was dark and leathery from too much time in the sun. He rapped on the window and said, "Ya looking for somebody?"

Geez. How obvious could we be? But given the newspaper bag slung over his shoulder, maybe he could tell us a thing or two—without leaving an electronic trail behind.

"Just hoping to get in touch with whoever lives here." Jacob nodded toward the house.

The guy followed his gaze. "Nobody lives there."

I stared stupidly at the house that was supposedly vacant. "But their TV was on last night."

"Must've been another place," the guy said.

"No," I insisted. "It was here."

With a shrug, the guy said, "Couldn'ta been. No one's lived there since Harris Tucker blew his brains out at the kitchen table."

CHAPTER 11

As my stomach bottomed out, squeezing painfully at half-chewed danish, the newspaper guy gazed at the GhosTV house and rambled on. "Yeah. Must've been twenty years ago now. My sister owns a housecleaning business but she couldn't bring herself to do the cleanup. The bank offered good money, too. Prob'ly not as much as they ended up paying some specialist from Des Moines—but eight, ten times what she'd normally get."

"Why the bank?" Jacob asked.

"Family didn't want it, I suppose."

"So who owns the property now?"

"No idea." The guy scratched his armpit philosophically. "All I know is that if you're looking for Harris, you're shit outta luck."

We watched the guy make his way down the block, flinging newspapers in the general direction of a few porches, until he turned the corner and was gone.

"The GhosTV was on last night," I said. "Even if I hallucinated the part about seeing through the wall, there was definitely light coming through the mini blinds when we got here."

Jacob nodded once. "I saw it, too. And then it turned off." We both shivered. "Is it possible a spirit can control the TV?"

Poltergeists are staples of old horror movies, but as far as I knew, that's all they were. Fiction. I'd encountered plenty of ghosts since that fateful day I saw the bus crash, but I'd never run across any that could move physical matter.

Unfortunately, there's a first time for everything.

I said, "Whether or not Harris Tucker can spin the TV dial himself, no way is it just a coincidence that a suicide and a GhosTV are right in the middle of a town where weird shit's going down."

Jacob didn't argue. "They must be connected."

"Fat chance figuring out how without letting the office know about it. We can't even do a freaking web search without tipping our hand."

"Maybe not...but it's a small town. People talk."

"Fine." I nodded toward the end of the block where the paperboy had ambled off. "Then let's go put the thumbscrews to that witness and see what else he knows."

Easier said than done. When we turned onto the next street, the guy was nowhere to be seen. We'd stumbled on the small commercial district of Mom-and-Pop shops abutting the park, places I might poke through on a lazy weekend morning, if I wasn't on assignment from the FPMP, and the town wasn't likely haunted. "So much for your small town," I said. "Our guy could be anywhere. How do we know where to...start?"

Before I was even done complaining, my eyes fell on the lettering stretched across a nearby awning: Tucker Books. As in, Harris Tucker. The suicide.

Jacob didn't gloat. As far as he was concerned, being right was its own reward.

We headed into the shop. It was stuffed to the rafters with used paperbacks, most of them older than me, with the cheap wood pulp paper so yellowed it was more like orange. First impression? Good luck spotting a ghost among the visual cacophony.

But that concern was quickly obliterated by the urgent need to sneeze.

Normally, I'd get it over with and let it rip. But normally I'm not within range of a GhosTV that can turn itself on and off—a GhosTV that's left my subtle bodies loose and sloppy.

I clenched up, not that I thought my spirit could fly out my ass, more like a reflex. And I squinted hard, as if that might do something to ward off the sneeze.

"There's no public toilet here," said a voice that was just as dusty as the shelves.

A wrinkled guy with a huge shock of white hair, plaid shirt, suspenders and dungarees shuffled out from the back, challenging our right to browse his crumbling wares.

Jacob didn't miss a beat. "Actually, I was looking for someone and noticed the name on the awning." The old guy went slightly less leery, and Jacob said, "Tucker Harris."

It must be habit that makes Jacob say things that are somehow technically true while still being bald-faced lies. If there'd ever been another telepathic lie detector like Carolyn, I'd never met 'em. But I supposed it didn't hurt for him to keep in practice.

Lie, truth or something in between, the statement still hit the old guy like a smack in the head. He flinched—evidence enough that he knew Tucker—and Jacob swooped in to finesse the conversation in the direction he wanted it to take.

"He probably won't remember helping me out." Probably not, given that they'd never met. "It was years ago—I must've been in grad school. Ran out of gas out in the middle of nowhere." Something that could have really happened at some point,

given the vagueness of the claim. He shrugged his most charm-
ing and self-deprecating shrug. "Is he around?"

The old man's shoulders slumped. "You're twenty years too
late. Tucker's passed."

While I blinked back the looming sneeze more forcefully,
Jacob pretended to digest the information as if it came as a
surprise. "I'm sorry for your loss."

"It was a long time ago," the old man said, though his resignation was still tinged with sadness.

Instead of prompting the man, Jacob picked up a thriller
from the counter, turned it over and read the back cover—
though even he would admit they're all pretty much the same.
He then slid it toward the cash register, further greasing the
wheels. And as he rang up the purchase—whoa, seriously, ten
bucks for that beat-up thing?—the old man spoke again. "That's
how he was. Always trying to help people."

"And look where it got him," snapped another voice from the
back room. An old woman lingered at the threshold, as dusty
and faded as the shop, as him. She hugged a thin cardigan
around her shoulders despite the oppressive August mugginess.

Thankfully, I wasn't the only one who could see her.

"What do you mean?" Jacob asked—as if he didn't already
know.

The woman sniffed a humorless laugh. "If Harris wanted to
help people, he should've been a plumber."

"Virginia," the old man chided, but without much force. I had
the sense that this argument was nothing new.

"Or an electrician. Or a mechanic. Anything but what he was."

With a sigh, the old man said, "Or anywhere but here."

Virginia added, "Why anyone would want to be a cop, I'll
never know. If the scumbags don't kill you, the stress will."

Huh.

"I'm so sorry," Jacob said gently. "What happened?"

He must've hit just the right tone. The man's eyes went soft in that way they do when people turn inward to focus on their memories. "Our son.... He cared too much—that's what happened. Some people just can't be helped, but Tucker, well...he had to try."

"Did he?" the mother asked bitterly. "Those women at the truck stop, going from rig to rig, selling themselves for drug money—there is no helping someone like that. They're like weeds. Pull out one and before you know it another one fills in the gap like it wasn't even there. Tucker had a headful of ideas from some psychology class about rehabilitation, when what he should've done was lock 'em up and throw away the key!"

"Virginia," the father said, with the weariness of someone who was tired of revisiting the same damn argument, one that no one stood any chance of winning.

"He was even involved with one of them," she spat. "Though at least she had the common sense not to come sniffing around his funeral looking for money. If I ever find Rosa—if that even is the whore's real name—she'll be sorry."

And with that, she stomped off into the back room.

Her husband watched her go, and when the footsteps receded, he said, "Tell Rosa I'm sorry—that's what the note said. Not Mom and Dad. Just Rosa. If only the jackasses he worked with hadn't gone and blabbed about her being a prostitute, we never woulda known. His mother wouldn't have to live with the whole...." He waved a hand helplessly.

"Where is Rosa now?" Jacob asked, the picture of sympathy, using his tone, his looks, his charisma to keep on pressing for more details.

"No idea. Probably for the best she never showed her face."

It was clearly a painful topic, but Jacob wanted to keep probing. Maybe the old man would have let him. But when I abruptly shoved my forearm into Jacob's hand and said, "Hold on," the spell was broken. The fact that I then sneezed hard enough to flutter the calendar on the wall didn't help, either. But at least we escaped from the situation with my subtle bodies all intact.

CHAPTER 12

"Look at it this way," Jacob told me. "People don't like talking about suicides. And chances are we understand Harris Tucker better than his own parents do."

Maybe so. He wouldn't be the first cop I've known to take the brutal way out. Clenching hard, I blew my nose, sneezed again, and blew it one more time for good measure. The white sedan hit me with cool, filtered air that smelled like new car, and I turned my head toward the vent, hoping to flush out whatever particulate I'd inhaled in the bookshop. "Still—suicides are sticky. Maybe after Tucker pulled the trigger he changed his mind."

"And what?" Jacob asked. "Came back to solve one last case?"

"Weirder things have happened." Especially with a GhosTV involved.

"Maybe I'd buy that theory," Jacob said. "But how does it connect to the stripping?"

What if Tucker had more nefarious reasons for keeping an eye on the local working girls? And what if now he was...what? Haunting women until they stripped for him?

I frowned. "No idea."

"Here's what I think," Jacob said. "Chance and Burke planted that GhosTV in a known suicide house so that when they finally found a medium, they'd be able to run their tests. The question is, if that place is empty, who's turning it on?"

Without waiting to see if I was on the same page, Jacob pulled a U-turn, heading back toward the GhosTV.

We pulled up to the curb and I peered through the windshield to take a better look at the house. Tall weeds poked up from cracks in the driveway, and they looked like they hadn't been disturbed in quite some time. "No cars." The paint was peeling and there were dozens of wispy trees sprouting up in the gutters. "And if someone does live here, they aren't big on maintenance."

Jacob drummed his fingers on the steering wheel. "If we were looking into this place under the auspices of the FPMP, we'd have years of official records on our phones in ten minutes flat. But doing it ourselves? Without a computer? On a Sunday?" He shook his head in disgust.

"We were both cops, once. That's gotta count for something." Though other than a really firm door-knock, I wasn't sure what.

"Even if we were still on the force, we're not only out of our jurisdiction...we're out of state. If we were cops, maybe we could expect some professional courtesy. Now, though...." Jacob shrugged helplessly. "But the fact that most people don't even know what the FPMP is? Not helping."

True. Not to mention the fact that if we dragged in the local PD in any official capacity, we might as well send F-Pimp National an engraved invitation to come see what we were up to.

But there was one thing we did have from all our time on the force that we hadn't surrendered with our titles and our badges—and that was our connections.

Bob Zigler had seen some shit in our time together at the Fifth—shit most people only see in horror movies. He wasn't quite the same after the whole zombie basement debacle...but when Carolyn was recruited by the Fifth Precinct, he decided to stick around to be her Stiff. Must've been refreshing to have a partner who always told the truth. Even if she did wield it like a baseball bat.

"It would be perfectly normal to call Zig on my cell," I said. "Right?"

Jacob cut his eyes to my phone. "He's an official PsyCop Stiff. He's probably being monitored." For his own "protection," no doubt. "But I did see a pay phone at the truck stop."

The Filling Station was doing brisk business by the time we got there, with its lot full of cars with out-of-state plates and a small line waiting for the women's restroom. It was overly bright inside, with fish-eye mirrors mounted every few feet on the ceiling to ensure no one would shoplift a Twinkie or a Slim Jim. The pay phone was mounted on the wall between the beer cooler and the showers. Thankfully, it was still in service.

Pay phones nowadays take debit cards, unlike the phones of my misspent youth—but swiping a card through the reader would obviously negate our whole attempt to stay off the radar. The checkout clerk was less than thrilled about providing me with quarters, but since I bought a pack of gum, she grudgingly acquiesced.

I headed over to the phone with my handful of change. Jacob positioned himself to block me from the overhead camera while I pulled up Zigler's phone number from my contacts and poised myself to punch it in the other phone. "Two dollars just to connect?" I said. Not that I expected it to still cost a dime. But jeez, talk about inflation.

My quarters disappeared into the slot, one after another, dropping into the phone with eight metallic clinks, and I put in Zig's number. The act of dialing a number felt just as foreign as feeding cash money into the phone, and I found myself second-guessing my ability to key it in correctly.

But just as I started to worry not only if I'd hit the right buttons, but whether or not he'd even pick up a random out-of-state call, he answered with a curt, "Zigler," and my shoulders unhitched. Because Zig was a smart guy. And if anyone could help us out, it was him. Zig was a cop. And police databases are pretty forgiving. Plug in what little you do know—names, aliases, part of an address—and you can dredge up a good list of potential targets.

Easy peasy...if you're in the right jurisdiction.

"It's me," I said unceremoniously. "I was hoping you might have a connection who can find out if a property is vacant or not."

"Okay."

"In Iowa."

"You'd need a federal database for that." He was keeping his tone neutral. Even so, I thought I heard, And you're the fed, not me.

"Maybe you know someone," I suggested. "What about McGuire? Didn't he move to Iowa?"

"St. Louis." Iowa, Missouri. Same difference. "As much as I probably don't want to know what you're up to, I hope you're not gonna do anything stupid."

"Who, me?"

"Because you wouldn't have called if you're not desperate."

"Desperate is a pretty strong word."

The sound quality on the line changed, and my heart skipped

a few beats as I wondered if the whole pay phone system was under F-Pimp surveillance too. Then an electronic woman's voice said, "Please deposit fifty cents for the next two minutes."

I fed in the quarters and told my stomach to stop doing flip-flops. Zigler was still talking. "Investigating a property that might or might not be vacant...tell me you're not considering a B&E."

"That's a pretty big leap of logic," I said, annoyed that he'd managed to zero in on my only idea pretty much immediately.

Zigler went on to tell me exactly what he thought of my investigative technique. Working with Carolyn must've rubbed off on him...and apparently, I liked him a lot better when he wasn't so direct. He criticized my impulsiveness, my caginess, and my inability to color inside the lines—then summed it all up with, "Even if you could drum up some probable cause, you're not a cop anymore. Get caught, find yourself on the wrong side of a badge, and then what? Not to mention how easy it would be for a squatter to whip out a gun and put a hole in you."

"Forget I even asked," I said, as the electronic lady came back on and repeated, Please deposit fifty cents for the next two minutes as a random quarter pinged to the floor. I had enough quarters to attempt to defend myself for at least another four minutes, maybe six if the runaway hadn't rolled too far...but what was the point? "I'm going now," I said, and hung up.

I'll say one thing for an old-fashioned telephone handset. They're really satisfying to smack down into the cradle.

Jacob didn't need to be a detective to deduce I'd struck out with Bob Zigler. He tilted his head toward the diner portion of the truck stop and said, "Come on, let's get some real food in us before church lets out."

You know Jacob's got stuff on his mind when you order a bacon double cheeseburger with extra fries and he doesn't remark on the sodium or cholesterol. As for me, I had plenty to think about myself. Because if my ex-partner found me that predictable, the behavior experts at the FPMP must be having a field day with me.

Maybe I had no business trying to outmaneuver Big Brother. It wasn't as if I was perceptive or analytical, or even particularly clever. Talking to ghosts was all I've ever been good at—but I wasn't particularly eager for Harris Tucker to try and bump me out of my own skin. Especially when the GhosTV had me falling out already without anyone else's ghostly encouragement.

As I was trailing my last french fry through the remaining dregs of ketchup on the plate, our server—same one from the night before—came by to warm up our coffee. She was a sturdy, forty-something Caucasian woman in a Filling Station baseball cap and a green polyester apron with a name tag proclaiming her to be Kathleen. A few buttons were pinned around her name tag, the type of flash that used to mainly have bands on them. But hers were custom jobs showing a trio of smiling kids and a golden retriever.

"Can I get you fellas some dessert?" Kathleen asked. "Cobbler of the day is blackberry."

"I'm all set," Jacob said distractedly.

Last night's peach cobbler had been fairly underwhelming... but the fact that she remembered our order however many hours later definitely piqued my interest. I've never worked in foodservice, so I can only imagine how much brainpower it must take to make the right order show up at the right table before it congealed into a cold lump. Your average person doesn't take much note of details, something that becomes clear when you take statements from witnesses that describe the same person as "short...or maybe tall" and ranging in age from twentyish to 65.

But every once in a while, you'll strike gold and run into someone observant, like Kathleen.

"What else is on the dessert menu?" I asked, mainly to keep her talking.

"Apple pie, cherry pie, rhubarb custard and lemon meringue. Donuts—cream filled or jelly. Cinnamon rolls. Pumpkin bars. Cake—chocolate or vanilla. And soft serve ice cream, though it can't hold a candle to the ice cream stand by the park."

I considered asking more about the pie, but we were on a strict deadline. "Say, you really seem to know your way around Beauchamp."

"Lived here all my life," she said with an easy shrug.

"So you know about all the...stuff...going on." Smooth.

"Commercial company?" she said. "Forty-sixty-eighty."

Cops throw around codes all the time, and in my lingo, four-sixty is simple battery. Which I'm pretty sure she wasn't talking about. At all. I must've looked as confused as I felt, because Jacob was quick to say, "We'll just take the check."

But I wasn't done talking yet. People who actually pay attention to their surroundings are few and far between. "Hold on—before you ring us up...how well do you know Baker Street?"

Kathleen's look turned guarded. "Well enough, I suppose. Like I said. Born and bred."

"There's a property there next to a vacant lot, looks to be abandoned." Could I pass myself off as someone hoping to make a real estate deal? With the suit—maybe.

Unfortunately, Kathleen was no longer interested in chatting. "Sorry. Can't help you. Have a nice day." She slapped a check down on the table and hurried into the kitchen, leaving the door swinging forlornly on its two-way hinge behind her.

Jacob leaned in, lowered his voice, and said, "She just propositioned you. Forty-sixty-eighty is the cost for oral, intercourse, or both."

Which made it phenomenally creepy that I followed up her invitation by bringing up the suicide house. "Who knew your Twelfth Precinct experience would come in handy today?" I said, doing my best to shake off how spectacularly I'd just botched contact with that potential witness. I grabbed the check off the table and said, "I was too full for cobbler anyhow."

CHAPTER 13

While Jacob hit the little boys' room, I headed over to settle our bill, hoping the middle-aged guy at the register wouldn't offer me any more trucker codes to completely misinterpret. Although "was everything all right?" sounded innocent enough, even through my now self-conscious ears.

As I scrawled a signature on my credit card receipt (totally overthinking the tip) I replayed the exchange that had just taken place. Kathleen hardly looked like the sort of person who'd give a BJ to a passing trucker, but looks can be deceiving. No judgment on my part—my past had its own fair share of anonymous hookups. But it was a risky game she was playing. Sex workers went missing every day. Most of the time, no one ever went looking for them, either. Though thinking back to the flair on her apron, she did have family. Not that it would be any help if some sicko left her dead in a ditch.

And speaking of family—I thought a wedding band was supposed to protect me from getting propositioned. Though, to be fair, the sort of guy who'd solicit a hookup at a truck stop probably wouldn't much care whether he was married or not. He wouldn't be looking for a relationship, just ten minutes of fun.

The guy handed back my copy of the receipt and I stuffed it in my pocket, still annoyed with myself for screwing up my chances with Kathleen, when I turned around and nearly tripped over the person standing behind me: the woman from the car rental place.

"Well, if it isn't my friend from Public Management!"

Ruth was resplendently middle-aged in a stars and stripes top, white pedal pushers, and sparkly gold flip flops...and she seemed awfully glad to see me. Hopefully she wasn't about to offer me a four-sixty. "Yup. Here I am. With my partner. Eating food. And, uh, paying for it."

She eased up closer. I managed a half-step back before the corner of the cash register counter prodded me in the kidney. "Any headway on those properties? My friend Jan said the music was so loud last night she could hear it even with the windows shut and the AC running. She called in a noise complaint—and they said they'd get to it. But they never do."

"Anyways. I'm on the clock, so I'd better get going." I headed out toward the car, walking quickly with extra-long strides, then had to wait there for nearly two minutes while Jacob figured out where I was.

"What was that all about?" he asked.

"The usual. Our buddy Ruth making sure we take care of the neighborhood hooligans."

Jacob beeped open the locks. "Why is it we keep running into her?"

"In a town of what, a couple thousand people?" I shrugged. "It's lunchtime now, and like you pointed out, there are all of two restaurants."

"I suppose." Jacob started the car and the AC blew hot for a few seconds, then cool. "Now what?"

I wouldn't go so far as to say that by warning me not to do anything stupid, Zigler inspired me to case the joint, and perhaps see if the back door happened to be open—maybe with a bit of assistance from me. Risky? Sure. But we were running out of time. Between our suits and our I.D.s, we could drum up some kind of official-sounding reason for what we were doing. Besides, if no one lived in the GhosTV house, (as everyone claimed) it wasn't as if we'd be interrupting anyone's Sunday brunch.

Luckily for me, my husband was down with the plan—probably because he was hoping to use brute force on more than just the back door. But we would cross that bridge when we came to it. Hopefully without Jacob smashing that bridge—and the TV—to smithereens.

When we got to the house, I kept hold of the crowbar—just to be safe.

Since lurking around looking shady would only draw more attention to what we were doing, Jacob and I strode up to the house like we were perfectly entitled to be there. All that was missing was a clipboard—though we decided that the guy at the motel's business center was unlikely to lend us his, since we'd already made off with his tape.

By day, the property looked more abandoned than it had the night before. Spiderwebs hung between most of the porch spindles, heavy with dandelion fluff and insect husks. Thin tendrils of climbing weeds wound around the gutters and the handrails by the steps. And there was a patina of dust on all the windows—not to mention the fact that they were all closed, with the weather in the low eighties and no air conditioner in sight.

It was quiet. Then again, all of Beauchamp was quiet

compared to Chicago. Even our residential neighborhood had an auditory backdrop of angry traffic, thudding music, and the occasional gunshot. Here, the noisiest thing going on was birds chirping in the trees overhead, some raucous kids playing Wiffle Ball a couple of blocks away, and the whistle of a train passing somewhere in the distance.

Idyllic. If not for the fact that we were casing a suicide house with a GhosTV inside.

A big part of the job involves acting like you belong wherever it is you need to go. Despite the fact that I hadn't procured a clipboard, I strode confidently up the drive. The tire iron was clamped under my arm beneath my jacket, but I doubted anyone would notice. It balanced the shoulder holster on my other side.

Behind the house, we found an overgrown yard devoid of lawn furniture and a back deck that was sun-faded and peeling. It felt empty and isolated.

A good spot to break into a house. Unfortunately, judging by the massive reinforced deadbolt on the back door, we weren't the only ones who thought so. Jacob planted his hands on his hips and glared at it. "That's not going anywhere. We'd need a battering ram to break this door down."

I mirrored his stance and craned my neck to take in the crappy little house. I wouldn't normally advocate crawling in through one of the windows, but without the owner, it was either that or a locksmith.

The kitchen window was too high up to crawl through without a ladder, but I could just peer in if I stood on tiptoe. Other than blue gingham curtains, there wasn't much to see…until I staggered forward and found myself sprawled on a linoleum floor.

I was disoriented, but only for a couple of seconds this time. (Though hopefully "falling out of my body" wasn't something I'd ever really get used to.) Sound came from beyond the kitchen door and I crept out carefully, trying not to overthink that fact that creeping was entirely unnecessary, given the fact that sports commentary was blasting from the living room... and my ghost-feet were barely touching the ground.

No suicide cop—not exactly sure how I felt about that, but didn't want to dwell on it. As for the house? Minimal furniture. A card table and some folding chairs in the kitchen, and the thrift store couch and recliner in the living room. That, and a GhosTV so big it needed its own zip code.

It's been a day full of ups and downs on the green, and now it all comes down to one final putt...

I'll say one thing about the massive console—those speakers sure packed a punch. The tone was calm and sedate—golf seems designed to put people to sleep—but the volume was cranked high. I supposed it wouldn't be the first time Jennifer Chance picked a weird tape to play. She'd needed to camouflage the fact that the tuner no longer received a broadcast signal. The set she'd exposed me to back during the whole kidnapping fiasco had been playing basketball in October.

Maybe I could have just floated into the room, but just because I was taking one of my subtle bodies out for a spin, it didn't mean I actually thought of myself as a spirit. And if the GhosTV was playing, there was always the possibility that whoever was watching it could actually see me. I dithered at the living room threshold for a moment, second-guessing the wisdom behind coming back to this house in the first place.

A commercial for car insurance came on, way louder than the sedate golf-announcer. Still couldn't see who'd turned on the TV. Hopefully, though, if they tried to exorcise me, I'd snap back into my physical body instead of blundering across the veil. Though I was in such uncharted territory, there were no guarantees.

Back to the wall, I sidled my way into the room with my entire nonphysical body clenched up tight, begging I wouldn't be spotted, while dreading the possibility of finding someone looking right at me. But when I turned the corner, the room was empty.

Relief. But I wasn't about to tempt fate.

The house was small, just the single story—one bedroom, maybe two if they were small. But not having the lay of the land, I didn't know if the three doors I spotted led to a closet, a crawlspace, a bedroom or a bath. And whoever'd turned on that TV could be behind any one of them.

Another ad came on, startlingly loud: Sunday! Sunday! Sunday! Monster truck rally! Get your tickets while there's still time! It was Sunday, I realized. And the date flashing on the screen was today's date.

How was it playing an actual broadcast? Hadn't those particular TV guts been repurposed to play the ghost channel?

I needed to get a better look at that TV, though first I'd obviously need to figure out who else was in the house besides me. I tried a door—or at least attempted to. My hand went through the knob. But when I tried to stick my head through it and peek inside, I overthought everything and just ended up mashing my face against the wood. I'd often wondered why spirits didn't fall through the floor and keep going until they reached the center of the earth. Maybe this was why. They were bound to some sort of baffling ghost physics. Either that or the limitations of their own thoughts.

I tried the doorknob again, focusing harder now on turning it, and still, my hand sailed right through. Maybe I'd better not think too hard about why I wasn't falling through the floor, I decided. I might end up in China.

Meanwhile, the TV chattered away. Ask your doctor about Provalica today! Side effects include dry mouth, constipation, weight gain, rash, and suicidal thoughts....

I sniffed the door. No smell—and the house was old and dusty enough that there should have been one, however faint. Why did some of my senses work, but not others? It's not like I had physical eyes or ears, but I could see and hear what was going on around me just fine.

I shoved against the wall again, remembering what it felt like when I'd been astral projecting back at PsyTrain. I'd been able to fly around and pass through walls. But my astral body felt different, floaty and a little buzzy. Whichever subtle body this might be—my ka, for lack of a better word—it felt a lot more like business as usual. Except when I tried to move something and had no effect on it whatsoever.

My hands looked solid enough to me unless they were passing through the doorknob. No mirrors, so I wasn't sure if I was visible. Then again, when this happened before back on the front porch, Jacob felt the zap, but he hadn't been able to see me. So hopefully I'd be invisible to any of Jennifer Chance's minions.

Hopefully.

Keeping one eye on the door, I sidled over to the TV. It had seemed hefty when I'd peered at it through the window, but now? It was utterly gigantic. The console was a chunky wooden monstrosity, walnut with gold acoustic fabric covering the speaker panels. The tube itself was small by today's standards, maybe thirty-two inches. But no doubt it weighed more than every set in our house put together.

I prodded at the cabinet, and again, my hand passed through. Though I did get a little tingle off my proximity to the tube. When I was a kid, I got a kick out of feeling the static when our old living room set warmed up. Maybe, with my subtle bodies rattling around loose inside me, I felt that kind of thing more than your average person.

The golf game flashed up on the screen, showing a closeup of a white guy putting, a commentator remarking on it, and a bunch of stats in the lower third. Again, this was markedly different from astral projection, where writing and numbers looked like a bunch of unfathomable squiggles. I could comprehend what was currently on the TV screen...if I cared enough about golf to read it.

I edged around the console, really not expecting much. The other sets I'd encountered had all the experimental stuff hidden somewhere inside the cabinet.

Not this one.

This one had a series of electronic devices strung together between the cabinet and the outlet. If I'd been in my physical body, my heart would've been hammering inside my ribcage, but all I felt was a disorienting queasiness, some grave distress of the soul. Had the GhosTV invention evolved into some kind of plug-and-play add-on that would work with any tube TV? And if so, what would keep the Dr. Chances of the world from plugging them in anywhere and everywhere? Bad enough I had to deal with all those intersection repeaters. Now I'd need to worry about falling out of my own skin?

And yet, there was something familiar about the gizmos behind the set, and once I calmed down, I realized they were no more exotic than a cow in a cornfield.

An antenna. A digital tuner. And a timer.

The GhosTV had been turning itself on and off—with the help of whoever'd plugged it into the timer.

The house really was vacant after all.

My relief was so profound, I hardly registered that I was floating through the walls, no problem, in my hurry to go tell Jacob what I'd seen. The house was empty, and once we found a way in, we could make off with that TV without anyone being the wiser.

I sailed right through the outside wall, thinking it was only a matter of convincing Jacob to keep it. But I'd cross that bridge when I came...to...uh....

The deck was empty.

Shit.

Where the hell was Jacob?

Where the hell was my body?

Don't freak out. No doubt they're just looking for another way in. Except my subtle body was moving fast—fueled by panic—and I'd zipped around the whole place in no time flat, totally unhindered by the overgrown briars between the GhosTV house and the duplex next door.

I went around one more time, just to be sure I hadn't managed to lap myself. But, no. My husband—and my physical body—were totally gone.

CHAPTER 14

Don't panic.

The rental car was still right where we'd left it. Jacob and my body weren't currently in it...but they couldn't have gotten far.

Unless F-Pimp National had rolled up, yanked a pair of bags over their heads, bundled them into an unmarked van, and hauled them off to a secret "facility," never to be heard from again.

Shit.

There had to be some way to figure out where my body was. A silver cord, for instance, like in the astral. Unfortunately, a quick glance at the perfectly readable street signs nearby reminded me I was most definitely not astral. I waved my arms around my head like I was fending off bees, hoping to find a psychic filament attached to my third eye, something to link me to my physical form.

Nothing.

How it's possible to be sick with worry when there's no physical stomach to fill with butterflies, I'll never know. But I was positive now we'd been abducted. If not by National, then by one of Jennifer Chance's people, some psycho who'd been skulking around this final safe house for the past two years just waiting for their moment of glory. And the worst part was, I wasn't sure which one was worse. The cult-like following of a mad scientist or the nameless, faceless bureaucracy. Either one would be more than happy to lock us up somewhere and throw away the key.

I could do this, I told myself. I'm an investigator. Fucking investigate: walk the grid, keep my eyes open, and hopefully spot something that shed some light on which way we'd gone.

Beauchamp was tiny by Chicago standards, small enough that we could print out a detailed map on six sheets of letter-sized paper—and one of those sheets was mostly truck stop and cornfield. Thanks to the evidence board we'd taped together, I got my bearings right away. I'd check the main thoroughfares first, such as they were, then zigzag back through the side streets.

I was sort of walking, sort of floating, propelling myself with great purpose down the street as I frantically scanned for two tall guys in black suits. Everything looked normal, at least at first glance. But then I'd notice a fifties brick ranch-style home with a massive oak tree growing through it, and I knew we weren't in Kansas anymore. Or what I'd considered to be Iowa up until now, anyhow.

Looking harder at my surroundings, I saw the roofline begin to shift and change as the residue of Beauchamp's past overlaid its present. It hadn't occurred to me that buildings might have etheric forms, but evidently they did. Maybe that's what kept everything non-physical from dropping down into the ground like it was made of quicksand.

The second story winked out on one house, but flickered back in as I faced it head on. An old barn disappeared and a modern apartment building took its place. Luckily for me, the streets of Beauchamp were still in the same general spot where they'd been a century ago, and the residential part of the town hadn't much changed. And so I wasn't wading through the ghostly remains of a Pony Express route or a slaughterhouse.

There was no time for sightseeing. I did my best to ignore the acid trip going on around me and focus on figuring out where the hell my husband—and my body—had gone. I reached the end of the road, literally. Across the street was the edge of a cornfield—and the cornfields in Iowa go on approximately forever. I doubled back, chose a cross street, and plowed along full steam ahead. The panic I'd been hoping to quell by sticking to a logical plan was starting to rear its ugly head, though, and the longer I went without finding us, the more likely the kidnapping scenario became.

I stumbled across the park from the night before. It was more populated than the residential streets, with several people out walking their dogs and some kids skateboarding in a parking lot across the way. I swerved to avoid a tree, only to realize at the last moment that it wasn't actually there in the physical. Not anymore. But as I stumbled out of its way, I managed to career into a cocker spaniel chasing a frisbee.

I sailed right through the dog with that spiderweb sensation of passing resistance—and the dog apparently felt it too, given the way it jolted and changed trajectory. It forgot all about the frisbee, dropped down onto its butt, and began vigorously chewing a spot on its haunches.

The other dogs saw me too, I realized. Or maybe not saw, so much as sensed. Big dogs, small dogs, serious dogs and goofballs. They lifted their heads, sniffing the air as I scrambled past. But unless you knew to look for it, they'd seem like they were just checking out some distant barbecue.

Maybe one of those dogs would know where my body was. But unless I could speak their language, it wouldn't do me a heck of a lot of good. I scanned the crowd for a couple of fed-types, found nothing but dog-walkers in T-shirts, shorts and flip flops, and forged ahead. Up the street, down another, every one more agonizing than the last. Because with each passing moment, my certainty grew that Jacob and I would live out the remainder of our days strapped to an exam table, locked away somewhere in a dark basement lab.

And then I turned a corner, and there it was: my body. I'd recognize it anywhere. Not just because it was tall and skinny, and dressed in a sharp black suit—but because Jacob was standing next to it. Frankly, it was disconcerting to be looking at myself from any point of view besides head-on in a mirror. As much as I'd deny it up and down, I must pose for myself, at least a little. Seeing myself from this angle was disturbing, to say the least. I really could stand to gain a few pounds.

Good thing we were in line at the ice cream stand.

Seriously, though? Ice cream? Now?

Jacob must've felt the same way. He was standing in an exasperated pose, feet planted wide and hands on hips, speaking to me with quiet desperation.

My body? Looking intently at the menu and strategizing my order.

I hurried over and shoved myself in. It clicked, briefly—long enough for me to say, "Jacob—"

But when I tried to turn and face him, my physical shell stayed exactly where it was, and my subtle body spun out of alignment.

"If you can't tell me what's going on," Jacob ground out, "at least give me some kind of hint."

If there was any good way to convey that I'd slipped my physical confines (yet again), I sure as hell couldn't figure out what it might be.

Jacob crowded closer. While he mimicked my stance and tried to look natural, he continued to grill me. Very quietly, but with growing anxiety. "Did you see something back there? Are we being followed?"

Good question. I glanced around just to be sure, but no one else seemed to notice that I was nothing but an empty shell. Then again, why would they? Your average person wouldn't be privy to the existence of other planes, and had only five senses to perceive their surroundings.

Jacob, however, had more. If only he could figure out how to plug into sense number six.

At the front of the line, someone walked away slurping a milkshake, and everyone moved up a couple of steps. Jacob was trying to look casual—just a guy waiting for ice cream—but I knew him well enough to see the lines of tension in his shoulders and the subtle leap of a muscle in his jaw. The red veiny talent was nowhere to be seen, though. Not until I shifted my perception. And even then, it was subtle. Just a glimmer. Almost like it was lying dormant under his skin.

But my talent and I were old acquaintances, and I knew how to power up. White light. I visualized it beaming on down from the heavens, just like I always do. Except here, in this weird out-of-body state, I could actually see it taking shape.

It was less like a ray of sun and more like a moonbeam, soft and glowing and hauntingly ephemeral. I was so surprised by the fact that I could perceive it in this way, and not just in my imagination, that I almost lost it again. But all my floundering attempts at training myself—those hours of yoga and breathing and tweaking my brainwaves on the phone app—must've done me some good. The training kicked in and the white light stopped scattering.

After all these years of just guessing whether or not what I was doing had any effect, the visual feedback was fantastic. The light amplified and filled my subtle body. I felt strong. Even hopeful.

When I shoved into my body again, this time the spiderweb resistance felt like something more. Fragile and slippery, yes, but at least now it was tangible. I sucked down hard on the white light and focused on fitting myself back into my shell. I prodded my head into place first, then followed with arms and legs, fingers and toes, like I was sliding into a full-body glove.

It should have been easier, given that I'd been riding around in that body for forty-odd years. But my subtle bodies had always been a bit too loose. And the proximity of the GhosTV was wreaking havoc on whatever normally stuck them all together.

I just about had it when my body lurched forward one more place in line. Thanks to the white light, it didn't leave my spirit behind, though I was pretty disoriented for a few seconds until I got my bearings again.

"Whatever you need," Jacob whispered, "just give me a signal. I'll be watching."

If only it were that simple. I needed him to watch energetically. But now that I'd seen the difference in the white light—actually seeing it, versus relying solely on my imagination—I finally appreciated what Jacob had been struggling against, trying to train a talent with absolutely no feedback to guide him.

Poor Jacob. Not only did he have zero idea what the talent was supposed to be doing—he had no idea whether he was doing it at all. None of the other psychic talents came with an instruction manual, but at least they had some quantifiable effect. Jacob had successfully Hulked out only a handful of times. Tearing a habit demon from my throat. Astral projecting at PsyTrain. And trapping Jennifer Chance's ghost inside her physical cadaver.

And he'd done these all under the influence of a GhosTV.

If only he could focus on his energetic power now, instead of following my dumb body around and waiting for my signal. I tried to talk, but my mouth wouldn't engage, and my tongue felt like a clumsy hunk of meat. I'd taken my body by surprise before, but now it knew I was struggling for control—and it was resisting me all the way.

Why the hell was I so fucking stubborn? I'd always thought it was one of my better qualities—the thing that kept me alive through the loony bin and Camp Hell and the police academy and beyond. But right now I'd give anything to be a little more easygoing so I could get my bodies lined up where they belonged.

Another step forward. I struggled to stay put. It was no use. At best, I was pantomiming the actions of my physical shell, and until the GhosTV shut itself off, I was literally just going through the motions. Discouragement is hardly a quality I'd care to cultivate, but in realizing that my current course of action was no use, I had a moment of surrender. One in which my spirit eyes settled into my physical eyes, and I saw what was really driving my body.

The flavor of the day: Double cherry chocolate chip.

Don't worry, I promised myself. You'll get your damn ice cream. Just let me talk to Jacob for a second.

I may be pretty good at lying to myself—but deep down inside, I do know the score. If the ice cream was that important to me, then I wasn't about to stand in my own way. Not when I could practically feel it dripping down my wrist.

My body let me take the steering wheel. Just for a second, but a second was all I needed. "Grab my arm," I told Jacob urgently. And hallelujah, he did—immediately, no questions asked. I focused there, on the anchor of his hand, on the spot where my subtle body had snapped perfectly into place in the physical shell. My white light leapt between us with a zap, and talking was still a struggle, now that my dumb physical body realized what I was up to. But I managed. "Don't let go."

"I won't."

"Now power up."

"How?"

"However you do it—but do it fast."

I've always suspected things would be a lot easier if we didn't get in our own way. Jacob was a master strategist, which was usually an asset. But when it came to his talent, he overthought everything to the nth degree. My urgency let him bypass his normal impulses and simply act. And with my subtle body's heightened perception, when Jacob started focusing on powering up, I felt his particular brand of energy push back and staunch the flow of my white light. Now that the leak was plugged (or at least slowed down) I could pull harder and form better words. "Whatever you're doing—it's working. Just don't let go."

"I won't," he repeated emphatically.

"The GhosTV turned on—it's on a timer—and I keep trying to project."

"I thought I felt something shift back at that house!"

He tugged at my arm to pull me out of line. "Hey, what're you doing?" I whispered.

"Going back to the TV," he said, as if it should be obvious.

"Hold your horses." Evidently, I had to come right out and say it. "One of us isn't going anywhere until it's had its ice cream."

CHAPTER 15

I'll say this for my physical body—once its needs were met, it was perfectly willing to turn over the reins and let me drive. I had Jacob keep hold of my arm anyhow, just in case. I didn't want my body to take off after a frisbee—or, God forbid, strip naked on Main Street in full view of the fine folks of Beauchamp.

"How is it possible for your body to function without your spirit inside?" Jacob asked.

"Apparently the carcass doesn't need as much guidance as we thought."

Jacob found the whole scenario profoundly disturbing. "We need some kind of signal."

"Like what? Knock knock, who's there?"

"I have no idea—but I need to know when it's actually you I'm dealing with."

I licked all around the perimeter of my cone—a really assertive power-move resulting in a massive mouthful of ice cream—to keep it from christening my suit. "Don't worry," I said through the ice cream, "it's still me—just trying to make sure I don't end up wearing it."

Jacob gave me the side-eye.

Once I swallowed, I said, "It's not like I was possessed. I mean, yeah, I wasn't really calling the shots. But it was still me. Kind of."

"Oh, that's a comfort," he said dryly.

"There are more subtle bodies than we know about. A bunch of inner selves stacked together like nesting dolls. Whatever frequency that TV is playing, it honed in on a specific one and knocked it loose."

We walked back to the house—drawing a few funny looks, what with the ice cream eating and arm-holding—and when we got there, I did manage to dissuade Jacob from kicking down the back door. "Let me get another look at it before you do anything that can't be undone," I said.

"Now you want me to let go??"

"It's the perfect opportunity." I gestured with my cone. "My body will be busy taking care of this."

"And how am I supposed to know when all your nesting dolls are back in place?"

"I'll tell you," I said…though I wasn't a hundred percent sure I could trust my physical body not to say whatever it took to get what it wanted. Still, there weren't a whole hell of a lot of options. I handed off the ice cream cone to Jacob just long enough to slip out of my jacket—then thought better of keeping my shoulder holster on and ditched that, too.

While my body lapped up the rest of the ice cream and started on the soggy cone, I let my spirit fall loose and head back into the house to do more recon on the GhosTV. The level of white light surged as soon as Jacob let go, and I went with it, topping myself up while I had the chance. I went through the back door with ease, and while I was on a roll, stepped through one of the interior walls too. It was easier now that I'd resigned myself to being etheric, and it allowed me to determine that all reports of the house being vacant were, in fact, true. There was minimal furniture—just enough to keep the TV from being the only thing in the house—but no food in the kitchen, no clothes in the closets, no sign of anyone actually living there.

Unfortunately, the TV took up the better part of the room all by itself. I peered behind it to check out the timer and see how much longer I'd be relegated to my ghost state. I'm no expert in electronics, but in my time as a beat cop I'd seen an illegal grow operation or two. It was just a matter of figuring out exactly how this specific timer was set while the world's loudest weather forecast blasted away my focus.

I may have been perfectly capable of reading in my disembodied state, but the timer itself was a byzantine thing with a dial and a bunch of levers, the whole thing peppered with tiny little numbers I could barely see. I leaned in to get a better look... and grossly misjudged the velocity I was capable of when I was unhindered by my own physicality. I tipped into the timer, and sparks flew from the electrical socket. The sudden silence in the room was quickly obliterated by a rushing in my ears as I landed back in my physical body with a jolt. My right hand was sticky, and my stomach was full. My tongue was sweet and tasted of cherries, and a headache was brewing. Not my typical one-eyed psychic strain headache, but brain freeze.

"I'm back," I said simply. Hopefully that was enough of a safeword for Jacob to stop giving me the hairy eyeball.

"The volume cut out all of a sudden."

"Yeah, about that. I zapped something. Maybe the timer, maybe the TV itself."

Jacob's eyebrows hitched up in surprise. "At least we don't have to worry about you randomly projecting anymore."

It was good of him to resist gloating over the possibility that

I'd just accidentally put the final GhosTV out of commission for good.

I took back my sidearm, but ejected the cartridge and handed it to Jacob. "You hold onto the bullets until I'm a hundred percent sure I'm the only one in charge of my trigger finger."

Jacob blanched. "I don't like you being unarmed without any backup."

"You're my backup," I said firmly.

He pocketed the ammo.

As I pulled on my jacket, I said, "Even if we broke down the door, maybe the two of us could wrangle the TV cabinet to the other side of the room, but it would be too heavy to maneuver it through the back door and down the stairs. And even if we did manage that, we can't just throw it in the trunk."

"I knew we should have gone for the SUV."

"Even then, there's no way it would've fit. This thing is twice as big as the last one. We'd need a moving van..." and good luck getting one anonymously when the rental car lady could spot us at five hundred yards. "Or a hearse."

The crazy plan clicked into place like an etheric body reseating itself in its physical host. Amy Grace had access to a hearse. And a gurney capable of transporting not only a massive body like the oversized dead guy I'd seen in the embalming room, but the hefty hardwood casket he'd be buried in, too. Plus, Amy had that whole funeral home at her disposal, with space enough to stash the GhosTV out of sight until we had a chance to come back for it.

I sketched out my ridiculous plan to Jacob, expecting him to talk some sense into me. So, naturally, what he said was, "Great idea. Let's go."

Whereas Grace Funeral Home had been hopping the night

of the viewing, today it was totally dead. No way for us to lose ourselves among a crowd of bereaved distant family members paying their respects. But we'd run out of options, so we stuck with our plan.

The place was locked up tight, but a discreet emergency number was posted in the window. Jacob, being the people-person that he was, made the call and got Amy's father on the line. Jacob then spun out some nonsense about needing to do some estate planning before he left town, laying on the charm shamelessly thick, and Mr. Grace agreed to meet.

"Once we're inside," Jacob said, "you find Amy and talk her into stashing the TV."

As if I'm capable of talking anyone into anything. But since it beat bluffing my way through my own funeral arrangements, I'd have to give it a shot.

Mr. Grace joined us in a hastily-donned suit with a tie slightly askew, not nearly as put-together as he'd been the night before, and ushered us into the funeral home. It felt quiet inside. Peaceful. Which was probably the idea behind the subdued lighting and understated decor. But for me, it was something more—the knowledge that Amy Grace had been making sure nothing straggled behind on the wrong side of the veil.

We came to the office, and I announced I had to use the can—except I called it the washroom this time, much to Jacob's obvious relief. Mr. Grace called out directions to me, craning his neck to make sure I forged off in the right direction, but Jacob inserted himself between us and proceeded to take up all the attention in the room so that I could wander off with as little fanfare as possible.

The funeral home basement was slightly less scary today than it was the night before. Not only because I knew Amy had cleared it of ghosts, but because I knew my way around now. With any luck, she'd be down there, and not off doing whatever it is morticians do in their time off.

A wet slurping noise sounded from the embalming room.

I sure as hell hoped it was Amy...although I dreaded seeing exactly what was being sucked up.

I rapped on the door and the slurping stopped. Amy opened the door in full PPE. She peered at me through the clear plastic visor and narrowed her eyes, then greeted me with, "Was there something else you needed?"

"Actually...yes. Can we talk?"

She stood aside and let me into the room—where the obese guy was splayed on a slab with a tray of bloody instruments beside him. A machine purred at his side, a machine that had just been sucking out fluids. At least it had caused his boner to deflate. I did my best not to stare at the ex-boner—but it was impossible not to at least cop a quick glance, and wish I hadn't.

Turning away from the body and trying to unsee the dead dick, I said, "Look—I know this is a big ask, but since the talk we had, I figured if anyone was likely to help me out, it's you."

She gave me a dubious frown. "Didn't you get whatever you were looking for last night?"

"Here's the thing—there's a certain, ah, piece of equipment—"

"All of our equipment meets Mortician Protocol standards. I double-checked it myself."

"Let's drop the whole professional spiel, okay? We've figured out what's going on here, and your projections aren't random. But we can get them under control, and I've got a plan. All we need is a transport for something in the neighborhood of four to five hundred pounds—roughly the size of a coffin, especially if we can unscrew the legs from the cabinet, which I'd imagine we could do without disturbing any of the electronics. Then somewhere to stash the thing—not for long. Two, three weeks. A month, tops. You've got plenty of storage—so, what do you say?"

Amy considered my request for a good, long moment, then flipped up her clear plastic visor, looked me square in the eye, and said, "I have absolutely no idea what you're talking about."

CHAPTER 16

Jacob was nodding appreciatively at a bunch of wood finish samples in the undertaker's office when I made the world's hastiest exit from my totally botched meeting with Amy Grace. Not only didn't she remember our out-of-body discussion last night. But she thought the "projections" I was talking about were some kind of business-related mumbo-jumbo.

Jacob disengaged a lot less awkwardly than me, but Mr. Grace did look a bit baffled as the two of us hustled ourselves out the door. I flung myself into the passenger seat, gestured out the windshield, and told Jacob, "Just drive."

Once the funeral home was out of sight, Jacob said, "Is it you talking, or just your body?"

"Oh, it's me, all right."

"Then I take it your talk didn't go well."

"Amy had zero memory of our conversation last night. None. And now she's not only suspicious that I'm not actually with some mortician protocol organization, but she probably thinks I'm crazy, too."

Jacob considered. "Maybe it's like astral projection. A few different people at PsyTrain could do it—especially with the

GhosTV playing—but most of them didn't remember afterward."

It was as good an explanation as any. "And now, without Amy's help, we're shit outta luck."

"Maybe it's a sign to let sleeping dogs lie. Look at it this way— since you disabled the tuner, there's no reason for National to start poking around in Beauchamp. This might all work out for the best."

Normally, I'd reluctantly agree...except Jacob was just a little too keen on selling his bill of goods. Which meant he really planned to drive out here again by himself later and take a sledgehammer to it.

But maybe taking it apart really was a viable solution. The GhosTV in Con Dreyfuss's office had worked just fine even without its cabinet, and we could pull out the tube and ship it to ourselves tomorrow morning—right from the FedEx counter in the car rental place—bright and early, before our ride even showed up. "Maybe we can't move the cabinet, not without causing a big stir and drawing attention to ourselves. But we can grab the tube."

"So you think we should break in," Jacob clarified, as if he thought there'd be a catch.

"We've gotta do something." I said. "We'll just need to pick up a few tools first."

While everything was closed on a Sunday afternoon in small-town Beauchamp but the truck stop and the restaurant, there was a SaverPlus just three miles out of town—an expanded SaverPlus with a grocery section, optician and pharmacy—and the conglomerate was doing pretty brisk business.

Shopping is one of the go-to ways Jacob and I communicate when we're worried our handlers are listening in. While stores these days are full of security cameras, there's a certain anonymity there too, a crowd of other shoppers where we can lose ourselves. Given how often we'll take a stroll through the hardware section, you'd think we would've built ourselves a second cannery by now. But we don't generally buy anything. It's just easy to make lots of noise pawing through buckets of nails and rolls of chain link fence.

This wasn't our usual store, but the hardware aisle smell was familiar, even comforting. Rubber. Wood. Galvanized metal. While we might be looking for something to drill out the lock—ideally without the whole neighborhood hearing us do it—walking down the home improvement aisle together put us both in a reflective state of mind.

"So," Jacob ventured. "Back there at the ice cream stand. That was actually you...just without your normal waking conscious-ness running the show."

"I suppose."

"Then you weren't possessed."

"No." I said this with some relief. "Most definitely not possessed."

"All the other incidents of people taking off their clothes, then...temperatures are high, and it's incredibly muggy. What if they're just bodies reacting to the weather?"

And if a man took his shirt off in public, no one would find that particularly remarkable, at least if he did it outside, which would explain why the phenomenon only seemed to be affect-ing women. If that were the case, that it was just bodies reacting to heat, then disabling the GhosTV would solve everyone's problems once and for all. But Jacob hadn't been angling to make me agree with him, for once. Just struggling to under-stand what was going on.

In moments like these—being with Jacob, doing something

that was so mundane on the surface, but so dangerous underneath—I found myself longing for a normal life. A life we'd obviously never have. I could pretend sometimes that we were just a couple of guys doing normal guy things, but that never worked for long, and it only left me feeling vaguely sad.

I was gazing at a set of socket wrenches, wondering how we'd managed to end up in this place, when someone nearly sent me flying out of my body by calling out, "Well, if it isn't my pals from the FPMP!"

I spun around, heart pounding in my throat, only to find the car rental lady standing at the top of the aisle in her American flag T-shirt with a big smile on her face.

I was speechless—Jacob too, for once—but Ruth didn't take any notice. She marched up the aisle in her sparkly flip-flops and said, "Good thing I ran into you fellas. I was just talking to my friend Colleen over by the Starbucks kiosk—didja try the salted caramel cold brew yet? Coffee and salt don't go together all that good if you ask me—anyways, she said one of those drug parties was in the works for tonight. There's a beat-up blue pickup truck that always shows up an hour or two before with the speakers for their loud music, and she saw it over by Parkway and Vine."

When I blinked stupidly, she added, "Three houses down on the south side of the street. The windows are all boarded up. Can't miss it."

"We'll be sure to check it out," Jacob said with the utmost fake sincerity. "Thanks so much for your help."

Once Ruth shuffled away, I turned to Jacob and whispered, "Second time could've been a coincidence. But even though half the town is shopping here—no way do I buy that we just so happened to cross paths." Sure, this woman seemed harmless enough. But I'd been trained in undercover work by someone who could pass herself off as anything from a boring middle school history teacher to a frazzled barista to an alderman. No doubt the folks at F-Pimp National were just as good. If not better. "Plus, now she saw us in the hardware aisle."

A muscle leapt in Jacob's jaw as he chewed through our next move. "Maybe it's for the best. I'd have no idea how to drill out a lock without looking it up on YouTube first."

If I just tipped Jacob in the right direction, he'd fold. Call it a day and walk away. I can always tell when he's teetering on that point of surrender, probably because it's so rare that he ever gives in. But instead of taking the easy win and encouraging him to abandon the GhosTV, I only found myself more determined to break into the damn house.

Must be the contrarian in me.

I planted my hands on my hips, scanning the aisle for inspiration...and my gaze landed on a five-foot folding stepladder. Casually, I said, "Nothing says we need to go in through the door."

It was a cheap thing, and lightweight, too. We paid in cash and I walked it out to the car, carrying it easily with one hand. It would even fit in the trunk of the rented sedan. But despite the fact that he was getting his way, Jacob was distinctly unmollified. He slammed the trunk a little too hard and said, "How the hell does Ruth always know where we are?"

I took a deep breath, not really wanting to fan the flames, but not willing to sugar-coat it either. "If she's from National—"

"You think National's already here?"

"If she is, then it's just a matter of tracking our phones."

Jacob immediately pulled out his phone and powered it down. "I might not know how to drill out a lock, but Pete showed me how to pull out the phone batteries. Let's head back in and grab a little screwdriver."

I wasn't a hundred percent sure that our phone trackers didn't have an emergency backup power source that Garcia wasn't privy to, but he was the surveillance specialist. And Jacob trusted him.

Once our phones were taken care of, we headed back to the GhosTV house. It was mid-afternoon, the sun was high, and the sky was hazy with humidity. We pulled into the overgrown driveway between the house and the duplex, all the way in, out of view of the street. Turned out the kitchen window I'd spied earlier had bars on the inside, but a single slender window in the alley was within reach of our stepladder.

Jacob fixed the ladder in place—its feet sank into the moss—and squared his shoulders, raring to go.

With a sigh, I said, "Come on, mister, you and I can both see you'll shred yourself squeezing through that hole. I'll do it."

It was surprisingly easy to break the window. None of the neighbors seemed to notice—then again, the loud window-unit churning away next door easily camouflaged the sound of me rapping a paving stone against the glass. It broke in big shards, easy to clear out. As I knocked the pieces loose, I marveled at the fact that it had taken me this long to break into a house. Given what a punk rock derelict I'd been as a kid, one would think I'd be an old pro at something like this.

Better late than never.

I draped a mildewy welcome mat over the sill just to protect myself from any straggling shards and heaved myself up, wishing I'd done less yoga and more pull-ups. But my foot found purchase against the rough asphalt siding, and graceless as it might've looked, I flopped in up to my waist. The flavor of cherry ice cream filled my mouth as the sill drove into my diaphragm. I swallowed it down, chastising my body for insisting on the double-scoop cone, but knowing it never really did anything by half-measures.

Flailing, I got my bearings. It was a mechanical room of some sort—dim and shifting with shadows. I'd been so worried about getting my physical self inside that I hadn't thought much about the metaphysical. Someone had offed himself in this house and it had been vacant ever since. A blueprint for a haunting if ever there was one.

On cue, a shape loomed in the corner and the taste of cherry I'd burped up went sour.

The salt in my pocket wouldn't do me a hell of a lot of good when my hands were busy scrambling for something to hold onto and pull my ass the rest of the way in. I told my body to go for the salted caramel frap next time, whether salt goes good with coffee or not.

White light thundered down in that way it does nowadays when I start to freak out, sudden and intense, followed by a bright jab of pain behind my right eye. I threw up a shield (and another mouthful of ice cream) and gave one final, big heave that propelled me all the way into the room, flopping like a fish.

I flipped onto my back, swallowing down cherry flavoring and gasping for breath. There, from my vulnerable supine perspective, I got a good look at what had startled me....

A water heater.

To be fair, the pipes coming out the top were casting a really weird shadow.

My head throbbed harder as adrenaline that had just squirted into my system coursed through my body, accentuating both my back-of-the-eye psychic strain and whatever pathways the brain freeze had lit up. Nearly bested by a water heater. But eventually, I'd prevailed.

And now I was inside...of a suicide house.

Just me and the final GhosTV.

CHAPTER 17

Just because the water heater couldn't chase me didn't mean I planned on letting my guard down. I pulled in more white light and eased open the mechanical room door. Normally, I would've drawn my sidearm. The house had been empty when I'd scanned it before, but someone could've entered the premises while I was out stuffing my face. But you don't draw a gun unless you're prepared to use it. And unless I wanted to lob my unloaded Glock at a potential threat, it wouldn't do me a hell of a lot of good.

I paused in the doorway, looked and listened. Nothing.

The kitchen held a card table and a couple of folding chairs. Hardly any counter space, but without any of the things you'd normally find in a kitchen like a dish drainer or an armada of small appliances, it still felt unused.

You know a place is spartan when I think it needs a little clutter.

I hustled over to the back door, where I found no alarm panel—not that I'd actually expected to—so I turned the dead-bolt and let Jacob in. Relief flooded my veins to have him by my side again. My gut did a queasy, post-adrenaline somersault.

I signaled toward my eyes and then to the kitchen door, indicating I'd cut right. He gave me a quick nod, drew his sidearm and cut left, and the two of us moved through the house like a well-oiled machine.

There wasn't much to scan. The place was hardly bigger than my crappy old apartment. I paused at the bedroom, where the closet had no door, just a shabby curtain hanging askew. The bed was an oddball size, not quite a full, with nothing underneath but an old candy bar wrapper.

"Clear," Jacob called from the living room.

"Clear," I echoed, but I found myself frozen in place, staring at that stark bed, wondering what would have happened if Roger Burke had decided to take me here instead of the weird B&B in Missouri. Well, Vic, there's no motel for miles around, but I did find an Airbnb just down the road in Beauchamp. Very minimal—you'll love it!

The floorboards creaked as Jacob paused in the doorway while I flashed back on the feeling of Amytal rushing down my arm. "Everything okay?" he asked.

"Fine."

"No ghosts?"

Not really. Just the ones of my own past. "It's fine."

"Then let's get a better look at that TV."

Maybe Jacob was right. Maybe the world was better off without an invention worth abducting a PsyCop for—worth killing and dying for. I followed him out to the living room where he was bent over the set, peering at the jumble of electronics behind it. "A vacation timer," he said. "But why?"

"No clue."

"Maybe it needs to be warmed up every so often. Or maybe she was testing the effect of an intermittent signal."

Jennifer Chance hadn't been playing with a full deck, but there was always a method to her madness—though I wouldn't risk poking around beyond the veil to ask. "We'll probably never know."

If there's one thing Jacob loves, it's solving a problem—especially if everyone involved acknowledges his cleverness. The TV was no exception. He poked around at the outlet, then commandeered a lamp from across the room, plugged it in, and clicked fruitlessly.

While he tinkered, I headed back to the kitchen to idly paw through the mostly-empty cabinets. A handful of plastic forks and spoons. A couple of mugs. Cheap instant coffee, bricked with humidity at the bottom of the jar. Everything dusty, stale and unused, like it hadn't been touched for months, or even longer.

And yet the final GhosTV had played on. At least until I crossed its path.

I was marveling at the ugly contact paper in the drawers when Jacob called from the utility room, "When you zapped the TV, I think you only blew a fuse. I'll swap it with one of the others."

I personally wouldn't have touched that old fuse box with a ten-foot pole, but Jacob seemed to know what he was doing. There was space for four fuses, one of which he'd already removed. He unscrewed one of the others like a lightbulb and screwed it into the empty socket, and the GhosTV roared to life again. The sound cut in and out a few times with digital glitchiness, then settled into a commercial for hearing aids—and then I realized that while I was heading toward the TV, my body had paused in the utility room doorway, blocking Jacob inside.

Sonofabitch.

I tried to step into my body, but just ended up behind the

shadowy water heater. "You're probably right about getting rid of the TV," it announced blithely, leaving Jacob wondering what the catch was. "I'm so sick of all this shit, the sneaking around, the waiting for the next shoe to drop. Aren't you?"

"I don't see that we have much choice."

My body took the fried fuse out of his hand and set it on top of the furnace. "We need to look out for ourselves."

"Agreed," he said carefully.

My body fit itself against his, and from my outside perspective, I could practically see the two of us click together. "We should ditch the GhosTV. And the Program. And take off together, just the two of us."

"If only it were that simple," Jacob said, though clearly he thought the idea had some merit.

"Oh, come on," I muttered.

My body backed him against the wall. Jacob grunted as our groins butted together. My body said, "You looked pretty hot bent over that TV when you were looking at the plug."

"Are you kidding me?" I demanded.

It angled its face into the crook of Jacob's neck, pitched its voice low, and said, "You know what would be even hotter? If I was underneath you with my legs in the air."

Jacob released a shuddering breath.

"Give me a freaking break," I yelled. "In what universe would I ever say anything even remotely like that?"

"I'd love nothing more than to plow you into the cabinet," Jacob said—and yeah, he totally does talk like that. Especially when his pupils are blown and he's thinking with the massive hunk of meat between his legs. "But it's too risky."

I dropped a hand between us and cupped him through his pants. "Then how about in here? We'll suck each other off. You know we can do it in two minutes flat."

Jacob hesitated.

"Don't tell me you're actually considering it!"

"We'll take this up later," Jacob said decisively, and his voice was smoky and full of promise.

But apparently my body wouldn't take no for an answer. Even a sexy no.

"When I see you moving through a scene, all buff and in-charge, how can I think of anything but how you are in the sack? How you own my ass...how you obliterate the rest of the sorry world until I forget about everything but you."

Heaven help him...Jacob was gonna cave. The body up against him may not have talked like me, but it looked like me, felt like me, and apparently, that was good enough for him. All of Jacob's intensity was directed at the idiot pinning him to the wall. Between the eager flush and the flaring nostrils, he was just about ready to make my dirtiest wishes come true.

Except...they weren't even my wishes. Sure, the big lug had looked pretty choice when he was bending over the TV, but there's a time and a place for everything. The time was not now and the place was not here.

My body had all the sense of a lightweight plastic stepladder, so even though it was the worst possible time and place we could get it on, it kept right on pushing. Which really should've been another red flag that Jacob wasn't dealing with the real me, since my typical M.O. is to quit arguing at the first sign of resistance and go stew about the fact that I didn't get my way.

The body nuzzled Jacob's perfect cheekbone and felt him up from thigh to shoulder. Greedy bastard. "We spend so much time making sure everyone else is okay, protecting everyone from the monsters. You took care of the monsters everyone knows about—the rapists, the pedophiles, the sickos who get their rocks off by preying on regular people. And I got to handle all the monsters no one else can see. But what about us? When do we get to just do what we want?"

"I didn't know that's how you felt." Well, that made two of us. But I guess I didn't exactly disagree. "You are my top priority, Vic. Us. And if that means taking another look at what we're doing and why, then that's what we need to do. All I ask is that you wait until we're not right in the middle of this so we can think it all through."

Jacob caught the hand that was trying to pinpoint his nipple through his suit jacket and brought my fingers to his lips—and I spotted my chance.

I flung myself at the pair of them and sailed right through me, but Jacob's chest stopped me cold. My spirit head snapped into alignment with my physical head and it registered as the type of jolt you get when you catch yourself falling asleep during a boring meeting.

And I wasn't the only one who'd felt the jolt.

Jacob stiffened. He might've let go, but I squeezed his hand hard and said, "Hold onto me—I'm having trouble keeping it together."

"Wait a sec—just now, that wasn't you?"

"We'll hash it out later. Just turn off that TV so you can make sure the person you're dealing with is really me—all of me."

I let go of his hand and released him from the pin, and he was quick to disengage. Without him there to hold me together, my subtle body rattled around inside the physical. It was like trying to run in an unlaced pair of shoes one size too big. The body stayed in place. But it felt one hasty step away from falling off again.

Not only that, but my vision was skewed, with everything glowing funny and Jacob swirled through with red energy. I pulled down white light and the room lit up brighter, but it helped me stay seated in my body well enough to follow Jacob into the living room.

The GhosTV glowed like a searchlight. If it were physical light, it would be so bright I'd never be able to look right at it without burning out my retinas. But the light was metaphysical, and it didn't hurt. Though it did make the physical world feel like maybe it was fake, and the overlay I'd seen while I was walking the grid was actually the real Beauchamp.

Jacob had paused in front of the cabinet to puzzle over the knobs on the TV set. Could we be sure the on/off really did what it was supposed to, or had Jennifer Chance rewired it to do something nefarious like dissolve my consciousness and leave my physical shell to stumble through the rest of its life fucking my husband and eating ice cream?

We were better off when the fuse was blown. I was about to tell him to just yank the plug out of the outlet when someone barreled in through the front door—without opening it.

And that someone was Amy Grace, in all her Egyptian-goth ghostly glory.

"Thank the gods I've found you," she told me. "I need your help."

"Jacob, wait," I barked out before he cut the TV signal.

He snapped around to look at me and narrowed his eyes. "Tell me why."

Super, now he thought the body was running the show. "Because Amy Grace showed up and she's got something to say."

Jacob stepped away from the dial, though he kept the TV cabinet well within reach.

It was tempting to make a remark about how Amy hadn't been very helpful to us from inside her body, but now that the shoe was on the other foot, she expected us to jump to her assistance. But I supposed it wasn't her fault if her talent didn't let her remember her projections. "What's going on?" I asked.

Amy gave me a pitiful look, then buried her face in her hands and said, "I lost my body."

CHAPTER 18

Once I relayed Amy's issue to Jacob, I expected him to shift into problem-solving mode and pinpoint exactly where Amy's body would've gone. He was sharp as a tack and saw connections between things long before anyone else did, and his mundane skills of observation were so astute, that they came off more like extrasensory perception.

But instead of leaping to Amy's assistance, what he did was go back to the TV and say, "We're not doing anything until your consciousness is secure."

"Wait," I said hastily. "If you pull the plug, what happens to Amy's ka?"

Jacob and Amy both whirled around to look at me. "What do you mean?" Jacob demanded, while Amy said, "Why would anything happen to my ka?"

I gestured toward the TV as yet another commercial played, this one for denture adhesive. "We have no idea where the body's gone off to—for all we know it could've hooked up with a trucker and it's halfway to Nebraska by now. Without the body, what if the ka isn't strong enough to stick around on its own once the GhosTV stops broadcasting its signal?"

"My body wouldn't just 'hook up' with a random trucker," Amy muttered. "At least, I hope not."

Jacob was none too keen about leaving the TV on if my spirit wasn't locked in. "There must be some way to shore up the connection between your consciousness and your body. What about a natural psyactive like mugwort tea?"

I said, "We didn't bring any—and I'm guessing it wouldn't be too easy to find around here." Amy regretfully nodded her agreement. "Besides, psyactives only make my subtle bodies loosen up."

Jacob frowned. "Then an antipsyactive. Alcohol."

The antipsyactive properties of booze were mild, at best. And, lucky me. My mediumship was so strong, all hitting the sauce did for me was lower my inhibitions—so where I was concerned, it had the opposite effect. "I'd rather keep my wits about me."

"What else have we got at our disposal, then? Candles, Florida Water, salt?"

"Let's not go hauling out the exorcism kit. I might accidentally flush out my own spirit."

"What about silver, then? Isn't there some property to it, some kind of vibration, that ghosts have a reaction to?"

I shuddered when I thought of the bodies in the zombie basement falling still when the milagro touched their foreheads. "Actually, you'd better keep any silver out of arm's reach until I've got a better handle on the projections."

Jacob huffed in annoyance. "So everything we know—all our experience and training—we've got zero options here?"

Before I could mumble some sorry excuse about this being uncharted territory, Amy announced, "Well, what you need is to get grounded."

"Grounded how?" I asked.

Jacob turned to look where I was looking and said, "What does that mean?"

"Hold on," I said, "can you hear her?"

Jacob paused. Blinked. Furrowed his brow and said, "Well, no...."

"Because it sounded like you were having a conversation."

"Of course not. I just inferred what she was talking about based on your reaction." So he said. But he didn't sound entirely sure.

Most of the time I can see a ghost like it's right there in front of me. But not every psychic experience is as vivid as the bus crash that sent me on a two-year Thorazine vacation. Sometimes they're just a fleeting glimpse. A cold spot. A creeping sensation across the back of my neck. "Maybe you were just connecting the dots. Or maybe you were listening from another place."

"And he could obviously tell you a thing or two about being grounded," Amy said. "I've never seen a ka seated so firmly in its physical body. You could hit this guy with a ten-ton spirit sledgehammer and he wouldn't even budge until he was good and ready."

"How would you know?" I asked.

Amy shrugged. "I can sense these things. Sometimes the deceased are way too attached to their dead bodies for their own good."

When I looked at Jacob with the TV playing and my vision shifted—searching him the way I would search the room for a straggling repeater—faint traces of red energy pulsed along his brow and twined through his fingers. Jacob might be notorious for stealing my white light, but he was tapped into a power source I knew next to nothing about.

Great. All I needed to do was forget about the white light I'd been powering up with for however many years and switch over to red energy. No problem.

"How do you go about getting grounded?" Jacob asked. He read up on all things psychic, but had never needed to master that particular topic, since Stiffs need grounding like a corpse needs an ice cream cone.

Amy said, "I've always focused on the higher chakras—the pineal gland and the crown. Those are the ones to activate if you want to travel through the world of the dead. To do the opposite though, to ground yourself among the living? You'll want to feed on your base chakra, at the bottom of your tailbone."

Oh, the bottom of my tailbone was already primed from all the dirty stuff my body said to Jacob before Amy showed up.

"The Base of Set is the primordial part of yourself, the part that's concerned with staying alive. You need to fill it with the power of earth."

"Okay," I said—sounding just about as hopeful as I felt.

"Connect with the soil. Shed your clothes and lie down on the earth, and drink up her energy. She's got plenty to give. A lot more than you'd ever be capable of drawing out."

"Lemme get this straight—you're saying I need to go lay down outside? Naked?"

Jacob was well acquainted with the tone of voice that preceded the point where I gave up and chalked up the whole thing as a loss. "What about just your shoes?" he suggested. "Stand outside barefoot. That shouldn't be too bad."

"You've seen the yard," I grumbled, "I'll probably step on a used syringe." But I had no time to piss and moan. The longer it took us to start tracking down Amy's body, the farther away it could end up.

We headed outside. I focused on my pelvis as I walked, trying to stay firm in my body. Hard to say if it actually did anything—which was how Jacob felt about his powers all the time. Goes to show how easy it was to forget what psychic abilities felt like when they were untested and new.

There was a spot in the yard where the buildings and a sagging fence protected us from prying eyes. I took off my shoes, then my socks.

Nasty.

My feet are my own business. I'm just not a barefoot kind of guy. Even flip-flops are a no-go, since the thought of traipsing out in public with my toes on display for everyone to see is something I'm patently unwilling to consider. Not that they're gross or anything. I keep my toenails trimmed. But they're pale—obviously from their constant confinement—and the dusting of black hair on each foot only makes them look that much whiter.

Even so, I dutifully exposed them, in all their fishbelly-white glory, and allowed my feet to touch the earth.

It would be great if I could say that I'd suddenly found the silver bullet, the magic pill that would solve all my problems and power me up to the next level. Unfortunately, the only thing I felt through the soles of my feet was crunchy grass, dirt, and maybe a bit of gravel.

Jacob knew my tone of discouragement...and he knew my "this is useless" face, too. He toed off his shoes. "I'll do it with you."

While I appreciated the show of support, I'd already written off the whole thing as an exercise in futility. "Don't bother, Jacob—I don't feel anything. We'll need to move on to plan B."

Amy said, "Not so fast. You haven't even tried feeding your

base chakra yet. There'll be some visualization involved. Are you any good at calling up a mental image?"

My inner optimist (which is usually about as sun-starved and atrophied as my toes) perked up. I told it to calm the hell down. "I can probably manage."

"Good. Then close your eyes and follow along with me."

Amy led me in some guided imagery, and I repeated it aloud, for Jacob's benefit. "Stand with your feet firmly on the ground and take a deep, cleansing breath. Now imagine that it's not your lungs you're breathing with, but your ka. And imagine that it's not air you're breathing, but energy.

"Everything is made of energy. Even the substance that makes up the physical shell has more space between the atoms than matter. While your body breathes air, imagine your ka taking in energy.

"Now think about the Base of the god Set, the bottom of your spine."

"The muladhara chakra?" I asked.

"That's what it's called in Sanskrit—very good. Focus on that base—become that base—and breathe energy in."

It might be tempting to balk about breathing with my ass, but with my eyes closed and a GhosTV churning out energy waves on the other side of the wall, it was alarmingly easy to think of my body and my consciousness as two separate entities. Bodies had things like lungs and toes and an itchy spot where I'd spent too long in a plaster cast. I felt my consciousness, though, as the space between the atoms. It didn't need to breathe with physical lungs. But it could definitely take in energy.

"The Base of Set," Amy repeated, more urgently this time. I opened my eyes and found I was three feet above the ground, peeking over the fence into the neighboring yard where a filthy plastic play-house sat mired in a rotting pile of last year's leaves.

I scrambled down into my body, thankful it wasn't scratching its balls or wandering off to go take a nap. It felt loose and somewhat ill-fitting.

"You're pulling in through the Crown of Horus," Amy told me. "Getting your ka ready to journey. You need to do the opposite—to ground it in your physical shell. Stop using your crown and focus on your base."

I thought harder about my ass. Hard to say if I was activating my lowest chakra, or if simply cutting off the flow of white light was keeping me on the ground.

"Think about the color red," Amy said. "Imagine the bottom of your spine is lit up and glowing with a steady red light."

As I repeated the words for Jacob, the image was already playing full-throttle in my mind. I always got stuck on which way the chakra was supposed to be spinning, much to my yoga teacher's complete exasperation. But the mental image of lighting up red was easy-peasy. I cracked one eye open and my line of sight was back below the fence where it was supposed to be.

"Good," Amy said, "really focus on the color red, and think about breathing into that primal seat of power. Go beyond the passive desire for security and expand into the empowering drive of creation."

My root chakra was plenty well acquainted with my sex drive, thanks to the Stiff that gave it a regular pounding. Maybe with all the crown chakra work I did, my sex life was the only reason I didn't just up and float away.

Funny, though. Being with Jacob never seemed to drain me—not unless he was actively stealing my white light. If anything, he augmented me.

I'd always thought of my own psychic energy as coming with an on/off switch. Either I was pumped up on white light with a one-eyed headache, or I was shut down on Auracel and walking through intersection repeaters without so much as a shiver. But I was never quite sure if psyactives made me more vulnerable to psychic attack, or less.

Maybe I'd been looking at it all wrong.

Maybe the flow of white light wasn't the only piece of the puzzle. What if it was possible to be buzzing with white light and grounded at the same time?

But pulling white light came so easily to me that I probably did it in my sleep. The red energy felt ungainly and strange.

I thought I'd cracked this code already, back at PsyTrain when I first saw Jacob pulsing with red energy by the light of the GhosTV, but the knowledge had been slippery. Apparently, if you don't use it, you lose it. Instead of cementing, the skill had sifted through my fingers like so much backyard dirt. Now the visualization felt like make-believe, and I doubted my ability to power up that way at all.

After struggling with the mental image for a good, long while, I finally had to admit, "I can't hold onto it."

"You just need practice," Jacob said.

"There's no time for practice," I snapped. "There's too much at stake."

Amy—who had the most to lose—was surprisingly calm about the whole thing. "If you get angry with yourself, you'll only make it harder. Your ka is strong. You're perfectly capable of doing this. You just need to focus."

Amy's ka was pretty full of itself, so the fact that she saw something in mine ignited a spark of hope. I had all kinds of evidence that the stuff most people are blithely unaware of is all real. If I couldn't make my subtle bodies do what I wanted, who could?

"Okay," I said. "So I focus on the base of the spine."

Amy nodded. "And the color red. Imagine it soaking into you. Imagine you feel heavier. Like you're saturated. Imagine the Base of Set anchoring you to the earth."

I did as she asked. I felt heavier. Maybe. Or maybe it was my imagination.

I must've been screwing up my face, despite my best efforts to look like I had everything under control. "Picture yourself as a tree," Amy suggested. "Your head is the tree canopy, your arms are the branches, and your legs and body are the trunk. Focus on your feet. They're the part of the root that's aboveground, the part we're always tripping over."

Could I picture myself as a tree? I did my best.

"Imagine your roots extend below the ground, deep into the earth. While your canopy takes in energy from the sun—your Crown of Horus—you can't survive without water, your energy from the earth. You need both. You've been using both. Just acknowledge the energy you normally take for granted."

As I picture my tree roots pulling energy from the ground, I experienced a fleeting moment of disorientation as my subtle bodies shifted in my shell. Whichever body connects me to the planet didn't ooze down through the soles of my feet and drain into the dirt—thankfully—but it did seem to stretch. I did a little mental scramble to hold onto it.

I must've made another face, because Jacob said, "You've got this."

"You've been walking on the earth for decades," Amy reminded me. "You've already got a feel for her energy. Just open up to it."

If you've ever seen someone grab a water bottle and shoot a

stream of water into their mouth—say while they're weaving a bike in and out of traffic in a crowded intersection on Lawrence while you're trying to get to work on time and attempting not to hit them—you know how easy it looks. Until the next time you're confronted with a similar water bottle. And you end up looking like you're competing in a wet T-shirt contest.

No doubt I was calling up earth energy. But most of it probably ended up scattered all over the backyard.

The crunchy grass rustled as Jacob eased close and said, "You're always telling me to trust my gut—and you're right. Now it's time for you to do the same."

Annoyed that it was so obvious that this old dog was incapable of learning a new trick, I said, "But at least when I pull down the white light, I've got somewhere to put it—"

Who knows what the gesture I made with that statement was supposed to be. A flail. A flap. An arc of the hand to indicate the psychic reservoir that expands every time I see a ghost, panic, and fill it to the brim.

What I ended up doing, though, was smacking Jacob square in the neck.

Energy jumped. But instead of my carefully hoarded reservoir of white light leaping from me to him, it was a surge of grounding energy flowing from him to me. Jacob is strong—crazy strong—and he fills his tank just by going about his day-to-day routine. But he'd been doing the grounding meditation right along with me, and his power-up was turbocharged.

We both felt the rush—we each let out a gasp.

I had nowhere to put this energy, no reservoir to hoard it. If I'd been hoping for the zap to result in a full psychic battery, I'd be shit outta luck. Yet, the single moment of being so incredibly full made something in my understanding click. Feeling the sensation of what it was like to be grounded, even for half a second, at least gave me something to try for. It gave me the understanding I needed to shift my perception.

"Let's do this," I said...and proceeded to power up.

CHAPTER 19

I'll say this for being grounded: it's different. Apparently I'd been walking around half out of myself and half in the spirit world for my whole adult life. Even on Auracel, I wasn't connected to the grounding energy, just cut off from the white light.

Being firmly rooted in physical everyday reality would take some getting used to.

We locked up the GhosTV house, even though that meant I had to scramble back out the window. We left the set playing. Turning it off was a risk that Amy's ka would find the veil before it found her body and leave the plane entirely.

Jacob said, "Ask Amy where she last saw her body."

"The embalming chamber," she said.

Of course. I quelled a sigh and said, "Back at the funeral home. Let's go."

It's not that I think a dead body is anything to be afraid of. They're not gonna hop up and attack me—at least, I freaking hope not. But despite all my years in homicide, I'd never grown entirely numb to death in the way Amy obviously had.

Plus, with an active GhosTV in the vicinity, who knew what might happen?

Because Amy had a tendency to lock her keys in her trunk, she kept a spare in one of the planters out back. We let ourselves in. The funeral home seemed quiet. "My dad's car is gone," Amy said. "He must be at the grocery store. He'll be the guy standing in the middle of the aisle with his calculator out making sure he doesn't go over his budget, so he'll be occupied for a while."

Which meant it was just Jacob and me, Amy Grace's living ghost...and the body in the basement. As we headed downstairs, I caught myself trying to pull down white light—mainly because it felt like I was sucking Pepsi through a straw without taking off the paper wrapper first. Intellectually, I knew the funeral home wasn't haunted, and the body downstairs was just a body, but it took some effort to quell my impulse to feed my crown chakra all the same. I'd worked hard for my grounding, though. I couldn't piss it all away simply because I was in the proximity of a corpse.

Still, my heart was beating just a little bit faster when we let ourselves into the embalming room.

My tumescent friend from the day before was now fully clothed—big relief. Instead of the stainless steel table, he lay in a casket on a pneumatic metal gurney. He was positioned under a work lamp. Beside him, a table held a tray of makeup—a huge array of stuff with sponges and brushes, powders and putties. Enough gook to not only fill in his wrinkles and pores, but build him another whole face.

Under the glare of the work light, he looked vaguely waxy and a bit too tan. His lips were pulled into a grim line, and I couldn't help but stare at the seam, which was stuck together with some sort of mortician's artifice.

But at least I couldn't see the shape of his junk.

Amy said, "I don't know how many times I've told him—left hand on top."

"Told who?" I asked.

"George—he does all the heavy lifting around here. Obviously, I can't move the decedents by myself. He and my dad must've loaded up Mr. Norton after my body took off—and my father won't correct him. Too worried he'll up and quit, and we'll never be able to find a replacement."

I relayed this all to Jacob, who said, "I can't imagine it's easy to find someone willing to do funeral work."

"Someone relatively normal, anyhow," I said.

"Not in a town the size of Beauchamp," Amy agreed. "If you could just put his left hand on top."

As blasé as I might claim to be when it comes to dead bodies, when faced with the premeditated act of moving one around, I found I was none too eager. Sheepishly, I looked at Jacob and said, "She wants us to rearrange his hands. Maybe you'd better do it. I'd hate to find myself in the middle of an accidental possession."

"I thought you were grounded," he grumbled. But since he was the Stiff, any body-handling we might need to do really should fall on him.

His expression was stoic as he lifted Mr. Norton's arm and placed the other hand on top, but I did see a telltale muscle leap in his jaw as he suppressed an obvious wince.

Amy was none too thrilled. "And he's left off the wedding ring! If Mr. Norton shows up at the viewing without it, his wife will have a fit!"

We found the wedding band, along with a pair of wire-rimmed glasses and a medical alert bracelet, in a tray on the counter. Amy said, "Fold the glasses and put them in his breast pocket—the family always seems to like that—and get that wedding band on."

I relayed the instructions to Jacob. The glasses were easy enough (especially compared to moving around the body's arms) but the wedding band...not so much.

Jacob pushed—hard—and now there was no suppressing the wince. The dead body's hand hung in his grasp like an uncooperative piece of meat, and the wedding band seemed two sizes too small.

"They can be a little tricky," Amy said. "Put some lotion on it. But don't get it all over his suit."

Haltingly, I tried to advise—but Jacob clearly wished he was anywhere but there. He was looking a bit waxy himself now, and a sheen of sweat had formed on his usually unflappable brow. I took the ring from him and greased it with some lotion. He took the dead finger firmly in hand and gave the ring a shove... and it popped out of his grasp and pinged to the floor.

"Don't let it roll down the drain," Amy snapped, and I dove down to grab it. The concrete floor was slightly graded to slope down toward the drain, so that's exactly where the ring was headed. The slats on the drain were wide. I slapped a hand over it, and the rolling wedding band toppled to a stop against my pinkie. I did my best not to think about what sorts of fluids normally took this route and returned the slippery wedding band to my husband.

Eventually, Jacob had to raise Mr. Norton's arm and hold it in the air to let some of the embalming fluid settle out before he could finally cram the ring into place.

"I can see why Amy's employee left the wedding ring duty to her," he muttered, and headed over to a nearby sink to wash his hands.

I took my turn at the sink, and was scrubbing away the drain-cooties when a small, electronic funeral dirge sounded from the counter, where a phone sat in a charger.

"That's a text from my dad," Amy said, and her ka flickered and reformed by the phone. Forgetting she was non-physical, she reached for it and her hand passed right through. Luckily, though, she didn't screw it up like I had the TV timer. "He's always so long-winded! Can someone scroll this for me?"

She gave me her code. Dutifully, I unlocked the phone, pulled up the message and read.

"Big sale at SaverPlus on that toothpaste we like. You have to buy five to get the savings, but between you and me, eventually we'll use them. The bakery is out of cinnamon rolls so want me to get a crumb cake instead or should we try to be healthy and eat some fruit? I guess with all that toothpaste we can afford the crumb cake."

She wasn't kidding. I never would've taken Mr. Grace for such an extensive texter. I kept scrolling.

"Toilet paper is on sale too, so of course the shelves are completely picked over. Someone really needs to be better about keeping them stocked. The after-church crowd tears through the store like locusts but there's always a good lull after that."

I scrolled even more.

"And someone made a huge mess out of the microwave popcorn shelf. How hard is it to put similar boxes together? Also it looks like...tampons...are on sale." I felt my face go red. "Do you need any?"

"Physical bodies are so messy," Amy said. "Eating. Defecating. Bleeding. Text him back—nope, I'm fine."

"That's it? You answer War and Peace with three words?"

"He just likes to know someone's on the other end. Make

sure you use punctuation, though. Otherwise he might start to worry."

Once I texted her father back, I pocketed her phone. Civilian cell phones do leave an electronic trail, but only if Big Brother cares to look, and we might need that phone while we tracked down Amy's body. "Now what?" I asked. "It's not like you left a trail of formaldehyde footprints leading out the door."

Amy shrugged helplessly. "I'm at a loss. My body usually sticks pretty close to home."

"She doesn't know," I told Jacob.

He scanned the room, then said, "What do bodies want? Creature comforts. What if it's taking a nap?"

"I'll go double-check," Amy said, and her ka strode off through the embalming room wall.

I wasn't sure exactly how much time to ourselves it left us, but I took the opportunity to slip my hand into Jacob's anyway. There was no fear of white light leaping between us with that queasy zap you'd get from shuffling around on acrylic carpet for ten hours straight. Just the comforting squeeze of his hand in mine as I let him know we were alone again for the time being.

He let out a shuddering breath. "At least the body wasn't moving."

Unlike the corpse of Jennifer Chance in the FPMP morgue. I can only imagine how it felt when he pinned her spirit in place so I could send it across the veil where it belonged. Jacob truly gets off on being the Man of Steel, but the chinks in his armor do exist—and we'd just managed to locate one of them with a dead body's ring finger. "You did good." I squeezed harder. "It's gotta be all downhill from here."

I dropped Jacob's hand just as Amy's ka stepped through the opposite wall. "I rechecked the whole place—my apartment, dad's apartment, the funeral home, even the garage. I checked the caskets in the showroom, too."

"Good thing you didn't climb into one of those," I said. "You could have suffocated."

"Modern caskets aren't airtight. Bodies release gases. The caskets need to burp."

"Great image."

"At any rate, my body's still gone."

Then it was time to start walking the grid...and keep our fingers crossed that the body hadn't taken a fancy to a passing trucker. As we headed outside, we spotted the smoker guy who'd caught me snooping around the funeral home—the one who hadn't done a damn thing about it. Currently, he was pawing through the bushes at the far end of the building. "That's just George," Amy said. "Surprised to find him working at all without my dad here to make sure he doesn't slack off."

"He works here," I told Jacob.

Jacob squinted at him. "What's he doing?"

"Baiting the rat traps," Amy said.

"You have rats?" I demanded, fruitlessly attempting to quell images of them feasting on Mr. Norton's eyeballs...or other tender parts.

"We do not—because we're scrupulous about taking precautions. It's not enough to just poison them out here. You need to be sure to plug all the holes where they might come in. They have no collarbones—you'd be surprised at how small of a hole they can squeeze through."

Jacob said, "Never mind the rats. If we're lucky, maybe he saw which way Amy went." He strode off, full of purpose, no doubt relieved to be dealing with a living body now, and not a dead one.

"Excuse me, sir," Jacob called over as he approached.

George gave half a glance over his shoulder, then went back to what he was doing as if he was annoyed with the interruption.

"Sir?" Jacob repeated patiently as he approached. "I was wondering if you could tell me the last time you saw Amy Grace?"

Jacob reached for his I.D. as George finished snapping the rat bait into place, dusted off his hands, and only then deigned to turn fully around...with a giant tick of a habit-demon stuck to his cheek.

CHAPTER 20

I hopped back a step and pulled down white light. Or, more accurately, tried to. I was still grounded. And the white light still felt ephemeral and distant.

It was unlikely Jacob could see the habit demon too, but he saw my body language just fine. He eased sideways to subtly insert himself between this George guy and me.

Most people get all mushy and misty-eyed when their partners whisper sweet nothings or buy them fancy trinkets. But my cynical heart softened whenever Jacob tried to be my human shield.

Hopefully, it wouldn't come down to that. George's tick seemed pretty damn attached to him. He eyed us dubiously and said, "Whaddaya want with Amy?"

Jacob flashed his I.D. smoothly—long enough for it to be obvious that it was something very official and the photo it contained was definitely his, but not long enough to really puzzle through what the FPMP might be. Unless you already had some random association with the letters, I supposed, in which case it might work to his advantage. "I only need to ask Ms. Grace a few questions. Nothing that will take up too much of her time."

Jacob somehow managed to sound utterly authoritative and completely non-threatening. Even somewhat bored. A bureaucrat doing his job.

George was only somewhat mollified. His body language relaxed—slightly—but his frown lines deepened as his eyes narrowed. And on his face, the etheric parasite pulsed gently, like it was breathing. Or maybe feeding.

White light has been my defense for everything nonphysical from the moment I realized the white balloon trick actually worked...especially once Miss Mattie confirmed that it was more than just my imagination. I'd filled up with light so often—from working a homicide scene to walking the grid around the FPMP to navigating a startling repeater at a busy intersection—that the act had become second nature.

One could almost call it a habit.

Amping up my white light made me etherically stronger. But I suspected that in doing that kind of power-up, I also made my subtle bodies function independently of my physical shell. I already felt like my shoes were a size too big. I didn't need any encouragement to step out of them.

It took a stunning amount of effort, but I managed to stop myself from pulling down white light, and to focus instead on grounding energy. Instead of coming down from the skies, I pictured my power-up rising from the earth. Not through my ass, exactly, but up through my spine. Like the roots of a tree feeding the trunk.

Did it feel ridiculous? Of course—but no worse than the white balloon. Though it wasn't as if anyone else was privy to the thought. Unless George was a telepath. And then all bets were off.

"When was the last time you saw Ms. Grace?" Jacob asked.

"She was in the chapel when I got here. Early day. Had to haul all the flowers out to the grave site for the burial before the family showed up."

"And what was she doing in the chapel?"

"How the hell should I know?" George said.

"I was making sure no one left any valuables behind," Amy told me. "People are so distracted, both by their grief, and the prospect of seeing a bunch of people they haven't seen in years. You'd be surprised at the sorts of things they forget."

Meanwhile, George was still taking umbrage at Jacob's perfectly normal question. "I don't ask the Graces what they're doing or why. It's not my place. I'm just the guy who moves the dead bodies around. The stepin fetchit who hauls the flowers or pulls the car around or baits the rat traps. If that stuck-up bitch was working or praying or just standing there waiting for someone to boss around, no idea. But what it boils down to is, they say jump, I say how high? And that's all I know."

Normally, the piss-poor attitude would only make me want to lean on the guy harder and really give him something to bitch about, but I wasn't used to grounding energy, and I didn't want to risk that psychic carbuncle leaping from him to me.

"Thank you for your time," I said vaguely, and turned back toward the car. Taking my cue, Jacob followed.

Once we were all inside the safety bubble of the white sedan, Jacob said, "He seemed awfully hostile."

"That's like saying the Sears Tower is tall," I agreed. (I'd never been on board with calling it the Willis Tower and pointedly resisted doing so at any given opportunity.)

"That's just the way George is," Amy said.

I repeated it for Jacob, then said to Amy, "Are you okay? He said some shitty things about you back there."

She leaned forward through the gap in the front seat and said, "If I was in my body? Probably, then, I'd be offended. But as my ka, I don't seem to care as much about people's opinions in the physical world."

"But what about the—thing—on his face?"

"What thing?" Jacob demanded.

"Could you see it?" I asked Amy.

"The scarab?" She nodded. "I wasn't aware you'd pick up on it too."

"Yeah," I said wanly. "I see all the great things. What is it?"

Amy said, "I don't know much about the scarabs. Since I don't remember them once I'm back in my body, I haven't done any research. Honestly, I haven't really decided what they are. If they're travelers from another realm, or helpers of some kind, or something beyond my human understanding."

"She doesn't know," I told Jacob, "but it looked like a habit demon. A bloated tick of a thing, as big as my fist—right on the guy's cheek."

Jacob blanched. "An addiction might explain George's hostility. Tell Amy we've seen things like that before, things that belong on the other side of the veil."

Since she could hear Jacob perfectly fine, I just said, "It's a parasite. Plain and simple."

"She's seen them before?" Jacob asked.

"Every now and then," Amy said. "They'll come in on a decedent, but drop away by the time the embalming is done."

I translated for Jacob as the half-digested chocolate cherry ice cream did a queasy churn in my belly...and then I checked my forearm, which was itching like a habit demon was chafing against my skin.

Thankfully, there was nothing there but a red welt where I'd been scratching too hard.

Jacob said, "What if the habit demons are responsible for the stripping?"

I tugged my sleeve down over my wrist. "Habit demons can make people drink and shoot up and even bite their nails. Why not take off their clothes?"

Amy said, "But I don't think I was carrying a scarab."

I told this to Jacob, who said, "We don't know if they attach to the physical or the etheric."

"And if it's the etheric, how would you know?" I asked Amy, but thought better of adding, If it was on your face, you'd hardly be able to get a look at it. "Maybe it was somewhere you couldn't see. And you can't feel them, not exactly. They camouflage their impulses to feel like your own urges."

Amy said, "It's the physical body that comes into my workroom. And it's the physical body removing the clothing. If there were a scarab on my physical body, my ka would see it."

Maybe. Except her ka had precious little interest in what her physical shell was even doing...as evidenced by the fact that she simply let it wander away.

I said, "Whether or not there's a, uh, scarab involved...we still need to figure out where your body went. So, think. Bodies like what they like. Food, sleep, sex. Anything that feels good. Is there anything you normally miss out on because you're too busy working?"

"My father's a good cook, so I get plenty to eat at home. And I already checked my bed. I've been flirting with a guy on one of my professional message boards, but it's really nothing serious. Besides, he lives in Albuquerque."

We couldn't just make a quick call to F-Pimp to see if her body was on a flight to New Mexico without reinstalling a phone battery and letting National know exactly what we were up to. I checked Amy's phone instead, but it didn't appear as though she'd searched any flights. Plus her car was still at the funeral home.

And when I gave it some thought, the act of booking a flight, driving to an airport and flying halfway across the country for the sake of getting a few jollies seemed like an awful lot of trouble for a body to go through. Especially when she could just go proposition a trucker. Heck, she might even find herself with an extra few bucks for her trouble.

"What about shopping?" I suggested.

"You've seen what passes for fashion around here. I do get a kick out of the kitschy magnets at the Filling Station, but they haven't added anything new to that spinner rack in ages."

"Shopping is a no," I told Jacob.

He racked his brain. "There must be something she always means to do but never manages to make the time."

"Not that I can think of," Amy said.

I thought back to our first conversation—the one I'd had with the whole Amy, body and soul. "Didn't you say you wanted to go to film school? What if your body is at the movies?"

✦ ✦ ✦

Beauchamp's movie theater was small by Chicago standards, but it got the job done. The building squatted on the north side of town with cornfields on three sides and a car wash across the street. The lot was pretty full, probably because it was another muggy day and there'd be AC aplenty inside—plus, there wasn't much else to do on a Sunday afternoon.

I nearly bought us three tickets from the kiosk before I realized Amy's subtle body had a free pass. We headed inside and the smell of fake popcorn butter hit me right between the eyes. The lobby was pretty dead. There were only two screens, and both of them were mid-movie. The teenagers working the concession counter were all noodling on their phones, bored out of their skulls.

One of them paused in her texting to stir the popcorn, and the buttery smell intensified. Intellectually, I knew it was all chemicals and sodium. I also knew I'd had a big lunch just a few hours ago and followed it up with an even bigger ice cream cone. But the heart wants what it wants...or, in my case, the stomach.

Jacob was already striding purposefully toward the cinema door. "Hold on," I said, and he paused, turned, and cast a shrewd look across the concessions, as if he figured there must be something of interest in the non-physical.

I ordered a popcorn so big I had to carry it two-handed... though with some finessing, I was able to stabilize it in the crook of my arm so I could eat and walk at the same time. When I caught up to Jacob, he raised an eyebrow and asked, "How do you feel about sleeping with the lights off?"

"I'm still here," I reassured him. "But either I give my body what it wants, or I risk it going off on its own again."

Amy said, "That fake butter topping's got more preservatives than my workroom. I suppose the things we gravitate toward aren't necessarily good for us." No doubt Jacob would have agreed, though I didn't repeat it.

We headed into the first cinema, where a kids' animated flick was in full swing. Animation had come a long way since I'd been a fan of it. My childhood shows had the same background looping past repeatedly, like whenever Fred hopped into the Flintmobile and passed the same tree every 2.1 seconds. While the new computerized stuff was a lot more realistic, I wasn't so sure I liked it.

While goofy music assaulted my eardrums, up on the screen, a battalion of guinea pigs erupted from a pet shop and streamed down the sidewalk, on some sort of life-or-death guinea pig mission to rescue one of their own. You could see how it was gonna end from a mile away. They'd find the critter in the loving arms of its new owner, a cherubic kid who lavished it with hugs and treats, and they'd reconcile themselves to the fact that they'd all get adopted.

I supposed you could do worse than hugs and treats all day. Or maybe that was just my body's opinion.

I'd sussed out the movie plot in the couple of seconds it took us to walk up the aisle. Once fully inside, I turned to scope out what we'd actually come for—the audience—and found myself completely disoriented. "They have recliners now?" I whispered.

Amy said, "How long has it been since you went to the movies?"

Too long, apparently.

"Look for any adult sitting alone," Jacob said softly.

Sitting...or splayed out blissfully on one of those recliners. I realized the weekend was starting to catch up with me—the long drive, the strange bed, the late night. And then I realized how fastidiously I ignore my own exhaustion whenever I'm working a case.

If my body wanted rest, it should think about that when it sprang out of bed every morning at five-thirty sharp without an alarm, while Jacob blissfully slept through two or three snooze cycles. But somehow I doubted there'd be any reasoning with it. I tried to focus on my grounding energy, which felt like nothing more than my imagination. "Grab my wrist," I told Jacob. "And don't let me sit down."

With a popcorn vat cradled in one arm and Jacob holding onto the other, I scanned the crowd. Sparse. Which made sense, as most people would take young kids to the cheaper matinee times in the early afternoon. And most everyone there had at least one kid with them, except the teenagers making out in the back row. I checked all the adults just to be safe, in case Amy had somehow managed to score some random children on her way in. But if Amy's body was at the movies, it wasn't watching the latest and greatest computer-generated guinea pig adventure.

We headed into the second theater. The scene on-screen was dim, and my eyes took a few seconds to adjust to the darkness. Dramatic music designed to get the heart racing pumped through massive speakers and I felt myself start getting all charged up. Or maybe not myself, but just my body...which I wasn't so sure I necessarily agreed with anymore.

Onscreen, a pair of extremely good looking agent-types darted through a warehouse, slid around a corner and crouched behind some conveniently placed shelving. The female agent was tousled and glistening attractively with just the right amount of sweat, while her male counterpart had a small cut on his cheek that only accentuated how symmetrical and per-fect his features were.

They're always one step ahead of us, the guy said. How the hell do they always know where we are?

The camera obligingly zoomed in on something clinging to his back...an ugly, insectile piece of technology picking its way up his kevlar body armor. I shuddered as it crept up his neck and burrowed into his hair.

Jacob wasn't paying any attention to the movie, though he

did feel my reaction. He gave my arm a squeeze and muttered, "The place is packed."

And they were mostly adults. I wasn't so sure we'd actually find Amy without whipping out our flashlights and shining them in everyone's faces. I turned to her ka and said, "You've got the best chance of finding your body without getting thrown out by the ushers."

"They don't have ushers anymore, either," she said with a shake of her head, though she did high-tail it into the crowd to start looking.

Jacob helped himself to a handful of popcorn and said, "This is awful." And a few seconds later, he dipped in again as we waited for Amy's ka to finish looking.

While the agents onscreen dove beneath a table to avoid some sort of laser beam, I said, "I don't get it. This body, I mean. If you'd asked me whether I deny myself anything—other than, y'know, Seconal—I would've said no. Of course not. I eat what I want, sleep when I'm tired, and drink all the coffee my stomach can hold." Not to mention the fact that my sex life was a hell of a lot better than I ever dreamed it could be. "But suddenly my body's acting like a spoiled two-year-old throwing a tantrum."

In the dark of the theater, Jacob slid his grip down my arm until he was holding my hand. He gave it a gentle squeeze. "Our life is phenomenally stressful, but it's just crept up on us little by little—like the frog that doesn't realize it's being boiled alive. We can keep a better eye on the FPMP from the inside, but now we can also see how far their reach extends. We figure out more and more about our abilities, but only by grappling with things that leave us having nightmares. If you need more time in bed...I'll make that happen."

Leave it to Jacob to start off philosophical and end on a note that left me wishing we could go back to the motel and do the nasty.

Since I suck at flirting, I never know how to reply—not while all my subtle bodies are in place, anyhow—so I was saved from having to figure out what to say by the return of Amy's ka. "My body isn't here, and now your theory about going off with someone at the truck stop really has me worried. I don't think I'd do anything like that. But I've never really given it much thought, so how would I know for sure?"

"Let's not get ahead of ourselves. Your body's probably busy doing something a lot less drastic."

We checked the restrooms on the way out—no Amy—and since I was already sick of hauling that giant popcorn around, I dumped what was left of it into a nearby trash bin and grabbed a big wad of paper napkins to degrease my hands.

I said, "There must be something else your body would want to do. Something mundane. Some creature comfort you don't normally indulge in. We could check the restaurants—"

Amy made a sound of disgust. "You have one greasy burger, you've had them all."

"Or the ice cream stand."

"It closes at three."

"There's gotta be something fun to do around here. Lawn darts? Bowling? Even a park where you can take in the scenery."

"This county is flat as a pancake and it's 90% cornfields. There is no scenery—"

Amy's voice cut off abruptly as her ka winked out.

I stopped in my tracks, jerking my arm out of Jacob's grasp as I spun around to find her. "Amy?"

I'd sucked down white light without even thinking about it. From my grounded state, it felt clumsy, but it got the job done. My head went fuzzy and the familiar, almost-queasy sensation of powering up prickled along my neck. All that time I'd spent grounding myself to stay in my body, undone by a single moment of panic. Except, that ready-to-fall-out feeling I'd been struggling with was now absent...and not just because I was suddenly an expert at grounding.

Even powered up, I was still firmly in my body.

Which must've meant the GhosTV was off.

CHAPTER 21

Between Amy's sudden disappearance and the thought that someone was twirling the dial of the GhosTV—maybe even someone possessed by Jennifer Chance herself—I didn't realize we'd been followed until a middle-aged woman ambushed us right outside the door with, "You'll hardly put an end to the drug parties at the movies!"

Jacob and I both stopped cold—as did my heart, at least for the couple of beats it skipped. I've never been more terrified of a person in sparkly flip-flops in my life. Unaware of my inner meltdown, Ruth kept right on talking. "Everyone needs a break now and then, but this is the prime time to catch those delinquents in the act!"

Jacob recovered first. He pulled out the don't-fuck-with-me cop voice and said, "Ma'am? We'll need you to step away and let us do our jobs. You're at risk of contaminating our investigation."

Ruth blanched, then huffed, then hustled over to a shiny new SUV parked in a handicap spot, climbed in and slammed the car door.

My adrenal glands pumped hormones into my bloodstream harder than a teenager squirting movie popcorn with fake butter, and by the time we got back to the rental car, I was shaking. Across the hood of the car, I told Jacob, "I could buy her crossing paths with us at the restaurant. And SaverPlus? It's a stretch, but still possible. But no way did she just happen to show up at the movies right when we did."

"What are you saying?" Jacob asked carefully.

"She's from National." I waited until her SUV pulled out of the lot and disappeared around a corner, then said, "They were here waiting for us all along. Sent an operative here to scope out the final GhosTV to see who'd come after it, and here we are, blundering right into their trap—"

"What if she's not from National?" Jacob said grimly. "What if all this time, she's the one who's been babysitting the GhosTV?"

Movie popcorn churned in my gut. "Then, what? She's another Roger Burke?"

"He did have the whole helpful-guy routine down pat."

True. But Jacob had suspected him right from the beginning. Something about Roger just rubbed him wrong from the get-go. Then again, our interactions with Ruth were minimal at best, so maybe he hadn't really had the chance to read her.

We climbed into the rented sedan. Generally, we avoid saying anything incriminating in the car. Peter Garcia claims that no one's out there installing eavesdropping devices in the FPMP parking garage while we're busy at work...but he only knows what his own department is up to. It's not like National would consult him if they wanted to keep a closer eye on their agents in the Midwest branch.

Then again, if Ruth had bugged this particular vehicle, why would she try to upsell us the SUV, back when we picked up the car?

Unless it was all an elaborate scheme to make us think we'd

made a decision, when in fact, she knew we'd only double down on the sedan....

The only good thing about sensitive surveillance equipment is that it's easy to overload. Crushing ice in the blender, rattling chains at the hardware store, even blasting the TV. When we needed to have a delicate conversation, we did it very quietly, behind the camouflage of something loud and obnoxious.

Jacob turned on the radio and cranked up the volume...then cranked some more as no sound came out.

Neither of our cars is a spring chicken. Mine because I dreaded all the decision-making involved in replacing it. Jacob because Crown Victorias stopped rolling off the assembly line years ago, and the civilian model he drove was the closest thing out there to a Police Interceptor. Neither of our cars has a fancy touchscreen on the dash, so when we encounter one, it takes some getting used to.

What showed on this particular screen was not a radio station, not a backup camera, not a map, but the wall of text that had confounded me before. A bunch of terms and conditions. Only now, I realized I could scroll down, and there was an "accept" button at the bottom. Before I could jab it, Jacob caught me by the wrist. "Since when do you actually bother reading these things?" I said.

But he wasn't listening—something had caught his eye. "Section four. We agree that by using the CarStar XM Radio and Onboard Safety System, we understand that information regarding speed, location and fuel consumption will be transmitted to the CarStar system."

I stared at the words stupidly even as Jacob read them aloud. "But we never agreed to that," I said. "We didn't push the button."

Jacob cut the engine to shut off the spyware. "No...but we

signed a contract."

"An agreement to rent a car."

"Which we also didn't read."

I grabbed the thing from the glovebox, and lo and behold—there among the fine print Voter Rayon had so blithely signed off on was the same damn disclaimer.

"Goddammit," I snapped.

Good thing I'd given my ammo to Jacob—we need to fill out umpteen reports when we discharge a weapon. But the butt of my Glock made a really satisfying crunch when it smacked through the navigation screen.

Jacob cut his eyes to the screen with its deep spiderweb crack. "That's probably not where the tracker is."

"Felt good anyhow," I grumbled. Hopefully Laura wouldn't question me "accidentally" destroying it when the expense report reached her desk.

It was either abandon the car and walk, or proceed with the knowledge that our movements were being recorded. And we'd look pretty conspicuous marching around with a ladder, so we'd be noticed either way. Jacob turned on the car again. Warm air blew from the vents, followed by cold as the freon kicked in. The screen lit up just fine. Apparently all I'd managed to do was mess up the glass and stop the touch function from working.

"What about Amy?" Jacob asked. "If someone turned off the GhosTV, her spirit must've snapped back inside her body. Right?"

"Normally, we could call and see. Unfortunately, I've still got her phone. And even if she is all put together again, she won't remember our little scavenger hunt, so she won't think to track us down and let us know if she's okay."

Jacob drummed his fingers on the steering wheel. "We need

to find her. Beauchamp seemed like a safe enough place to let her body do its thing…until we met George."

Amy hadn't seemed particularly worried about George, so neither was I. Clearly, though, Jacob was. And he was the one with the gut instinct for reading people. If Jacob was worried…I should be, too. Hadn't I just been thinking about the fact that he'd spotted something was up with Roger Burke within two minutes of meeting him, while I blithely let the guy drug my coffee and transport me across state lines? "You think there's foul play?" I asked.

"I think there's an anger issue, and a power imbalance. George made no qualms about badmouthing Amy. It could just be a bunch of talk. But he sounds too much like all the perps I've interviewed that we can't just look the other way—like he's itching to 'put her in her place.'" He got that pensive look that came from too many years of seeing too many ugly scenes. "People think rape is about sex…but it's not. It's about power."

And we wouldn't be able to live with ourselves if it turned out George had been teaching Amy a "lesson" all this time—with or without her ka inside her body.

Jacob said, "Once he crosses that line, there's no turning back. And when he sees he's got nothing left to lose—that's when everything will really devolve."

"Then we go back and pay George a visit."

"If he's got Amy, he won't be keeping her at the funeral home. He'll take her somewhere he's in charge. But we've got no last name. No idea where he lives. And no access to the data we'd normally use."

"That's it, then." While we had nothing, someone back at HQ could dig up the info in a heartbeat. "There's no choice but to come out of dark mode."

"Not so fast." Jacob pulled an aggressive U-turn before I'd even had a chance to dig out my phone. I shot him a questioning look, and he said, "George could have taken her anywhere. But if we get Amy's ka back, she can tell us exactly what he did with her body."

CHAPTER 22

We peeled up to the GhosTV house, swung into the driveway, and dragged out the ladder. The sun was getting lower now. Even though we'd done this earlier that evening, in the low light it felt a lot more sinister. But if the neighborhood ignored us in broad daylight, it wasn't about to worry about us now.

I paused at the top of the ladder and listened through the broken window. Nothing but the distant thud of a bass line from some music next door drowning out their barking dog. The GhosTV house felt just as empty and abandoned as it had before. So, with precious little time to screw around, I launched myself up and through the narrow window.

The back door was just a few steps away, and it was a huge relief to let Jacob in. Not just because my sidearm wasn't loaded, but because he was my anchor. Literally. Even when my subtle bodies weren't in any danger of falling out.

Neither of us moved to turn the lights on—no sense in alerting the whole town that we were poking around in the vacant house. Just my luck, a bunch of kids would show up hoping for a "drug party." But with all the curtains drawn, our flashlights shouldn't attract any more attention than a GhosTV on a random timer.

We checked the hodgepodge of cords and devices behind the TV more closely. I said, "According to the timer, this should still be on. Unless some old daylight savings bullshit is throwing me off."

Jacob followed the trail of cords with his flashlight. "Must be the fuse again."

Some things really should be left to professionals. Murder investigations. Embalming. Electrical work. But Jacob seemed to know what he was doing—then again, even if he doesn't, he's never let that stop him. He unscrewed the fuse, held it up to his flashlight, and said, "Blown. Have you got a penny?"

I hate change. Nothing like grabbing for a bag of salt and coming up with eighty-seven cents instead. But I'd paid for my ice cream with cash, I realized. And when I got my change, my dumb body hadn't bothered to dump the coins in the tip jar. "Dare I ask what you need it for?"

"We can use it to complete the circuit."

"Gee, that sounds really safe."

"Uncle Leon did it all the time." And Uncle Leon was missing an arm—so I wasn't sure how much we could trust his work-arounds. "It's gotta be copper, though. Something old."

While it wouldn't power up the GhosTV anytime soon, it was probably for the best that all three of the pennies in my pocket were shiny and new. "Can't you switch out one of the others?"

Jacob inspected them with his flashlight. "The fridge is on a thirty-amp fuse and the plug takes fifteen amps...though I guess that's no worse than a penny."

"Before we burn the damn house down—with the GhosTV and us in it—why don't we try plugging into a different outlet?"

"The whole living room is likely on the same circuit."

"Then we try the bathroom. This house is not that big, and there's an extension cord on the coffee pot. Between that, the timer and the cord itself, I bet it'll reach."

Jacob nodded decisively. "Let's do it."

While I was right—the TV cord, the extension and the timer did daisy-chain to make a pretty long stretch—the bathroom outlet was placed as awkwardly as humanly possible. I pulled gingerly on the cord. "Can you give me like six more inches?"

It was ripe for a lewd retort...but with Amy's body AWOL, neither of us was in the mood to kid around.

"This thing weighs more than a refrigerator," Jacob grunted from the living room.

"Then don't lift it by yourself." Jacob might be in great shape, but he could still put his back out—and if he did, we'd be screwed.

Lift with your knees, not your back. That's what they always say. What that means in practice, I've never had any idea. No matter what I do with my legs, my arms and back take the brunt of the work. We only had to move the TV far enough to reach the outlet, though. And so I braced myself, and on the count of three, lifted.

Heavy did not even begin to describe it. But Jacob and I were desperate, and between the two of us, we managed to lift the thing and move it a half-step closer to the bathroom.

Though when we set it back down, it gave off an ominous creak.

I said, "Tell me that was the floorboards and not the console."

"There's only one way to find out. Plug it in and see if it works."

No doubt I should have been less cavalier about taking orders from someone who wanted to stick a penny in the fuse box. But with less than an inch to spare, I jammed the plug home.

Sometimes, if the light is low when I unplug my electric razor, I can see a little spark jump between the socket and the prongs. According to the internet, either it's perfectly normal and nothing at all to worry about, or we're all gonna die. Since I look homeless when I go too long without shaving, I've chosen to believe the former.

But when the extension cord attached to the GhosTV zapped me...I felt it.

Or did I? As zaps go, it was pretty mild. I'd done worse shuffling around on a cheap carpet. Heck, it was zappier whenever Jacob stole my white light. In fact, maybe I'd just imagined it all. The important thing was, we'd managed to turn the TV back on.

I heard the blip and stutter of a digital antenna finding a signal. And then the laugh track of a crappy syndicated sitcom.

I would've loved to turn the thing down, but we had no way of knowing if the volume knob was connected to more than just the sound. I focused hard on Amy Grace. "Amy?" I called out over the stilted banter of the sitcom. "Amy, can you hear me? We're back at the—" What—the suicide house? The GhosTV? Everything I'd been calling the place in my mind sounded ridiculous. "We're back where you found us before."

I paused to listen.

"Anything?" Jacob asked.

"Not a damn thing."

He brushed at a stray cobweb he'd picked up during our exertions. "We need to find her. Talking to George was incriminating enough. Add to that the fact that you saw a habit demon on him...well, I'll just never forgive myself if something happened to her right under our noses and we couldn't do anything to stop it."

And now it was personal for him. Try as you might to maintain a certain professional detachment to get the job done, now and then a case will get under your skin anyhow. I'd be lying if I said I wasn't attached to Amy myself. Sure, she was brusque inside her body and pedantic when she wasn't. But if I'd made a friend in my short time in Beauchamp, I'd have to say it was her.

Jacob dusted his hands together, then shook them off. "Greasy."

"What?"

"The TV."

I rubbed my fingertips against my thumbs, and felt nothing but a bit of residual stickiness on my right hand where I hadn't quite contained my ice cream cone. "Guess you ended up in the wet spot this time around. There's a dried-up bar of soap in the bathroom...though, frankly, I wouldn't go near that outlet if I were you. Just looking at it funny might cause the whole house to burst into flames."

Jacob waved away another cobweb and headed into the kitchen instead. As he scrubbed his hands with some dregs of generic dish soap, he said, "The way I see it, we've got a choice. Either we stay dark, stay off National's radar, or we plug back in and get George's info in two seconds flat. In other words, we've got to choose. The GhosTV—and potentially, our freedom—or saving Amy."

Of course, I cared what happened to Amy. I care about freaking everything, a hell of a lot more than I ever like to admit. But I wasn't about to serve us up to National on a platter when we couldn't be sure if Amy's body hadn't just wandered off to watch a nice sunset over the cornfields.

And then I realized there was someone else who could get us George's info almost as quickly as HQ. It might not be a dossier complete with his employment history, his arrest record, and even his traffic violations. But I'd bet we could get a last name and an address.

Ruth Parrish was surprised to hear from me, to say the least. Not as surprised as she would be once she saw what I'd done to her rental car, but still, she was pretty shocked when I called. Putting her off-kilter was good. Witnesses are more useful when they haven't had a chance to rehearse what they're going to say.

I put Amy's phone on speaker, dialed the number on Ruth's business card and got her on the line. "You're familiar with the Grace Funeral Home," I said, more like a statement than a question, since I was certain Ruth was familiar with everyone and every place in town.

"I...am. But I don't see what this has to do with the drug parties."

"I'm not at liberty to comment on the particulars of an ongoing investigation. The employee who handles the gruntwork there, George...?"

"George Stanton?"

"That's the one. Have you got an address on him?"

"Well, I...off the top of my head, no."

"It would really streamline the investigation."

"You think George is involved?"

You've gotta be firm or else witnesses will just walk all over you. "Ongoing investigation."

"Oh. Uh, right. Well, I'm pretty sure he still lives in the old schoolhouse apartments on Grandview. But the kids at these parties are in their twenties. Doesn't he seem a bit old to be involved?"

"Thank you for your help. I'll let you know if you can be of further assistance." I hung up without waiting for her reply.

I found the apartments with a quick search while Jacob

re-washed his hands. "Not to dash your hopes, Vic, but apartment buildings aren't exactly an ideal place to bring a victim. Too many prying eyes."

"Maybe so. But there are plenty of neighbors to canvass. They love to tattle on each other's comings and goings. And you've gotta admit, it's pretty refreshing to be asking around in a small town where everyone knows everyone else's business. If this were Chicago, we'd be shit outta luck."

Jacob scrubbed harder. "I doubt HQ could come up with anything more concrete than an address, not without checking all the local traffic cams. It's quickest to just head over there ourselves." He gave his hands a final rinse, and then a decisive shake. "Feels like we just dodged a bullet."

Maybe. But it was obvious we shouldn't count our bullets until they hatched.

CHAPTER 23

The schoolhouse apartments on Grandview turned out to be anything but grand. No big surprise, considering George schlepped around dead bodies and baited rat traps for a living. The building was solid, constructed to withstand the tread of generations of school-aged children. It was blocky in a particularly municipal sort of way, not to mention dull and worn around the edges. The vestibule hadn't been swept in so long, I spotted sidewalk salt crusted among the grit, gravel and maple seed helicopters. A dozen mailboxes hung on the wall, some empty, some overflowing with junk mail. A recycling bin was parked beneath them, also overflowing. The whole thing was pervaded with the smell of dirty laundry and boiled cabbage.

I rang the doorbell marked Stanton. No answer. Jacob tried the inner door. Locked. I then proceeded to try every other doorbell. Out of a dozen residents, someone was bound to buzz us in. Hopefully someone eager to speculate on their neighbor's comings and goings.

One by one, I pushed the doorbells...and not a single one fell for it.

"There's cars parked outside and lights are on," I said, annoyed.

"Maybe people are less blasé around here about letting in a random stranger than they are in Chicago."

Jacob was busy scanning a small billboard by the door. I read over his shoulder. A few yellowed flyers for some sketchy looking "business opportunities" and a notice that a service charge would be assessed for all late rent payments. Jacob pointed at the notice. "There, at the bottom."

Property Manager

Randy Wood

Sounded like a made-up porn star name to me. But there was a phone number printed underneath, so it couldn't hurt to try it. Though given the state of the lobby, I'd be lucky if he hadn't retired in 1992.

I put Amy's phone on speaker and dialed the number, and thankfully, he answered.

"Victor Bayne on official business from the FPMP." Not something I generally threw around, but it seemed to have some traction around here. Even if no one actually knew what it meant. "I'll need to access one of the apartments on Grandview."

To say Randy "porn star" Wood was flustered would be putting it mildly. "I can't just let someone into an apartment without 24 hours' notice."

"Official business," I repeated.

"It's just...people get testy when you invade their privacy. And it's so hard to keep the rental units filled."

"You've got ten minutes to get over here and let me in or I get a locksmith out here and do it myself—and bill all the charges to you."

As I spoke, the interior door opened outward, and a flabby guy in a Hawaiian shirt and cutoffs stood with a phone to his ear. "Let's not be hasty." His voice echoed from Amy's phone.

"They charge triple on a Sunday night."

I hadn't necessarily expected the guy to be on the premises. About time something went our way.

Randy Wood was in his fifties, Caucasian, average height and a few pounds overweight. He was paler than I was—and that's saying a lot. But he looked particularly doughy because he was completely bald, all the way down to the eyebrows.

I flashed him my I.D. "We'll need to see unit 208."

His shoulders slumped in resignation. "Fine. Follow me."

The hallways were brown—the carpets, the walls and the nicotine-stained ceilings—and the fluorescent light fixtures gave all of it an odd greenish undercast. Every few yards, a printed "painting" hung. A random landscape. A banal flower. Generic art from thirty years ago hanging faded and warped in cheap plastic frames.

The sound of a half dozen TVs competed with one another as we tromped up the hallway. We paused in front of 208 and Randy knocked.

No answer.

"Open it," I said.

"I'll need to call the tenant and let him know—" Randy said.

"No time," I told him. "We need to see the unit. Now."

I'd used my cop-voice, a tone I'd cultivated through my time on patrol—of telling knuckleheaded civilians to curb their dogs, turn down their stereos, and for God's sake, stop spray-painting random penises on the overpass. And as most civilians tended to do when I laid that tone on them, Randy obeyed and unlocked the door.

George Stanton's apartment wasn't much bigger than the white-on-white one-bedroom we'd lived in before the cannery, but that was where the similarity ended. My place had been in an older brick courtyard building, with hardwood floors and high ceilings. This apartment was flat and low, open-plan, with a galley kitchen and wall-to-wall carpeting.

My hand drifted toward my sidearm, but since I'd given my bullets to Jacob, I went for my flashlight instead. I shone it up the hallway as I headed toward the bedroom, hoping for the best (an unharmed Amy) but steeling myself for the worst. What I found, instead, was neither. Other than a rumpled bed and an overflowing laundry basket, the bedroom was empty.

That left the bathroom. If anyone had to dispose of a corpse in a place like this, the bathtub would be the only logical place to do it. It wouldn't be easy. But between that and the garbage disposal, a determined enough person could make it work.

Thankfully, the only visible organic matter in George's bathtub was a nasty infestation of dark mildew in the seams of the shower surround.

Back in the main room, Jacob was scanning the junk mail by the door while Randy tried to act accommodating, though mainly, the guy just sounded nervous. "Is this about the water pressure? Because I've explained to our tenants I dunno how many times that we have no control over the water mains, and they need to take it up with Public Works."

I took a better look around the living room. To say it was a bachelor pad would be putting it mildly. A TV tray parked by the couch held the crusty plastic remains of at least three microwave meals, and the couch was strewn with discarded socks, a T-shirt and a few wads of used tissues.

Jacob had paused in the kitchen doorway, where he spotted a trash can. People's garbage will offer up valuable clues as to their day-to-day routine. From fast food wrappers to various receipts, the trash is a goldmine that can divulge a bunch of useful information.

Or a swarm of fruit flies.

Jacob made a sound of disgust and fell back a step, waving the bugs away. (I'd say "frantically," but Jacob doesn't do frantic. Vigorously, though? Yeah, that description fit pretty well.)

I had the good grace to act like I hadn't just seen him get bombarded, and his voice was level when he asked me, "Seen enough?"

"All clear." I turned to Randy. "Are there any other areas of the building the tenants have access to?"

His tone was just a little bit too innocent when he replied, "Such as?"

"Storage? Laundry?"

He wiped sweaty palms on his Hawaiian shirt and said, "Again, I have no control over the water pressure—"

"Basement," I said firmly. "Let's go."

Cringing, Randy led us down two flights of stairs and into a lower level that didn't look much different from the second-floor hallway. Everything was brown and thirty years out of date. But while the upper floor was stuffy and stale, the basement felt cooler. The ambient smells were less pronounced, but the air had a certain mineral quality to it, as if the olfactory contaminants were being filtered through concrete. Amy's grounding meditation came back to me, the thought of red energy coursing up through the earth, and I pictured the grounding mojo flowing up through my subtle bodies. I felt solid.

How strange.

Maybe the reason I've always felt so uncomfortable in basements had nothing to do with the baby's repeater I'd stumbled across beneath my old apartment. Maybe the whole vibe in general simply felt weird, since I'd gone through so much of my life feeling anything but grounded.

As Randy scurried ahead, fluorescent overheads played across the smooth curve of his scalp. "Our laundry facilities are reasonably priced—just fifty cents a load higher than the local laundromat. And considering the convenience of having the washers right downstairs, I'd say it's well worth it."

Inside the laundry room, a woman sat on a battered lawn chair, scrolling on her phone as laundry tumbled in the dryers. When she saw it was Randy, she rolled her eyes, but went back to her scrolling without comment.

Obviously, no one would stash a victim somewhere so public.

Jacob shifted his shoulders uncomfortably, like he was hoping to dislodge some stowaway fruit flies. "Is there anywhere else in the basement that the tenants can come and go?"

He'd been asking Randy, but it was the woman on the phone who answered. "The storage lockers—total mess. And the fitness room, if you can call it that. Treadmill's been broke for the past two months."

"Treadmills don't grow on trees," Randy said defensively.

I doubted we'd find Amy in the fitness room, broken treadmill or no, but if the storage lockers here were anything like the ones at my old apartment....

"We'll need to see it all," I said. "Let's go."

We checked the fitness room just to cover all our bases. Empty, save for an elliptical, the broken treadmill, a couple of yoga balls and a weight bench.

The storage lockers were another story.

They were more like corrals than lockers, a couple dozen in all. They were arranged in two deep, narrow rows, with wooden slatted walls and padlocked doors. Easy enough to see in through the slats—even despite the shifting shadows. Some lockers held orderly stacks of boxes. Others were filled with seasonal stuff like skis and Christmas trees and even a kayak. But most of them were just dumping grounds for trash. Garbage bags of clothes ripped open with fabric pushing through the torn plastic. Cardboard boxes sagging, one of them with mushrooms sprouting where the damp wicked up from the floor. And shoved against the far wall at the end of the aisle, a mountain of crappy, outdated broken electronics lay abandoned by prior tenants, crap too heavy or cumbersome to recycle.

Jacob shone his flashlight like he was warding off something with a lightsaber. Dust motes danced in the beam. He nodded at some random trash on the floor. "This hasn't been disturbed in a while."

I'd have to agree, though when he hustled our bald tour guide out the door, I stood in the doorway for an extra moment, considering the detritus. There might not be any bodies here. But if you were looking to hide a GhosTV, you could do worse than stashing it among all those ginormous tube TVs from the nineties....

Jacob backed into the hallway, shaking off the willies. As he backpedaled away from the storage lockers, he spotted a door with a placard. "What about the mechanical room?"

Randy's eyes darted to the door. He somehow managed to look doughier without even moving. "Tenants aren't allowed in there. Safety reasons. And obviously, it's locked."

Jacob nudged the door with his flashlight and it creaked open an inch.

"It should be locked," Randy said. "When the weather is humid like this, the doorjambs shift around. It's not as if I can control the weather."

Maybe not, but everyone knows humidity makes a door stickier—and even if we were in opposite-land, there is such a thing as a dehumidifier. Still, while it would be satisfying to argue with him just for the sake of being right, finding Amy was way more important.

"Really, there's nothing interesting in there," Randy said. "You see one hot water heater, you've seen 'em all."

I sure hoped this guy didn't play poker—'cause if he did, he'd be flat broke before he even finished his first drink. A disturbing scenario spun out in my mind. Him and George in some kind of sick, sadistic pact. And maybe Amy wasn't even their first victim....

"Jesus!" Jacob scrambled back, boffing into me. I steeled myself for something bad—really bad—and angled past him into the mechanical room, swinging my flashlight beam in a sweeping arc.

I'd expected blood.

I'd expected a body.

What I didn't expect was the far wall to be teeming with insects the size of my hand.

No clue what they were. They looked a lot like cockroaches, but they didn't skitter away from my light beam like a roach would. Maybe in Iowa they bred their roaches big and slow. Or maybe, judging by the plinks and plunks of leaking pipes all around us, they were some kind of cockroach-adjacent water bug.

I'm no handyman, but even I could see the plumbing in this place was...creative. And not in a good way. Pipes criss-crossed the ceiling, with every joint wound with so much duct tape they actually bulged. Or maybe it was just the water pushing out against the tape. Everything was dripping so hard you could practically take a shower. And while there was a drain set in the center of the room, water was pooling in every dip in the floor.

Randy said, "That leak must be new. We have forty-five days to bring it up to code." The only way to bring this place up to code would be to bulldoze it into the ground. But while the mechanical room was nightmare-worthy in its own right, at least Amy Grace wasn't duct taped to the sewer line.

Nervously, he added, "People don't realize how challenging it is to manage a property. They see those shows on TV where things get remodeled in two days while the owners stay in a hotel for a weekend. What they don't realize is that there's a huge crew at work making that remodel happen. And they cut corners, too, believe you me. Just because it looks good for the camera doesn't mean it's quality work. They make house-flipping look so easy, too. Like all you need to do is slap on a fresh coat of paint, knock out the kitchen wall and you'll double your profit. It's all a bunch of lies. Real estate is not for the faint of heart."

Before Randy's babbling could go any farther afield, I swung my beam around, casually catching his eyes with the glare. "What can you tell us about your tenant in 208?"

"George Stanton?" He raised a pasty hand to shield his eyes while I answered with a bland look. "He works at the funeral home."

Obvious.

I waited.

Randy said, "He's lived here, five? No, six years. Pays on time, more or less. Quiet."

"So he's an ideal tenant," Jacob said.

Randy shrugged haplessly. "He's fine."

I could sense this guy was eager to take our focus off the

dubious plumbing, so if he knew anything worthwhile, he'd spill it if we just came at him from the right angle. "We might have some flexibility on those forty-five days…if you can tell us more about Stanton."

"I don't understand. Is George in trouble?"

"I'm not at liberty to comment on an ongoing investigation." I swung my light beam to a pipe bulging with dripping duct tape. "Forty-five days is nothing. The time goes by incredibly fast."

Randy groped for something to tell me that would buy his plumbing a reprieve. "I mean, you can't really blame him for how he is."

Bingo. "Go on."

I expected a litany of his mistreatment at the hands of the ruthless funeral home barons known as the Graces, something that would confirm our suspicions that George had snapped and made off with Amy to take his revenge.

And Randy went somewhere else entirely.

"I mean, to have a Beauchamp for a father…to watch your uncle piss away the family fortune…that would make anyone angry."

My flashlight beam dropped to the floor. "What's that got to do with anything?"

"And why didn't he take his father's last name?" Jacob asked.

Randy shrugged. "His mom was just a lot lizard who couldn't prove anything. But she swore up and down Leland was the father." Leland—the one who was purportedly slow. "Even if anyone believed her, it probably wouldn't have mattered. Roy Beauchamp didn't exactly disown Leland…but he acted like he had one son: Marlon. And Marlon was no prize, either. Blew the family fortune on a bunch of bad investments."

"What kind of investments?" Jacob asked.

"Businesses that failed within a year. A shopping center that never got built. When he died, not only was the Beauchamp fortune lost, but even his real estate portfolio was worthless.

"It was a great opportunity for a motivated buyer. My cousin made a nice nest egg flipping some of Marlon's old properties. It's a seller's market." He sighed. "And yet, while most vacant homes around here get snapped up within the first month, others sit on the market and rot—I swear, it's like they're cursed, and no amount of vinyl plank flooring or subway tile will change the buyer's mind. Just goes to show, if something looks too good to be true, it probably is."

CHAPTER 24

It was full dark by the time we headed back out to the rental car. Jacob shook out his pant legs before he got in, then cracked open a travel case he had stashed in the back seat. I might tease him about his Boy Scout-level preparedness, but when he handed me a protein bar, I devoured it in three bites. Dinnertime had come and gone, and while my stomach would usually lodge only a minor complaint about a missed meal, tonight my appetite was especially sharp.

"Got any more in there?" I asked.

He handed me the uneaten half of his, then pulled out a wet wipe packet and tore it open. "I will never unsee that wall of bugs," he said with a shudder as he went at his hands as if he could scrub away the memory. "My skin is still crawling."

I grunted my agreement through a mouthful of protein bar.

"And I think something dripped on me." He ripped open another wipe and gave the back of his neck a thorough going-over, then dug into a travel pack of tissues and blew his nose, hard. Good thing he was a Superstiff who didn't need to worry about blowing his ka out his own ass. "What's even worse, I'm positive I inhaled a bunch of fruit flies. I swear I can feel them burrowing into my sinuses."

Jacob looked at the used tissue—but he must not have seen anything with six legs and a pair of wings, because instead of brandishing it as proof, he just crammed it in his pocket with a huff.

We swung by Amy's apartment above the funeral home, hoping she'd turned up while we were trudging through the world's nastiest basement, but the lights were all off and no one answered the doorbell. And we narrowly avoided being spotted by her father, who came to the window at the sound of tires on asphalt in the parking lot.

"Now what?" I said. "God-knows-what's happened to Amy and we can't afford to keep dicking around."

Jacob ground his molars together a few times, then said, "George isn't at work. He isn't home. And you saw a habit demon on him."

"On his face," I emphasized.

Jacob shuddered again. "I didn't see any utility bills for a second property in the pile of paperwork on his counter, so where would he be? In his vehicle?"

"With Amy? That seems like a stretch."

"Maybe. But what if he's out trying to score whatever drugs he's on?"

"That's presuming it's something as normal as drugs feeding the tick, and not some kind of twisted proclivity for torture." I'd seen habit demons get off on ragged cuticles, after all. Who in the hell knew what their real deal was?

Neither of us held out much hope of finding George at Ruth Parrish's drug party, but she'd given us the location, and it was the only lead we currently had. I looked up Vine Street on Amy's phone, and the two of us kept our eyes peeled for the beat-up blue pickup truck. But we needn't have bothered. You could hear it from two blocks away.

"I'd figured Ruth was just being a busybody," I said as we pulled up to the nearest empty spot, a good hundred yards off. "But, shit. That music is vibrating the car windows from all the way down the street."

The party house was a small, single-family home, a postwar ranch style place with a For Sale sign out front. A red balloon tied to the sign bobbed listlessly on the meager breeze. The temperature had cooled down some, but it was still a warm summer night, and windows and doors were all open. Red lights glowed from the openings, giving the little house a decidedly hellish look. And the dance music inside thudded so hard it practically shook the sidewalk.

I've dealt with hundreds of noise complaints in my time as a patrolman. It's like riding a bike, I suppose. Muscle memory carried me toward the house at a good clip. I strode up the stairs, knocked on the doorjamb and announced myself—not that anyone could hear me. And not that I was even a cop anymore. But procedure is procedure.

The smell of weed hung heavy in the air and the place was packed. Teens and twenty-somethings, mostly Caucasian, and mostly zonked out of their minds. They flailed like noodle guys at car dealerships, oblivious to how ridiculous they all looked.

All the lightbulbs were red. It felt like a giant darkroom. The red light tricked my eyes and made the partiers glom together into a single, seething mass of humanity.

The place was tiny enough that two dozen people filled it up good—three, tops. And whatever space didn't have a flailing person in it was occupied by some kind of inflatable.

Red and black balloons bobbed through the crowd. Some

kids were batting them around, and some were just oblivious, completely zoned out, dancing with a staticky balloon stuck to their head. There was no real furniture, but a bunch of pool floats, loungers, and blow-up chairs were jammed up against the wall. Some held kids making out. Some held kids zoning out. And some lay flaccid, popped, and trampled.

Jacob and I stuck out like a couple of black-suited sore thumbs. Only some of the partiers noticed us, though. And even then, they didn't seem to care. I spotted someone doing lines off a unicorn pool floaty. It struck me as odd, because coke was about the last thing I'd expect at this hicktown balloon rave. But people are always seeing what they can shove up their nose, and pretty much anything was snortable if you crushed it fine enough.

Still, I'd seen my share of coked-out partygoers in my day, and that wasn't how this crowd was acting. These kids had a sort of inward-turned buzz that didn't jibe with cocaine. Oxy, most likely, or maybe ecstasy...whatever it was, they were definitely enjoying themselves.

My hand went to my throat where a habit demon I'd picked up at The Clinic had once hugged me like a turtleneck sweater. Addiction is pernicious. It's physical. It's psychological. And apparently, it can also be spiritual. Jacob had torn the thing in half while he was pumped up on psyactives and the red energy of our GhosTV—before National hauled off the device, anyhow, never to be seen again.

The little tickle I get deep inside my gullet, the flutter behind the root of my tongue that anticipates the swallow of a little red pill, is mostly dormant these days. But every now and then it rouses, just a touch, to remind me how good it would feel for that smooth barbiturate relaxation to spread through my veins again.

I cleared my throat and stepped deeper into the fray.

If I didn't quite fit into this crowd, the same would be said for George. Even if he'd changed out of his work clothes into something more casual, he was still a good twenty years older than anyone else. Then again, a pusher wouldn't really care, so long as he had cash in hand. Plus, the red light was playing tricks with my eyes. I kept them peeled for someone squinty and sinewy—someone ferrying around a habit demon—and pushed through the crowd.

It took a few minutes, but I eventually worked my way back to one of the bedrooms where a few kids were taking a break from the main action. The music here was just as loud, but the treble was somewhat blunted. No pool floaties. No dancing. A couple of kids earnestly tried to talk, shouting in each other's ears. Others just lay on the dusty hardwood floor, staring up at the ceiling.

Jacob plucked at my shoulder and shouted in my ear, "Habit demons?"

Thanks to the loud music and red lights thickening the air, I couldn't say for sure. Too distracting. I pulled down some white light, but the action felt blunted and strange. Good thing. Did I really want to be operating out of my crown chakra if there were habit demons here looking for their next meal? I wanted my subtle bodies to firm up, not float away. I didn't need white light. I needed red grounding energy.

The red light that had made everything feel daunting and alien before suddenly felt like an asset. I've always been visual to a fault, and with everything lit up red, focusing on that unaccustomed energy source was easy.

I was the straw sucking soda from a long, tall glass. I was the tree drawing groundwater from the earth. I was full of subtle bodies, and I held onto each and every one as I filled myself with red.

It was a totally different psychic high. Like ketamine versus coke. Not that I've ever been in the K-hole, but I've heard it can be a pretty sweet trip—unless you take too much, in which case you feel like you're dying. The floaty feeling I got on white light was absent. In its place was a solid sense of rightness. Maybe that sounds pretty boring. But as someone who'd always struggled to hold it together, I thought solid felt pretty damn good.

Looking at the world through blood-colored glasses did have its disadvantages, though. I didn't see the habit demon until I walked right into it.

The hand-sized tick hung in the center of the room at chest level like a spider in the middle of a web. In fact, once that analogy came to mind, the room lit up with a webwork of strands. Not in concentric rings, like an actual spiderweb, though. More like the protective laser field from that action flick playing at the theatre.

The habit demon didn't seem particularly drawn to me—huge fucking relief—and when I backed up a step, it simply continued crawling its way along one of the barely-visible strands.

"There," I shouted, though Jacob probably couldn't hear me. I pointed at it for his benefit.

Jacob tried to see it, but it was kind of like pointing out something to a dog and having it look at your finger instead. I jabbed my finger harder in its general direction to try and indicate it was a couple of feet away. Jacob's gaze overshot and went to the far side of the room.

The habit demon trundled off through the wall.

I sighed and shook my head.

The thing had been only half-visible to me, like a bad holo-gram. I could hardly expect Jacob to see it, especially when his active subtle body had never communicated to the visual center of his physical brain.

But he could probably feel it.

I jerked my head toward the door and went off to see where the habit demon had gone. The other side of the wall was a bathroom with a line of five kids waiting their turn. At least they weren't just pissing in the corners...but I supposed the night was still young. I flashed my F-Pimp I.D. at them and they all decided maybe they could hold it for a while, and melted back into the living room crowd.

When the bathroom door opened a few seconds later, I'd planted myself in the doorway, hands on hips, with my cop-face in place. Even in the john, the lights were red. There were two guys inside, and I doubted they'd been helping each other pee. One was maybe eighteen, still fighting acne, but the other was older, mid-thirties. He was dressed like everyone else, in shorts and an overpriced T-shirt, but the fat gold chain around his neck and the diamond stud in each ear marked him as the type of guy who liked to show off his bling...and the type of guy you'd duck into the can with if you had a few bucks burning a hole in your pocket.

I personally wouldn't have scored from anyone so flashy—seems to me they're just itching to get caught. But it made it a lot easier for me to sort out who was who.

I made no move to get out of their way. The kid seemed pretty freaked out, but the dealer puffed up and put on a tough-guy act. "Who the fuck do you think you are?"

While it would've been a great setup for an uber-macho reply like, Your worst nightmare, his dealing took a back seat to Amy's disappearance. "I'm looking for someone."

"Don't know 'em."

"George Stanton."

"You deaf, grandpa? I said I don't know 'em."

Grandpa? I put him at five years younger than me, tops. Any more than that—he needed a way better skincare routine. Then again, if he partook in his own merchandise, maybe he was aging in dog years.

"Think harder. Small town like this—I'll bet you've crossed paths."

"Don't. Know. Him." Bling accentuated each word with a poke to my chest. Talk about a pair of stones. He would've fit right in at the Fifth Precinct, where swagger was half the game. I was tempted to put him in his place, but a flicker of movement on the shower curtain reminded me to keep my eyes on the prize. Anyone could arrest this jerk. But only a high-level Psych would be able to clean up the etheric mess.

He shouldered past me as I tried to get a bead on the habit demon, and I let him go. Chances of him giving up George were slim to none.

The kid who'd just scored, however....

I crowded into the john with him, pulled the door shut behind me and twisted the lock. The kid swallowed so hard his adam's apple bobbed.

"What did he sell you?" I asked.

"Nothing."

The walls were plastic panels stamped to look like tile. There was a distortion in the grid behind the kid's head, roughly the size of the tick. I glimpsed it for half a second, then lost it again.

I spotted a shaving light and flicked it on. It was a fluorescent bar built into the cabinet, nothing they could change out with a red party bulb. The room went bright, even as I realized all the light in the world wouldn't help me get a bead on the habit demon. It wasn't moving through the physical world. It didn't reflect light or cast shadows. I'd have to look with my subtle body.

It took me a moment, reaching for white light down through my head, fumbling, switching gears, and drawing grounding energy up through my spine. But sometimes an awkward pause will work in your favor.

"I know George Stanton," he blurted out.

"Yeah? How?"

"He's my aunt's boyfriend."

How had I not considered the fact that George had a life outside the funeral home?

The kid was even younger than I'd first thought, maybe a gangly seventeen. Could've easily been me—had my social circle been my age instead of two years younger, thanks to my lousy grasp of academics forcing me to repeat both fourth and sixth grade. "I'll need her information. And yours."

His mouth worked.

I pulled out the dreaded notepad. "Now."

He gave me a name and stammered through what he knew about his aunt. A name. A phone number he retrieved from his phone. A description of her house.

Despite the fact that he reminded me of myself, I wasn't about to go easy on him. "You listen to me. I need to talk to George. And if you call ahead with a warning I'm coming...let's just say I'll make sure you go down hard for whatever you just scored. Are we clear?"

The kid nodded, looking like he was about to wet himself. The habit demon flickered into my line of vision, crawling past a hair-thin tendril—toward the wall, and away from the kid. Because it sensed he was about to flush his drugs down the toilet? That smacked of precognizance, but maybe time works funny when you're out of phase with the physical.

When I let myself out of the bathroom, the kid bolted past me like his ass was on fire. And while the lights were still red and the music still loud, the party had thinned out considerably. A couple of guys in black suits showing up'll do that.

Jacob was questioning a pair of girls over by the kitchen. They looked just as terrified as my witness had, and just as eager to make tracks. Good. There might not be much else to do in Beauchamp, but this party wasn't worth picking up a habit demon.

He cut the girls free—they bailed—and headed over toward me. As he walked, he batted away a red balloon that was bound and determined to stick to his jacket. "I've got a lead," I told him. "Let's go."

We were on our way out when a bedroom door opened and a shirtless guy with an eagle tattooed on his pecs barged out. Caucasian, early twenties, a thick build chiseled by some time in the gym. "You got a search warrant?" he hollered over the music. "I don't see no search warrant."

I had zero time for this—and normally, I would have just rolled my eyes and walked away. But Eagle Tattoo was faster than he looked, and he'd stomped over and put himself between us and the exit. If the dealer had balls the size of Beauchamp, this one's were bigger than all of Iowa.

"The door was open," I said blandly.

"Yeah? Who said you should invite yourselves in?"

I do my best not to touch anyone unless I absolutely have to. But when his hand twitched toward his waistband, I knew with a stunning clarity that not only was this jackass about to pull a piece on me—probably from the back of his sweaty underpants—but that in giving my clip to Jacob, I'd rendered myself defenseless. And so I used what I had at my disposal: my reach, my reflex time, and my training.

All those hours of having tactics drilled into my head really paid off. A grab. A pivot. And before he had a chance to put a hole in me, Eagle Tattoo was face up against the wall with an arm twisted behind his back. The only thing left to do was disarm him.

Except, the gun I was so sure would be stuffed down the back of his pants...wasn't there.

"What the fuck, man?" he said, high and wild.

Even Jacob looked startled. He reined it in quick, though, and told the guy, "Next time someone wants to leave, stand aside and let them go."

My adrenaline was high from strong-arming Eagle Tattoo, but it wasn't tempered with my normal white light headrush. I felt grounded. Solid. Strong.

I almost wished there had been a piece, so I could disarm him and show him who was boss.

When Jacob turned and cut through the crowd like a plow through a cornfield, I followed. As satisfying as it might be to continue our pissing contest, some small, niggling voice inside reminded me that every moment I wasted here must've felt like an eternity for Amy.

There was yelling behind us, indiscernible beneath the thumping of the music. And the volume cut, leaving everything suddenly silent—except for the one guy screaming. "Do you know who I am, motherfuckers? Do you know who I am? I'm Ben Carver's son—and when he finds out what you did here, you are so fucked!"

We kept walking. "George has a girlfriend just a few minutes away," I said. "And who the hell is Ben Carver?"

Jacob frowned. "Get in the car."

CHAPTER 25

Ben Carver, turns out, was the sheriff responsible for this shit show of a town. I called up this information on Amy's phone while I cranked up my side of the AC, hoping to blow some of the sweat-and-pot stink of the party off me.

Jacob, meanwhile, navigated toward the girlfriend's house with his hands gripping the wheel so hard his knuckles were white. "Are you okay?" he asked. "What the hell was that back there?"

Maybe I had let things escalate a bit. "I thought there was a gun down his pants."

"I had a clear line of sight. If he was armed, don't you think I would've done something?"

I twisted the blower to its highest setting, then gave it a few more experimental twists just to make sure I had it all the way up.

Jacob said, "First the GPS. Now this. I'm worried about you."

"And I'm worried about Amy. Look, maybe I overreacted. But what's good ol' Daddy Sheriff gonna do about that little standoff?"

"Hopefully nothing. But if word gets back to Laura—"

"Then we tell her we were looking to catch the next striptease in action."

Huh. Between the GhosTV and Amy disappearing, I hadn't actually thought about the strippers for a while.

What if the clothes were coming off because there was a habit demon crawling around on them? And since only the subtle body could feel it, the strippers were none the wiser as to what they were doing?

As I turned that notion around in my head, Jacob jerked the car to a stop and said, "We're here."

George Stanton may have lived somewhere too public to stash a victim, but his girlfriend didn't. Her home—the "blue house with the white flowers" her nephew had described—was a single-family cape cod with both a garage and a basement.

It was coming up on 2am by the time we cop-knocked on the door. Since Jacob had just brought up the GPS incident, I let him do the knocking, so as to prove I wasn't suddenly getting off on hitting things. Though the thought of giving something a good smack did hold a certain appeal.

Jacob banged on the door until the lights came on inside. A few seconds later, the door opened. George Stanton stood there, shirtless and squinting, with a statuette of a jaguar clutched defensively in his right hand.

At least I could be fairly certain he wasn't reaching for a gun.

I supposed I'd never live that down.

When he recognized us as the busybodies who'd bothered him at work that afternoon, he lowered the makeshift club and said, "What the fuck do you want?"

Jacob flashed his I.D., slid his foot in the door to prevent it from being slammed, and said, "We just had a few more questions."

"It's the middle of the night," he said incredulously.

"Who the hell is that?" a woman called from upstairs. "If it's my asshole of a brother, tell him to go sleep it off somewhere else!"

"It will only take a minute," Jacob lied, and George blearily stood aside and let us in.

The inside of the house was disturbingly normal. Cheap furniture, oversized flatscreen TV, and a bunch of mass-produced art on the walls—sunsets and barns and still lives. There was a typical amount of clutter—junk mail and too many remote controls—but overall, the place was just...normal. Then again, whenever a gruesome murder goes down, someone's always bound to claim that the killer seemed "so normal."

Jacob said, "Following up on Amy Grace—have you seen her since the last time we spoke?"

"A few hours ago?"

"Sir—just answer the question."

"No, I ain't seen her. I finished my shift a few minutes after we talked and came right here. That good enough for you?"

Jacob continued to grill him, essentially asking the same questions with slightly different wording to see if his story shifted. It didn't. While we questioned him, the girlfriend came halfway down the stairs to see what was going on in a skimpy pajama set with a man's plaid shirt thrown over the top. Her fried blonde hair was tangled from sleep, and she looked just as baffled to see a couple of strangers in suits as George did.

Not the look of someone with a woman trussed up in the basement.

Or a woman's body.

Damn it, if Jacob hadn't planted the seed that someone had abducted Amy, I would've figured she'd wander on home whenever she was good and ready. But if there was even a slim chance she was in serious trouble, I couldn't just let it drop.

And if foul play was involved, the possibility of finding Amy alive at this point was dwindling, fast.

"Who is that?" the girlfriend asked.

"Some kind of cops," George said. "But I already told 'em everything I know."

"Agent Bayne?" Jacob said, and I shook off the thoughts of all the gruesome ways we'd probably end up finding Amy. Jacob touched his cheek and said, "Anything else?"

Shit. The habit demon.

I did my awkward white-then-red-energy grab, then looked harder at George. But the creepy nonphysical tick thing I'd seen on his face earlier was…gone.

Great.

Not that I wanted to see a habit demon feeding off him. But like I always say, if something's there, I'd rather be able to see it than not. It's like swatting a bug off the bedroom wall and watching it drop into your pillows. Unless you find it, you're putting on new sheets, whether or not they happened to need changing.

"And approximately when did you come home?" I asked lamely.

"Six," he said. For the fourth or fifth time. "And we ate and we watched our shows and fucked and went to sleep. Anything else?"

I glanced over his shoulder into the kitchen and said, "Does that door lead to the basement?"

"Yeah? Why?"

"If you don't mind," Jacob said, motioning for him to let us have a look.

"What, you think Amy's in the basement?" George demanded. "If she was trying to get away from the funeral home, the last place she'd come is here."

His girlfriend was now seated wearily on the stairs. She lit a cigarette, waved it toward the kitchen, and said, "Just let 'em look and get it over with so we can go back to bed."

He didn't like it, but it was her house. With a scowl of supreme annoyance, he held open the cellar door and said, "Knock yourself out."

One of us would need to stay topside to make sure no one deadbolted us into the basement or pulled out a twelve-gauge. Though if there were a shotgun in the house, the panther statue would probably still be on the mantle.

Basement duty fell to me. I was none too fond of the task, but since I was the one who could see the spider falling into the pillows, I steeled myself and headed down.

As basements went, it was completely unremarkable. Laundry. Piles of storage crates. An exercise bike used as a drying rack for a couple of brassieres. No Amy Grace...in body, or in spirit.

We poked through the rest of the house, but the only ones there were George and his girlfriend. If they'd done something to Amy, would her ka stick around to tell me? Or would it just discard its body and move on to the next phase of eternity?

No clue.

But I did know how people acted when they'd done something that needed covering up. They'd get all affronted and start throwing up a smokescreen of explanations. These two, though? They just wanted to forget this all happened and go back to bed.

Well, that was it. I was shit out of ideas and I was positive the next time we saw Amy she'd be back in her workroom at the

funeral home...in a body bag. I was right on Jacob's heels when
he walked out the front door—so close that I nearly slammed
into him when he stopped cold at the top of the porch stairs.

Since I had spiders on the mind, when Jacob waved something off, I figured he'd just walked through the first long,
anchoring strands of a new web. But instead of powering on
ahead, he planted his feet and tried again to brush something
away while I dodged around him and kept on walking.

Then something twanged my awareness. A subtle, nearly
imperceptible flutter of apprehension. I turned and took a
better look.

It was a web. Though it hadn't been spun by any ordinary bug.

A single red tether stretched from somewhere inside the
house and out into infinity, and along that hair-thin tightrope,
the tick of a habit demon was creeping along...right in Jacob's
direction.

If anyone's got a built-in defense from unseen creepy crawl-
ies, it's him. In the heat of the moment, though, I didn't care
whether or not he was a True Stiff. For all I knew, the GhosTV
had catalyzed him somehow—made him more sensitive while
it left him vulnerable to attack. But the thing was coming right
upon his seven, and I'd strode off too far ahead to intercept.

"Behind you!" I jabbed my finger in its direction.

Jacob spun around...and swatted the thing off its tether.

I didn't hear the creature hit the ground so much as feel it—
through the soles of my feet, the point where my subtle bodies
met the earth. It had fallen gracelessly, taken by surprise, and
it landed on its back like a turtle.

But instead of legs flailing in the air, what I saw on its under-
side was a pulsating sucker of a mouth, a sickening maw lined
with rows of needle-like teeth.

"There," I said, pointing again. And in the heat of the moment, without time to think and over-think, to second guess his own talent, Jacob didn't look at my finger. He swung his focus directly on the habit demon....

Then reached out and grabbed it.

I backpedaled with the image of that horrible pulsing mouth seared into my brain. "Watch it!" I snapped—but, of course, he couldn't. Jacob couldn't see the thing.

But evidently, he could damn well feel it.

The creature didn't so much squirm as try to reshape itself, oozing out of his grasp like a slimy, tied-off condom. Jacob was half a step ahead of it, wrangling it two-handed now with his feet planted wide and grounding energy coursing through him.

I really wished I hadn't thought of the condom analogy when Jacob gave a final, hard push...and the habit demon burst.

It wasn't filled with goo, though—not like an actual insect, or a used condom. It was filled with energy. And in its death throes, I actually could see it, like a dusty black cloud erupting from the creature's body. It filled the air, exponentially bigger than the habit demon itself. The cloud didn't move like physical dust—it roiled around like it had a life of its own. Maybe it did. Maybe we humans weren't the only things with subtle bodies riding around inside us.

Though a habit demon inside a habit demon was a notion I didn't want to dwell on.

"It's a cloud now," I called out, which sounded supremely dumb even as the words left my mouth. But Jacob must have understood. He spread his hands wide like he was trying to scoop up the air. But his powers were too untested. Too raw. And the habit demon smoke rushed through his fingers and swirled away.

"It's gone," I said.

Good thing I'd been walking over intending to give him an encouraging bump of my shoulder. I was within range to grab him when his knees buckled.

CHAPTER 26

By the time I drove us back to the motel—a mere five minutes away—Jacob could walk on his own. He was wobbly, though, and would need to recharge his batteries. The two of us might not operate from the same chakras—we might not flow the same energy. But I'd tapped myself out often enough to know exactly how it felt.

"We don't have time to rest," he said. And I got where that was coming from, too. From the knowledge that I was the last line of defense, and if I couldn't pull up my big boy pants and step it up, there'd be nothing standing between everyone else and the abyss.

"You're no good to anyone unconscious, Jacob. Lie down and give yourself a few minutes to recuperate while I go raid the vending machine." In the past fifteen hours, we'd consumed nothing but a protein bar—actually, Jacob had only eaten half. I was feeling lightheaded and woozy myself, and I wasn't even the one who'd just made a habit demon pop.

The vending machine took plastic, so I was able to raid it on behalf of the FPMP with my company card. I grabbed anything that looked substantial and racked up nearly fifty bucks worth of snackage. Trail mix, granola bars, cheese crackers, and a mess of chocolate bars for quick energy. It was hardly a nutritious meal, but at least we wouldn't starve. And hopefully it would be easier to stay grounded with some food in my belly.

When I got back to the room with my armload of calories, Jacob, naturally, was not resting. He had our map of Beauchamp spread out over the desk and was staring down at it like he could burn a smoking hole with his eyes through the cheap copy paper.

He said, "It was harder for me to get a bead on the habit demon at that last house than it was at the party. We were farther away from the GhosTV."

He'd placed a starlight mint on the GhosTV house rather than marking it. Smart. If our map ended up in evidence, we wouldn't have to explain what it meant.

I'd expected all of our X's to form some kind of a pattern around the GhosTV. But they didn't. They were just a big, random swarm of pen marks. "Something's not adding up."

What I didn't realize was that while I was scanning the map (and plowing through a packet of cheese crackers) Jacob was scanning me.

"What?" I said, blowing out a few crumbs.

Jacob nodded at me with his chin. "What's with all the snacks?"

"That's what they had in the machine." Spread out on the bed where I'd dumped it all, it did look like a lot. "Who knows when we'll get our next meal?"

Jacob narrowed his eyes.

"This isn't an ice cream situation," I said.

He narrowed his eyes harder.

"It's not," I insisted.

"Look at how you're standing." He pointed to the mirror.

My right hand was holding a crinkly plastic packet with a few cracker crumbs at the bottom and my left hand was on my hip. My shoulder holster showed the butt of my empty gun. "Okay, I'll bite. How?"

"Your stance. It's nothing like it usually is. And it's been that way all night."

My feet might've been planted, it's true. But just to get a better look at the map. Because people do that, right? Plant themselves in front of something they want to study? "What are you saying?"

He stepped up and looked me square in the eye, so close I could practically see the wheels turning. "How do you feel about sleeping with the lights on?"

I tsked and tossed my wrapper in the trash. "I'm not my body. I'm me."

He looked deeper, totally unconvinced.

"I'm just hungry, okay? Normal hungry. Not weird hungry. Aren't you hungry, too?"

He glanced at the snacks again. "It's not just this. The GPS. The sheriff's son...."

"I'm not armed and I thought he was reaching for a weapon so I had to act fast—cripes, Jacob, it's me. Am I starving? Am I stressed out? Am I worried now we're gonna find Amy at the bottom of a dumpster? Sure. But I'm still me—not just some big, dumb body with nobody home."

He made to turn away, and I caught his shoulder, grabbed him by the jaw and turned his face toward mine. "Listen to me. I'll admit, I do feel different, but not because a piece of myself is missing. I've quit pulling down white light—"

"You pick now to stop shoring up your defenses? What about the habit demons?"

"That's just it. I can see 'em a lot better when I'm hopped up on light, but I don't think it's much of a defense. Not like being grounded."

"So you're not fragmented." He was part skeptical, part desperate to believe it was true. "You're grounded."

I considered myself. "I guess I am."

Jacob reached up and smoothed my hair back from my face, locking eyes with me so intensely it felt like he was trying to merge the two of us together. "I always thought possession was the worst thing I had to worry about—and that if someone else was riding around inside your skin, I would know. Beyond a shadow of a doubt. But what am I supposed to make of the fact that when you just shift your energy, you're like an entirely different person?"

"This is me," I told him. Gently. Letting the words play across his lower lip. "I'm still me."

Mostly. Though the me I'd been shaping and honing all these decades probably wouldn't have breathed all over Jacob with cracker-mouth, and he definitely wouldn't be turned on by the raw look in Jacob's big, dark eyes.

He pressed his forehead wearily against mine, cupping my cheek, and I felt a tremor of exhaustion course through him. "And you're still you," I said, "acting like you're made of steel." I guided him toward the bed. "Seriously, Jacob, lie down for a few minutes."

"A few minutes could be the difference between finding Amy dead or alive."

"Just long enough so the room stops spinning."

He must've felt pretty lousy to actually comply. I shoved the vending machine crap aside and eased him down with me onto the uncomfortable motel bed. "Just a few minutes," he murmured. "No more."

"No more," I said into his hair as I pressed a kiss into his temple....

And dropped into blackness like I'd been hit with a tranq dart.

I jerked awake to the sound of a rattling window unit. "Sonofabitch," I snapped, and Jacob snorted awake. I checked the clock—quarter to five. We'd been asleep more than two hours—two hours we couldn't afford.

I rolled across a miniature landscape of vending machine snacks and swung out of bed. My holster was digging into my side and my jacket was a wreck. Good thing it was black. You'd only know I'd slept in it if you looked really close.

I scrambled to get myself together with a finger-comb to my hair and a quick swish of mouthwash. But Jacob wasn't rushing around like me. He was standing in the middle of the room with his feet planted and his hands on his hips. He wore his sidearm at his belt, like most everyone else nowadays, and it rode there just below his trim waist. He'd had the foresight to toss his jacket over a chair when we came into the room, but his white dress shirt had picked up a major diagonal crease down the back. It was his confident stance, though, I noticed the most. The exact stance that he'd found so suspicious in me. But for him, it had always been second nature.

He was gazing off into infinity, shifting around all the puzzle pieces in his mind. "There has to be a connection," he said. "The strippers. The GhosTV. Amy."

The cobbled-together map was right where we'd left it, spread out over the desk. I put my finger on Amy's name, wishing I was some other kind of psych. A telepath, a precog—someone who could pick up an impression of where she might be by focusing on her name. But no. I was a medium. Like her.

"Vic?"

I blinked. "When Amy told me about shepherding over the spirits of the dead, she acted like it was business as usual. Nothing new. Whatever's going on in the etheric, she's predisposed to feel it. She doesn't need a GhosTV playing to receive the signal. So, what if we took her off the board?" I covered her X with my fingertip. "Then all the stripper sightings form a blob around the TV."

As much as I wanted a chance at a do-over with that goddamn hunk of screwed-up technology, I wasn't willing to let Amy pay the cost. Not if there was any chance she might still be alive. I scowled and said, "I hate to say it, but what if leaving the TV on is making everything worse? what if it's bumping Amy out of her skin so the habit demons are at the wheel? We've gotta shut down the GhosTV."

Jacob and I headed out to the car, where we nearly collided at the driver side door. "You want to drive?" he asked—and his tone said, since when? "It's still dark out."

"True. But you nearly laid yourself out dealing with that habit demon. And I didn't notice any intersection repeaters to speak of."

"Okay," he said, still a bit leery of my motivations, but not enough to argue about it.

Curious now, I kept my eyes peeled for repeaters all the way there. None. Because of the reasonable speed limit? Because the GhosTV signal had somehow wiped them out? Or because I'd been so grounded these past few hours that I just couldn't see them?

I wasn't even consciously thinking about the grounding energy, though when I shifted my focus to my tailbone and thought about my base chakra, I sensed it was still active. And being grounded? It felt fucking fantastic.

I wouldn't say I'd woken from two hours' sleep feeling totally refreshed, but I was definitely good enough to plow through the day. And when I tore through a granola bar (I can usually take 'em or leave 'em) I tasted every last grain and nut. Sleep was better. Food was better. And while I might not have had a chance to get laid while I was focused on grounding myself, I had no doubt the sex would be phenomenal.

Which then begged the question...who the hell would want to function out of their crown chakra when being grounded felt so good?

We coasted up to the suicide house and pulled to the top of the driveway. I clambered in through the window as quietly as I could and let Jacob in the back door. The TV was just as we'd left it, at a cockeyed angle to the living room wall with some piggybacked extension cords hanging taut to the bathroom outlet.

An infomercial for a miniature blender was playing, claiming a daily smoothie would be sure to revolutionize anyone's life, but it was obvious the tiny thing could never hope to pulverize a handful of fruit with much success. Jacob and I had burned through so many blenders to cover our conversations from prying ears, we now knew more about blenders than we'd ever imagined.

I paused with my hand on the massive console, wracked with preemptive regret. For everything I thought I knew about being a medium, I go and uncover some other facet that I never could have imagined.

Back when psychs were first discovered—back when our talents seemed like something we could actually control, rather than some aberration that ended up controlling us—researchers dreamed of abilities like the ones the GhosTV provided.

To be able to split off some fragment of yourself and travel unhindered was not only the stuff of spies, but explorers. Imagine having a subtle body crawl through the sewer and find a problem without tearing up a whole city block. Or sending one into a burning building to check for survivors. Or, hell, sending one out into the solar system to see whether or not Pluto really is a planet.

None of this has panned out.

Maybe that's what sonar and spacecraft are for, and humankind has no business getting too big for its britches. Or too small for its shoes.

There was still so much I could learn if I mastered even a fraction of what the GhosTV could do. If the only thing happening here had been the thing we were sent to investigate—a bunch of random clothing removals—I wouldn't have lost any sleep over fudging the truth. Nothing to see here. Definitely not worth putting the small Iowa town on the FPMP's radar.

But Amy's disappearance changed everything.

No way could we sweep it all under the rug with Amy's body gone missing—and the first twenty-four hours after a disappearance are the most crucial.

We had to call in the cavalry.

So we'd better dismantle the GhosTV before they showed up.

"It pains me to say it," I admitted, "but you're right, Jacob. Turning off the GhosTV isn't enough. We'll have to destroy it."

CHAPTER 27

While we all love being right, some of us put more stock in it than others.

Jacob had the good grace not to gloat. And since it would be impossible to dispose of the whole TV without a forklift and a moving van, pulling out the components Jennifer Chance had added, pounding them up with a brick and scattering what was left into a random cornfield would have to do the trick.

When we pulled the plug, I felt no difference. Not until Jacob started unscrewing the back of the console with a butter knife scavenged from the kitchen, and my energy shifted. The glorious groundedness I'd been reveling in began to subside.

It started with a small chill that played across the nape of my neck. I ignored it. But then something flickered in the kitchen—the kitchen where Harris Tucker had blown his own brains out—and I had to admit that the crown chakra had become my default setting for a reason.

What if my recent groundedness had nothing to do with Amy's visualization, and everything to do with the TV...and the ominous creak we'd heard when we moved it?

I tried to imagine the red energy flowing up through my

spine—and got nothing. Shit. It must've been the TV. It was painfully tempting to stop Jacob, to plug it back in and verify we'd somehow managed to set it to the grounding channel.

Another flicker from the kitchen.

A flicker I couldn't afford to ignore.

Leaving the TV to Jacob, I moved toward the flicker cautiously, so as not to startle anyone or anything, and edged down the hall to the back of the house where the cop had offed himself at the kitchen table. The current card table was probably in the same spot where the deed happened. Between the appliances and the doorways, there were only so many places a table would fit.

Gooseflesh crawled up my forearms as I considered Jacob's theory that Chance had chosen this particular safe house for a reason. It would hardly be efficient to test her invention in a house where no one had ever died. And the more violent the death, the better.

I didn't want to reach for the white light. But I didn't see that I had any other choice. If something was lurking around, I was better off knowing exactly what I was up against.

I pulled, hard, and imagined my crown chakra blown open wide. White light had been my drug of choice for so long, drinking it down at the sight of some half-seen flicker was like dry-swallowing a pill. Unpleasant. But doable.

Whatever residual grounding energy remained in me resisted like a parched throat, but I kept on swallowing until it relented. Every once in a while, a pill will really stick partway down—you can feel it burning your esophagus. But for the most part, once it gets past a certain point, it's smooth sailing.

The pill analogy turned out to be more apt than I'd anticipated.

One second I was struggling to ingest the white light, and the next it was sliding on down. I felt it first, like a headache you've just realized is nagging you. I ride my crown chakra hard, and my brainpan liked to complain. The only reason I even noticed now was the fact that up until now, I'd been blessedly free from the dull ache all day long.

It was easy enough to ignore, though. I'd been doing it for years.

The next thing to register was my sight, as white light sparked the visual part of my cortex. The room blurred as a second reality overlaid the first, then shifted ever so slightly out of alignment. Difficult to see unless I focused just right. The card table changed shape. And the empty chair pulled up to it was suddenly filled.

It was the silhouette of a balding man with his back facing me—and there was only one person it could be.

"Wait—" I said...as spectral blood splatter, fragments of flesh and bone and brain, sprayed me from head to toe, all lit up red.

It wouldn't have been quite so bad if I hadn't felt it. Even after the sensations faded, the memory of the gunshot stayed on my skin.

Harris Tucker had left one hell of a repeater behind. Can't say I recalled ever feeling them before. Then again, I did my best to dodge around repeaters, not just stand there gawking in the splash zone. As I turned toward the hall to let Jacob know we were no longer exactly alone, he said, "Did that work?"

"Did what work?" I asked, though my voice sounded oddly flat.

Then it also said, "Who knows? We don't have time for this, Jacob. We should just tear out the guts and get it over with."

And the second voice had the same feel as Jacob's—as if it actually existed in the physical room. Whereas the one I'd just spoken with was nothing but the mental construct of a voice.

Sonofabitch. Thanks to a certain someone plugging the damn TV back in—someone who apparently can't leave well enough alone—I'd been ejected from my body.

A body that was evidently full of opinions. "We shouldn't screw around with it. Even the tiniest nudge can have it doing God-knows-what. Like when we moved it into the hall. I think we changed the channel."

"To what?" Jacob wondered.

"Does it matter?" my body said. "You were right. It's dangerous. It needs to go."

"No, Vic, you were right. We might not be able to crack this whole thing without the TV. Before we do anything we can't undo, maybe we should try to recapture the settings that were playing when you first saw Amy. Maybe she's been trying to talk to us all this time and we didn't know she was here."

I brushed away the lingering sensation of repeater brains as I stomped into the living room. The TV was still at that odd angle, with the back removed and lying to one side, and the extension cord stretched to the bathroom. Jacob crouched with his pocket flashlight shining into the cavity while my body stood like it thought it was the boss of the world, hands on hips, scowling.

"So what's your plan?" it said. "Turn up the volume and hope Amy reports in? We don't even know which button does what. We should ditch it. Now."

"We've got time enough to get rid of it later. The tuner is at our disposal, if only for a few more hours. It would be a shame not to use it to our advantage."

My body rolled its eyes. "Don't forget, when Amy is back inside her body, she can't even remember whatever funny business her ka gets up to. She'd have no reason to get in touch with us. For all we know, she's in her bed right now, safe and sound."

It had a point.

"So we go back to the funeral home?" Jacob asked. "If she isn't there, what are we supposed tell her father?"

"No reason to start a panic." My body pulled Amy's phone from my pocket and keyed in her passcode. "I'll bet she's still got a landline. And here it is: home phone." My body hit the call button and held it to its ear. "Even if she's asleep, a call from her own cell should drag her out of bed."

"What the hell are you doing?" I yelled at the body, then turned to Jacob and demanded, "Aren't you gonna stop him?"

Jacob, however, just mirrored my body's Superman stance and waited to see what it would do.

A pause. Then, in my most bored and confident cop-voice, my body said, "Yeah, I found a cell phone and was hoping to get it back to its owner. Give me a call as soon as you get this message."

It hung up without identifying itself.

Which could actually work to our advantage. If this whole thing went sideways, the "found cell phone" argument would give us all kinds of plausible deniability...as long as no one thought too hard about how I'd gotten past the lockscreen.

"We could just leave it at that..." my body said, thinking hard. "But George knows we were looking for Amy last night. So if something did happen to her, this whole thing will blow up in our faces."

When it wasn't out getting ice cream, apparently my body was cognizant of some pretty heavy truths. Then again, survival was its main imperative. But what if it didn't grasp the full situation? What if it took some wildly decisive course of action—one that ended up getting all of us killed?

"That's not me!" I called in Jacob's ear. I might as well have been yelling at the wall. And when I tried to poke him, he took no notice whatsoever.

He said, "If Amy's not at home, then where is she?"

My body waved the phone. "We have her contacts list right here. We could go down the local numbers." It did a quick scroll—her contact list was even shorter than mine. "Looks like one of them is the local gym. They'd be open at an ungodly hour. I can't imagine any body in its right mind would be eager to hop on a treadmill, but maybe there's a hot tub or a sauna. And poking around a public place would cause less of a stir than dragging all her friends out of bed."

As wildly decisive courses of action went...it wasn't bad. All the yelling in the world wouldn't get Jacob to turn off that TV—not from my spirit body, anyhow. So, grudgingly, I left the GhosTV behind, followed them out to the car, and tagged along to the gym.

The gym might've been smaller than the one where Jacob pumped iron, but thankfully, they were still big enough to be open before sunup. Jacob and my body flashed I.D.s to a bleary minimum-wage employee at the front desk who had no idea whether Amy was there and couldn't figure out how to look it up. While they received the get-go to survey the place for themselves, I stepped through the desk and took a look at the computer. Some sort of proprietary software was running, connected to a card reader to check in the members. No help there. But a dog-eared list taped to the side of the monitor held a class schedule.

And we were just in time for Danielle-the-dancer's first spin class of the week.

Unfortunately, Jacob wasn't thinking about her, and neither was my body. They were too busy searching for Amy. They did a sweep of the main area, eliminating the machines and the weight benches, then paused at the women's locker room door. Or, more accurately, Jacob paused and grabbed my body before it could barrel into the room.

Jacob said, "If a couple of men go in, we cause a big stir."

"Then what? The only employee I see is the kid on the desk. Also male."

While they discussed the most unobtrusive way to get a peek inside the women's locker room, I walked through the wall and had a look for myself. Thankfully, I didn't end up glimpsing any body parts I shouldn't. It was a small room with some lockers and benches, changing stalls and a small shower. An athletic-looking woman was tying her sneakers when I came in. By the time I'd checked through all the nooks and crannies, she'd hefted her giant water bottle and was striding out the door.

I followed her out and found Jacob concocting some story for a woman he'd pulled off a treadmill. My body showed her a photo from Amy's phone. She gave it a quick glance—too busy checking out Jacob—then dutifully headed into the locker room to do their searching.

Too bad I couldn't communicate with them and tell them it was empty. Or could I?

They were talking, heads bent together, with my body saying, "We don't know exactly when Dr. K and Garcia will show up without turning on our phones."

"I've been thinking about that myself," Jacob said. As he started discussing the pros and cons of going on-grid again, the distance they'd need to travel, and the probability that we'd be safe for a few more hours...I stepped into my body.

And fell right back out.

Damn it.

I tried again, this time with less force. But with the slower approach, I noticed something. A mild push, like you'd get trying to stick together the same side of two magnets. I stepped in and tried to power through this repelling force, but it only grew stronger. I ended up sliding around it...and, again, back out the other side.

I only needed to get in there long enough to work my mouth, I reasoned. But jamming my head into place was just as fruitless as a whole-body takeover. Maybe even worse. It was like I was headbutting an opponent when I was the only one who could feel the impact.

Fucking body.

It was right about one thing, we really would need to hustle. Not only was time ticking down, but we didn't even know precisely how long we had.

They say two heads are better than one. I just wasn't sure who was technically the head in this situation.

But if I was stuck being noncorporeal, I figured, I might as well use it to my advantage.

CHAPTER 28

While Jacob and my body did a sweep of the public areas to check for Amy, I figured I should make sure no stone went unturned. I coasted through a staff door in the back of the building, where I found an office, a single-stall bathroom, an equipment room and a second locker room for the instructors. All empty, except the locker room…where the first striptease artist we'd interviewed was getting ready for her early-morning class.

I've never been one to stand up in front of a group and make myself the center of attention, so I can't say I blamed Danielle for doing a little primping. But she put her hair in a ponytail, then teased a few wisps out with a long fingernail, then pouted, pulled off her scrunchie, and started the whole procedure over again.

Three times.

"I don't suppose you have any idea where Amy is?" I asked. No answer.

I wasn't surprised. Even if the GhosTV had loosened up her subtle bodies, that wouldn't help her to hear me.

Once her hair was sufficiently subtly-tousled, Danielle paused to double-check her posture. She wore lycra leggings and a matching sports bra that left nothing to the imagination. I hadn't been exaggerating when I'd said her abs were better than mine. They weren't quite a six-pack, not like Jacob's. Apparently women can't get those without a crap-ton of work. But I could see the subtle lines of definition that I lacked, despite my negligible body fat.

Though when Danielle pulled out a compact and added a touch of contour...I began to realize why her torso looked so defined. Part of me thought, I can't believe she puts makeup on her stomach. While another part of me wondered if maybe sexier abs were within my reach after all.

Before I could go too far down the rabbit hole of wondering how it was possible to be of two minds about something while I was only a fraction of myself, Danielle bent down to re-tie her sneaker...and that's when I saw it.

A habit demon sitting right between her shoulder blades.

It was the same sort of tick-shaped demon as the one Jacob popped back at the party—the same type George had on his face.

I couldn't just stand there and do nothing. I might not be able to get back inside my own damn body, but habit demons didn't move through the physical plane. I opened up my crown chakra and white light poured in—way more than I was normally able to tap. Not only that, but the resistance I normally felt was absent. No loopy wooziness, no behind-the-eyeball headache. Just pure power.

Copying a move out of Jacob's playbook, I made a grab for the demon with visions of tearing the thing in half like a parking ticket I had no intention of paying. I was so hopped up on light, so sure of myself, that it took me a second to realize that my hand went right through the thing.

Mostly.

A wad of residue stretched between my hand and the bloated etheric bug, part smoke, part slime. Maybe ectoplasm? Aside its occasional appearance on my own hand, I'd only ever seen that clear goo when something moved between two planes—astral and physical. What if it wasn't specific to that? It could be the static that was created when subtle bodies from two different planes rubbed together—bodies that had no business veering into one another's lanes.

Like ectoplasm, the goop evaporated fast, as if it was on a time-lapse camera. But unlike ectoplasm, it was smoking while it disappeared. Or maybe it was more like the miniature dust cloud that puffed out when Jacob tore the tick in half. It was there and gone in a heartbeat, leaving me to wonder what the hell I'd just done.

But whatever it was, it hadn't dislodged the habit demon. And it was none too happy about being fucked with.

It pulsed. Its body flexed like a paper bag in the hands of a hyperventilating headcase.

Danielle's head jerked up. Not only was she lean and well-muscled, she was flexible, too. She threw a hand over her shoulder and scratched. Her physical hand passed through the habit demon like it was nothing. The demon crawled to one side. She reached over her other shoulder and scratched. Then she shifted her sports bra as if to reposition an itchy tag.

I drew down another pull of white light so I could take another swipe. But as I filled my well, Danielle plucked one final thing out of her gym bag: a bottle of prescription pills.

The habit demon sucked harder.

When she set the bottle on the counter while she knocked

one back, I craned my neck to get a look while avoiding the pumping bellow of the etheric tick. Dexedrine, an amphetamine they give you for ADD. And it wasn't her name on the label—not unless her real name was Brandon. They shared a surname, but that was about it. Son, nephew. Whoever it was, they were probably flunking out of trigonometry so Danielle could be nice and perky for her early morning spin class.

Though as someone who'd been under the influence of a habit demon myself, I had no business throwing stones.

When I gave the habit demon another shove, this time, it detached from Danielle and dropped to the floor with an etheric thud.

Because I was powered up enough to knock it off? Or because it was done feeding?

Either way, when it trundled over to a drain in the floor tiles and dropped out of sight, I wasn't willing to follow...whether or not my ghost-body was able to thrust its head down the drain. Who the hell knew what was lurking down there in the plumbing?

As Danielle gave herself a final primp and headed toward the door, I stared at the drain. The habit demons I'd encountered before stuck to their hosts. In some cases—like the late, unlamented Dr. Kamal—they'd even merged. But these particular creatures were ambulatory, and maybe that was worse. A single habit demon could wander around and feed off multiple hosts.

Then again, the fewer habit demons we had to contend with, the easier it would be for Jacob to crush them. Plus, he already took care of one back on the girlfriend's porch.

I followed Danielle out into the gym...and slammed right into her back. Hopefully it didn't mean I was getting used to being a ghost, that I now expected to be able to sail right through anything that stood in my way. But at least I had the decency to feel a bit startled when I saw what was in her sights.

Me.

She gave her hair another primp and headed over.

"Good morning!" she said brightly to my body. "I figured you'd be headed back to corporate by now—I'm surprised to see you're still in Beauchamp." Her voice turned ever so slightly flirtatious. "Hopefully that means you see something here you like?"

Judging by the look on my body's face, definitely not. But Danielle was one of those confident folks who stride into every personal encounter presuming everyone was predisposed to like them—not unlike the guy who steals my covers whenever the temperature dips below sixty-eight. She took my scowling in stride.

My body said, "I had a few more questions about the incident at the diner."

"Some things just can't be explained."

"How 'bout you try? You claimed you had an urge to move. A somatic impulse."

"A need to move. That's right. The body was designed to move, after all. Not sit behind a desk all day. Our sedentary lifestyles are a leading cause of—"

My body cut her off. "And you said you also heard music."

"It must have been inspiration. When you live and breathe your work, like me...actually, work isn't even the right word. More of a calling."

"Uh huh." Did I always look like such an asshole when I interviewed someone? "So there was a physical sensation. And then music. Anything else?"

"Like what?"

A deliberately casual shrug. "Maybe you saw something too."

Talk about leading the witness. And what the hell was I getting at, anyway?

"Well, now that you mention it, there was something. Like I was looking in a dance studio mirror. As I did each move, I was able to see it too—to get a really good look at the physiology of each particular motion and gesture. A few key muscle groups were engaged. If my husband hadn't blocked me from the pole, I'm sure it would've been a much more effective full-body workout."

What pole, I wondered...and then I recalled the mutant bunny rabbit taxidermy hanging proudly in the center of the restaurant.

Danielle said, "If you give me your contact info, I'd be happy to send you the latest research from the American Council on Exercise on the efficacy of pole dancing."

"Won't be necessary. I've got what I need."

When my body turned away with zero interest in Danielle's charms, a flicker of alarm crossed her face. But only for a moment. She steeled herself and trailed along after it, saying, "Beauchamp may be a small market, but the women here are ready for something exciting and new. You tell corporate we can produce the numbers, if you take into account the rest of the county. People will make the trip if they feel it's worth it. Think about it this way: anyone can buy an elliptical or stream a workout on their computer. But pole dancing requires both equipment and hands-on training. It's not like buying a yoga ball at SaverPlus and parking it by your desk. You need to come to the gym."

"Like I said. I've got what I need."

Jeez. What a dick.

Once it was obvious my body was well and truly done talking, Danielle's expression went dark. She looked daggers at its back as it strode off to rejoin Jacob and say, "We've seen all there is to see here. Let's go."

The sun was just pinkening the horizon as we climbed back into the white sedan—where my body nearly collided with Jacob again on its way to the driver side door. "I feel better," Jacob said. "I'm fine to drive."

"You sure?"

"Positive."

"Come on," I told Jacob. "You've gotta know something is up. Since when have I ever wanted to drive?"

Yelling at my husband while I was projected did me as much good as punching the GPS, so I gave up and climbed into the car. It was tempting to get in the front and see if the seat could help me align to my physical form long enough to get a message to Jacob. It would only take a few words. But the thought of that repelling sensation squashing me down into the upholstery—or worse, right through the bottom of the car—made me chicken out.

As Jacob buckled himself in, my body announced, "She's lying."

Jacob and I both did a startled take. "What makes you say that?" he asked, genuinely interested.

"Don't listen," I said. "There was a habit demon on her. I saw it."

My body either didn't hear me or didn't care. "The woman's story kept changing. All Psychs lean on a particular sense. I'm visual, Darla's auditory, you're tactile. But the more I pumped for information, the more she miraculously dredged up. First it was a feeling. Then there was music. And now, suddenly, she says she could see herself."

Well...it wasn't wrong.

Jacob seemed to think so too, though he couldn't resist playing devil's advocate. "But it's possible she's firing on a few different senses, isn't it? You're visual, but you hear things too. And you feel cold spots."

I gave a humorless laugh. "But I'm the most tricked-out medium since Marie Saint Savon."

And so humble, too.

Jacob wasn't at all put off by my body's bragging. "Wouldn't the GhosTV factor into it, though? With its signals playing in the background, maybe a low-level medium would gain the talent of someone a lot higher. Temporarily. But a few minutes is all it would take."

"People lie, Jacob. And when you think back to her video and compare it to the dog walker we came across, the moves were nothing alike. The girl in the park looked weirded out and desperate, but Danelle looked provocative, like she was putting on a show. She's an attention-seeker, plain and simple."

Jacob considered this and nodded. I couldn't say I blamed him. As much as I wanted to disagree with my body purely on principle, it did have a point. Quite a few of them.

But it hadn't seen the habit demon stuck to the woman's back.

I liked my body better when it was bitching about a nightlight or plowing through chocolate cherry ice cream. At least then Jacob stood some chance of realizing I wasn't really me. This theory about the fitness instructor made too much sense. That gut instinct you feel as a cop has to come from somewhere, and apparently my big dumb body wasn't so dumb after all.

So that was that. I was stuck here haunting my own life. And while I really wanted to be pissed off at Jacob for not noticing anything was going on, not only did the body look and sound like me, but it thought like me, too. And since I'd been swearing up and down that my aggressive stance was just a result of me being grounded, he had literally nothing to go on.

Jacob ran a weary hand through his hair. "Whether Danielle is telling the truth or not, Amy is still missing. Where does that leave us?"

"With the good possibility that we're combing through this town while Amy's in the cab of an eighteen-wheeler halfway to South Dakota. She could've snapped back into her body when the GhosTV went out of range. But if we want to canvas the night cashiers at the Filling Station and see if they noticed her taking off with a trucker in the middle of the night, we'd better do it before their shift ends."

Damn it. If my body kept coming up with plausible ideas, Jacob would never realize I wasn't working the controls.

Hopefully, once I was out of range, I'd snap back too. Like Amy.

Except...what if I didn't? What if my body headed back to Chicago without me and left me back in Beauchamp with no one for company but the habit demons and a suicide repeater?

Jacob started the car and said, "Aren't you gonna put on your seatbelt?"

My body shrugged like it was beneath him, but he'd deign to do it for the sake of keeping the peace. When it clicked the latch, its hand brushed my sidearm. It wriggled the gun from the holster and peered down the empty cartridge. "You can gimme my clip back."

Jacob raised an eyebrow. "Why now?"

"Because if there's prostitution at the truck stop—probably dealing, too—someone's bound to be carrying. I'd be going into a potentially volatile situation without any backup."

The car coasted to a stop as Jacob cut his eyes to my body. He stared at it for half a second, then peeled into a sudden U-turn, muttering, "I'm your backup."

"What the hell?" my body demanded. "The truck stop's that way."

Jacob didn't answer. He was too busy burning rubber, rushing us back to the GhosTV.

CHAPTER 29

We swung into the driveway so hard and fast I was surprised Jacob didn't take out the garbage bin on the neighbor's curb. But the rental car had some decent brakes on it and we jerked to stop between the houses with a crunch of crumbling asphalt.

"What is it?" my body asked. "If you've got an idea, share it with the whole class!"

Jacob ignored it. He slammed the car door loud enough to set the dog next door barking and stomped up the rickety stairs of the back deck.

"Oh shit," I muttered—at the exact same moment as my body—as Jacob reared back and gave the door a good, solid kick. It was a well-placed strike, but unfortunately, not only was the lock new, but the doorframe was made of sturdy stuff. Hopefully my husband wouldn't end up in a plaster cast of his own. It took two more kicks—and a few more barking dogs—before the doorknob gave, and Jacob could tear the door open and barrel toward the GhosTV.

"I hope you know what you're doing," my body said.

"Pretty sure he does," I told it, touched by the fact that when the chips were down, Jacob found a way to come through.

We hurried through the kitchen—through a spray of spectral blood and brain as Harris Tucker shot himself on an endless repeating loop—and dove down the short hallway. Wedged in the hall halfway to the bathroom, right where we'd left it, the GhosTV was playing the morning news. Jacob jerked the cord from the wall so hard I was worried he'd tear it right out of the TV. Disorientation as the room lurched around me. And then I was looking at the inside of the house from a completely different angle.

And if that wasn't enough to tell me I was back in my body, the heavy drag of physicality sure was.

I was starving to the point of lightheadedness. My lower back was twinging with sciatica from sleeping in a strange bed and skipping three days of yoga. And the inside of my mouth tasted exactly like you'd expect from scarfing down a wad of cheese crackers without brushing my teeth afterward.

All in all, after being unencumbered for so long, finding myself back inside a physical body pretty much sucked. Frankly, the only thing this body currently had going for it was the lack of my signature crown chakra headache.

No doubt I'd remedy that soon enough.

This was my body. I wasn't about to let it go off and fuck everything up without me.

"I'm here," I said as Jacob whirled around to face me. "I'm me."

He looked wild, wide-eyed and rumpled, with his normal I've-got-this confidence totally stripped away. "Are you? When is your birthday? And how do you feel about my mother's Spanish chicken casserole?"

I closed the gap between us and took him by the shoulders, massaging small circles on either side with my thumbs. "My body would know those things just as well as I do." Maybe it would be quicker to disparage Shirley's more questionable recipes...but since I'm a grownup, I'm perfectly capable of maneuvering around the olives—then burying them under some uneaten mashed potatoes. "Jacob, I promise you. This is me. All of me."

He stared deep into my eyes as if somehow he could see through me and check whether all my nesting dolls were in place, but that wasn't a talent he'd ever possessed. Could he feel it with his etheric telekinesis, though? Maybe. If he'd trained for it. Hopefully this wasn't something we'd need to practice from now on.

I gave his shoulders a solid squeeze, focusing there, on that spot where our physical bodies connected. Anyone who's ever seen a superhero movie might think it would be amazing if they could be invisible and walk through walls. But at the end of the day, if I couldn't touch this man—couldn't put my arms around him and mash my lips to his—those crazy powers were worthless.

We kissed. Him tentative, me desperate. Regretfully, I broke the kiss, though I did pause to trace his cheekbone with my fingertips and remind myself exactly what he felt like.

"Listen," I said. "While you and Asshole were scoping out the gym, here's what I found out."

I told him about the staff locker room, the Dexedrine, and the habit demon on Danielle's back.

Jacob's shoulders unhitched as he began to trust that without the GhosTV's interference, I was now really me again. "Good to know. But your body had me convinced that she'd conflated the whole striptease."

"I hate to admit that it might've been right...but I think the rest of me is in agreement."

"Then where does this leave us?" Jacob asked. "If the habit demons are making people strip, and Danielle had one on her back, then what reason would she have to lie?"

"People do unfathomable shit all the time." Unfortunately, that knowledge did us no good whatsoever. "But I think we can both agree that the GhosTV stays off from here on out."

Everything was pointing to the truck stop, whether it be Amy hitching a ride out of town or a pillhead looking for their next fix. We headed over and got there just as the sun peeked over the tassels in the nearby cornfields, a few minutes shy of 6am.

While the rest of Beauchamp had been drowsily rolling out of their beds, making coffee and checking their phones to see if anyone had liked the photo of their Sunday dinner, the Filling Station was already in full swing. Big rigs chugged down diesel at one set of pumps. At the other, travelers with out-of-state plates scraped bugs from their windshields as their gas tanks filled.

People streamed in and out the door—to pay for gas, to top up their coffee, to avail themselves of the diner, to pee. It was a typical slice of Americana.

Aside from the habit demon perched above the doorway.

"Twelve o'clock," I said with a nod.

We both paused at the front of the car. Jacob's eyes followed mine as if he hoped that maybe, this time, he would be able to see it...if only he were to look in just the right spot. But the GhosTV was on ice and he was just his usual Superstiff self. Ghost Teflon, but not exactly brimming with red veiny energy.

Although....

"Before we go in there," I said, "maybe you should ground yourself."

He cut his eyes to me dubiously. "I'm already grounded."

I warmed to the idea. "I do basically the same thing every time I suck down white light—I amplify what's already there. Why not do the same?"

"I've hardly got time to learn a new trick—" he said.

But I knew my idea was solid. Maybe I had a gut feeling about it, thanks to my big dumb body. Whatever the reason, I knew it couldn't hurt to try.

"Don't let impostor syndrome stop you from using everything you can to your advantage, Jacob. Take two seconds and do Amy's meditation. Imagine the grounding energy. Imagine your body pulling it up like tree roots. And, for crying out loud, close your eyes. I won't let anything sneak up on you."

If Jacob kissing me back there in the suicide house didn't prove that he thought I was really me, the fact that he'd close his eyes in proximity to a potential habit demon hangout definitely did.

While I'm hardly the guy to guide anyone through a meditation, there was no one else to do it. "Think about the energy you'll be tapping into. Red. Glowing. Coursing around beneath our feet like an underground river."

A pretty good image, I thought...but a line formed between Jacob's brows. "This is a waste of time."

"No, it isn't. It's red," I emphasized—as if he hadn't heard me the first time. "Red grounding energy."

He shook his head in frustration.

"If you'd just stop worrying about how it won't work and try to see it for half a second—" And that, I realized, was the problem. Jacob probably couldn't see it.

But he could feel it.

"You got this," I told him gently. "I promise."

With a subtle sigh, Jacob closed his eyes, leaned his butt on the hood of the car, and listened.

"You know how it feels when you steal my white light? Imagine that tingle, that zap, whatever it is. But, uh, different." Nice. Expecting me to describe something without mentioning what it looked like was like shooting a gun without ammo.

I did my best.

"The stuff you're tapping, it's not light and bright and spar-kly like crown chakra mojo. It's a deeper, more solid thing. It feels different. Like...the blender. When we push all the various buttons and the vibration changes."

That's right. I'd just compared the channeling of grounding energy to a kitchen appliance. But as I was about to agree with him and admit that grounding him was a stupid idea to begin with, I saw the crease between his eyebrows begin to ease.

I seized on the whole vibration idea. "Get really still and focus your attention downward, below your physical body. That energy, it's there—it's always there—and there's plenty of it. More than you'll ever be able to hold. Enough for you to tap into whenever you need. Imagine yourself—feel yourself—reaching down and pulling that energy in. Imagine your subtle bodies thick and strong. Solid and anchored. Because you're a freaking badass, Jacob. And you know it."

Whether or not this meditation of mine was working, I couldn't really say. Not without a GhosTV playing in the back-ground. The corner of his mouth quirked, though, when I called him a badass. I supposed that counted for something.

With me brimming with white light and Jacob (hopefully) fortified with red, we headed into the Filling Station. I scanned first for Amy. But while I spotted the kitschy magnets she'd said her body was drawn to, she wasn't currently there. I wasn't really surprised. She'd been missing all night. And there's only so long a spinner rack of magnets will hold anyone's attention.

Next, I looked for habit demons. Without the GhosTV playing, it was a lot harder than I thought it would be. Even when I pulled down another big volley of white light, even when my tank felt full, I couldn't be sure if the place was clear—or if I just couldn't pinpoint them atop the visual clutter of the grocery shelves.

We'd paused there, Jacob and me, beside the spinner rack with its googly-eyed corncob magnets. I turned to Jacob, expecting him to tell me that he'd been right all along. That meditation was useless, and without the GhosTV, we were S.O.L. But Jacob wasn't paying any attention to me. He was standing there with his eyes closed. Listening. Feeling.

"There's something here," he murmured.

I could've used more specifics—but something was better than nothing.

I scanned the mini mart again, encouraged by the fact that Jacob thought there was something to find. White light thrummed down as I focused on the various people. The ladies' room had a line, with one preteen girl clamping her knees together desperately. The coffee pots were busy. So was the microwave, where a couple of portly truckers argued good-naturedly while their breakfast burritos warmed through. Regular people doing regular things. And any one of them could have a habit demon riding around on them.

Though when I heard a ragged cough behind the counter...I realized where I should be focusing my search.

CHAPTER 30

The coughing cashier who'd snagged my attention was a twentyish Caucasian guy with a long, wispy beard and hollow eyes. His Filling Station polo shirt—a bright, cheerful blue—hung awkwardly from his bony shoulders. As he rang up his customer, a guy who couldn't figure out how to swipe his card at the pump, his eyes darted nervously, tracking something behind the counter.

I grabbed a box of donuts from an endcap and got in line… even though the other cashier was wide open. "Sir?" the woman at the other register said. I ignored her. "Sir?" she repeated, like I was phenomenally thick. I kept on ignoring her, focusing instead on the sketchy clerk.

He looked greasy. Which didn't automatically make him a criminal—especially since he was just finishing up a night shift. But if I had to pick between him and the stout, corn-fed woman barking "Sir?" at me and say which one was dealing uppers, I'd go for the skinny guy with the shifty demeanor.

Try as I might, though, I couldn't get a bead on any habit demon. Not with a chrome cigarette rack right behind the guy reflecting the movements of the customers over by the coffee and fooling my eyes.

Jacob joined me, centering the clerk in his sights. "Do you see something?" he whispered.

"The lighting is tricky." I wasn't about to admit that without the GhostTV, the habit demons were a lot less substantial, since that would only make it harder to dismantle the thing when the time came. Instead, I pulled energy through my crown chakra. Ahh…there it was, the one-eyed headache.

And still, no telltale bending of light.

We were standing a person-length away from the counter, me staring at the clerk, Jacob staring at me. Someone behind us huffed and went to the "Sir?" lady. The greasy guy glanced up, watched us with little interest for a couple of seconds, then said, "Uh…did you wanna buy that?"

Awkwardly, I stepped up to the counter and let him scan my donut box. If he thought I was looking at him unusually hard, he gave no sign of it. His hands were pale and he had a homemade tattoo of an infinity symbol on the meat between thumb and forefinger. But no habit demon.

Maybe, though, if I got him to turn around. "And…a pack of smokes."

He stared at me blandly for another beat, then said, "Okay. What kind?"

He was asking the guy who'd smoked one cigarette—once—and didn't even finish the damn thing. Were Marlboros still cool? Apparently they still sold them. But holy shit, twelve bucks a pack? Maybe that was for a carton. No, that couldn't be right…. "Marlboros." The guy continued staring. I cleared my throat. "Reds."

He turned around and plucked a pack out of the display. The only thing on his back was a stray hair.

"You know what? I changed my mind. Just the donuts."

"Quitting, huh? Good for you. Glad I never started. My only vices are video games and Mountain Dew."

And now I saw the nefarious thing behind the counter that had been vying for his attention was an open comic book.

Great. If ever there'd been a cautionary tale about profiling someone based on their appearance....

Thankfully, Jacob had drifted away during that scintillating exchange. He stood at the magnet spinner rack, just a bit too still to be casual. I was wondering if we'd end up giving his family a bunch of corncob magnets for Christmas—or just intend to, but forget about them by the time winter rolled around—when I realized he wasn't actually looking at them. Not unless he was looking through his closed eyelids.

When I approached, he cracked one eye to make sure it was me. "I think I feel something."

Without the GhosTV playing? Not very likely, but at least he hadn't just set his sights on someone whose big weakness was caffeinated soda.

Jacob's brow furrowed as he concentrated. "Back at the party—even back at George's girlfriend's place—I felt something. Faint. Like a cobweb."

"A tether," I murmured.

"You saw them? I wasn't sure they were really there." But now that his impression had been confirmed, he was even more determined that he'd felt something.

I doubled down on my crown chakra and looked for the telltale shifting of light, and saw nothing. Then again, maybe it wasn't white light that made those tethers visible. Maybe it was red energy. "Jacob, stop reaching out for a second and reach down instead. Charge your batteries first. Then see if you can feel something."

Jacob's expression scrunched up as he tried. Then he took a slow, careful breath, exhaled, and extended a hand out in a languid sweep. He opened his eyes and said, "There."

I looked...and saw nothing. "Where? By the automotive section?" If a habit demon were lurking around somewhere in the mini mart, I'd expect it to be at the beer cooler. Even the coffee bar. Not lounging there among the air fresheners.

Psychic powers are tricky, though, and the grass is always greener. Those of us who wished it all would just go away were bombarded with extrasensory perceptions, while people who desperately wanted to be psychic concocted impressions where none existed.

Not to say Jacob had no talent. Just that he didn't know how to use it quite yet.

Though he did fall into the category of desperate wanting.

"Everyone gets a false positive now and then," I began.

But Jacob was already shuffling toward automotive with his hand extended and his eyes shut.

I figured it would be easier to help him. He'd never accept defeat until he saw for himself he was wrong. "You're clear for another three yards," I said. "Stop. Newspaper rack to your right." He felt it. "You can either jog to the left or take a ninety-degree right."

With a sweep of his hand, Jacob went left. We navigated up the aisle (with the trail mix calling my name the entire time), past the beef jerky and through a motor oil display. Jacob paused, thinking hard. Or maybe calling up earth energy through his shoes. But before I could try to console him by claiming we all made mistakes, he pointed to a narrow door half-hidden by a promo poster hawking a refillable coffee mug and said, "It leads there." He frowned. "At least...I think it does."

I tried the door. Locked. "I'll get a clerk to open it up." No doubt the broad who kept barking "Sir?" at me would just love to accommodate my request.

But Jacob, being Jacob, ignored my suggestion. He leaned in, raised a fist, and rapped gently with his knuckles.

I rolled my eyes—but the joke was on me. The door I'd taken for some kind of storage closet opened a crack, and a face filled the gap in the door. "Can I help you?" a guy in a blue polo said in a tone that was so inflectionless, the blandness must've been deliberate.

He was maybe thirty, Caucasian, average, clean-cut and unassuming. But judging by the way Jacob slid a foot in the door, this guy was anything but boring.

There were two ways to handle this situation. Either act like we were in the market for some pills, or pull out the F-Pimp license and get bossy. Jacob, however, did neither. He simply stood there in the doorway...and closed his eyes.

A sure way to get shot if ever there was one. And me and my empty gun as his only backup. But as I was reaching for my useless sidearm, Jacob cocked his head, furrowed his brow, and pointed. "There," he said, jabbing a finger toward the corner.

To call the room an office was generous. More like a glorified closet covered in sticky notes. An old computer on a crappy desk hugged one wall, and a bank of battered filing cabinets lined the other. There was nothing more than an aisle between them, so narrow that the manager probably couldn't even stretch his shoulders without smacking himself on the filing cabinets. The third wall, opposite the door, was floor-to-ceiling shelves.

They were groaning with product, all sorts of random crap,

from dented cans to a pile of old magazines to big cubes of toilet paper. Jacob was currently pointing at an open cardboard box, but I doubted he wanted to call attention to the inventory.

Not with a bloated habit demon clinging to its side.

It didn't look solid, not like it would have if the GhosTV were playing. But even though it was more of a transparent overlay, I saw it well enough. It was the same gumdrop shape as the others, but bigger. And this one had a tail hanging off the back.

Or at least I thought it was a tail. Until it grew.

Did habit demons shit?

The manager was talking now, babbling something about the office being private—and we weren't from the home office, were we?—and actually his shift was just ending.

But Jacob was too focused on the habit demon to pay him any heed, and I was too busy trying to keep down my mostly-digested cheese crackers. Because the tip of the long turd had broken off and dropped down onto a filing cabinet....

Where it proceeded to trundle away.

"Sir?" I said in my best pissed-off cop voice. "Stay seated and place your hands behind your head. Lace your fingers together. Eyes forward."

The manager had gone whiter than the glaze on my new box of donuts...which I no longer had any desire to consume. "Up there on the cup lids," I whispered in Jacob's ear. "Stuck to the right side of the box. And it's not exactly alone."

If it were me, I would've asked what in the hell that was supposed to mean. But maybe Jacob already knew. He was a telekinetic, the rarest of all the psychic talents, bred for multiple generations by a researcher with a God complex who tricked a bunch of patriots into doing their civic duty during the cold war. And Jacob's talent was focused in a nonphysical plane.

Not only that, but he'd been loading up on grounding energy like I mainlined white light.

My skin prickled as I realized he and I were standing way too close, and I had no way of knowing which way the mojo would jump if we brushed up against each other. I always bitched about him grabbing my white light. I'd hate to steal his grounding energy.

I dropped back a step, and Jacob lunged forward. The manager flinched as this menacing guy in a black suit crowded into the tiny office with him. Before I could tell Jacob to watch himself, he was already making a grab for it. I couldn't see whether or not his eyes were closed, but he snatched that habit demon off the box like he could damn well see it himself.

And then the energy jumped. Not from me to Jacob like it usually does, but from Jacob to the habit demon. The creature solidified—at least, it looked that way to me, as if Jacob had picked up a particularly ugly beanbag—while undeveloped pieces dropped off the swinging tail and pattered to the desk, rocking and pulsing.

I wanted to warn Jacob that it was drawing energy from him but couldn't find the words. Fortunately...I didn't need to. Because the habit demon wasn't the one flowing the energy.

Jacob was.

The bloated tick of an etheric parasite popped like an overfilled water balloon. The goopy, smoky insides flared dark against the fluorescent-lit wall, hung there for a moment, then dissipated in a cascade of dark sparkles.

The manager was babbling something about being only one of many people who used the office, so he couldn't be responsible for its contents.

Obviously not. The GhosTV was.

While the guy demanded to see his lawyer—and did we happen to know of a lawyer?—Jacob smacked down a hand on the desktop, startling us both. Sticky notes fluttered. Luckily, he didn't crucify himself on the receipt spike a couple of inches to the right. Working with your eyes shut might be good for focus, but the real world still mattered.

The biggest baby-segment, the one that was developed enough to be ambulatory, was now an etheric stain on the desktop. And Jacob, I saw, even as he shook the residual etheric goop from his hand...finally looked like his good ol' smug self again.

CHAPTER 31

When we went back out to the rental car, there was no question as to who would drive. Sweat glistened on Jacob's brow and he was shaking like a blender on the puree setting. Was it exactly like a white light hangover? Probably not, given how different our talents were. But the feeling of being depleted—of being psychically used up, wrung out and hung up to dry—was something you don't soon forget.

While he collapsed in the passenger seat and caught his breath, I grabbed my salt from the trunk, then filled him in on the gory details. Mostly, he was proud of what he'd accomplished. But he was also concerned about cleaning up the baby demon-shits before they developed into full-fledged adults.

"When you think about it," I said, "we couldn't have hoped for a better smokescreen. Laura will authorize cleanup in aisle seven. And dealing with these habit demons will buy us some time to stick around and look for Amy." I turned on the cabin light and got to work snapping my phone battery back in. Lucky for me, the FPMP models were designed to be changed in the field with relative ease. I managed to do it without dropping anything important down the console.

Jacob had used the momentary reprieve to sit with his eyes shut and catch his etheric breath. Actually, I wouldn't have been surprised if he'd started snoring, which is where things usually end up for me when I have the urgent need to rest my eyes. But eventually, he surprised me by speaking, instead.

"Here's the thing I still don't get. If the habit demons were making people strip, and the fitness instructor had a habit demon on her back, then why was she faking?"

"To drum up business for her pole-dancing class? Look, for all we know, she did do a legitimate striptease at some point, but in a place where there was no one around to see it—and that's what gave her the big idea to begin with."

But now that he mentioned it, the more I thought about everything, the less it added up. Not to mention the fact that Amy was still unaccounted for.

"Let's take another look at our map," I said. Jacob dug it out of his pocket and spread it across the dash.

"The GhosTV is here." I pointed to the spot we didn't dare mark with an X. "And here's the diner." I put my thumb over Danielle's X. "Even if Danielle is the outlier, not Amy, it still puts the GhosTV right in the middle of the blob."

Jacob smoothed his beard in thought. "Hold on. What if we eliminate them both?"

Jacob covered Amy's X with his thumb...and the loose blob of X's clustered around the GhosTV shifted before my eyes. Not in the same way a shifting shadow would resolve itself into a repeater, but damn near close. What was once a vague shape was now a circle. Only it wasn't the GhosTV at the center.

It was the party house.

"Vine Street," Jacob said urgently. "Hurry."

We'd been operating under cover of night for the better part of the investigation, but it was a bright, sunny Monday morning now and the tiny town of Beauchamp was rousing itself from a lazy summer weekend. I couldn't blow through all the stop signs since there were other cars to avoid. And the sense that we'd been right on top of the place a few hours ago and missed something was making it seem twice as far away.

While the GhosTV house was isolated enough for us to break in (what—three, four times now?) the party house was too exposed. But it was currently for sale, and a lockbox with a realtor key hung from the doorknob—a very newfangled contraption that looked way too technical for the likes of me. Even Jacob was stumped. I sent a photo of the device to HQ, and was told to download an app—one that allowed me to put my phone up against the sensor and access the key. I'd been none too eager to plug back into F-Pimp, but I had to admit... the technical expertise was nothing to sneeze at. Frankly, the hardest part about the whole operation was making sure my Bluetooth was on.

The party house seemed bigger now that it wasn't filled with balloons, red lights, and a bunch of stupid Millennials. But the smell of weed lingered, along with shreds of red latex and an empty vodka bottle on the windowsill.

As we crept deeper into the house, my sense of dread deepened. Jennifer Chance and Roger Burke had left their mark on Beauchamp, that much was certain. What if they'd set up more than one safe house?

I pulled down white light, and it settled in my head with a sickening throb. Whatever refreshment I'd felt from my grounded power-nap was long gone, replaced with the brittle fuel of desperation and adrenaline. I considered my sidearm, knew it was useless in more ways than one, and shifted instead to ghost mode. Pocket flashlight in one hand, salt in the other. And Jacob at my side.

He closed his eyes and listened, or felt, or whatever it is he does. But without an obvious habit demon to zero in on, there wasn't much for him to find. He swiped a hand through the air and said, "I think the cobwebs here might just be cobwebs."

"And I'm no help. Without the GhosTV playing, I can't see the tethers either."

I checked the bedrooms, bath and kitchen. Nothing, nothing, nothing. Meanwhile, Jacob stood stock-still in the center of the living room, hands on hips, scowling.

"Maybe there was no circle on that map," I said. "What if there weren't enough data points to prove anything at all, and we were so gung-ho about finding Amy, we just saw what we wanted to see? We drew a connection with the party house because we'd been here before. Not because there was anything here to find."

Not sure if Jacob heard me or not. He was too busy sliding off his necktie.

"Jacob?"

Ignoring me, he tied it around his eyes.

It should have looked ridiculous, like an impromptu game of "Pin the Tail on the Donkey." But even with his eyes covered, Jacob looks like the badass he is. Broad-shouldered. Intense. Determined...and fearless.

And since I'd never be able to live with myself if I crapped out on him now, I managed to find my second wind, too. It wasn't pretty. But I forced open my fatigued crown chakra just a little bit more and pulled down another surge of white light.

We'd both gone still—looking, searching, feeling. It was so quiet I could hear the distant thump of a car stereo and my own pulse thrumming through my ears. In a seller's market, vacant homes stayed vacant for a reason. There had to be something here—there had to be—but for the life of me, my talent was coming up with nothing. Not even a wispy repeater.

Nothing at all...until the gentle scrape of stone on stone reached our ears.

And it was coming from the basement.

I considered saying that maybe it was just a rat—but no one's ever accused me of being optimistic.

Jacob whisked the tie off his eyes, drew his sidearm and angled through the kitchen. "Clear."

I clutched my salt baggie and followed, kicking myself for not insisting on getting my clip back the second we unplugged the GhosTV.

The basement door, directly off the mudroom, was locked from the inside. Jacob had it open with just a single kick—either it wasn't as sturdy as the exterior door on the GhosTV house, or he was getting good kicking things down. Since we'd obviously lost any potential for surprise, we went into the whole, "Federal agent! Weapons down!" routine that would hopefully keep us from being shot as home invaders.

Turned out we were wasting our breath. The only one in that basement was Amy Grace—and she'd totally succumbed to that impulse to strip. But that wasn't the part that worried me the most. Not only was she flat on her back in her underwear, but her limbs were bloodied, flailing against the concrete floor.

Jacob was at her side in a heartbeat. "She's having a seizure!"

Etheric projection was finally taking its toll. Hopefully this wasn't in my future too, and my persistent headache wasn't a precursor to a full-blown grand mal.

Contrary to popular belief, people can't actually swallow

their own tongues during a seizure, and any attempt to stick something in their mouth to prevent it will only end up with you getting chewed on.

Jacob and I had enough training to handle the situation. While he turned Amy on her side, gently cradling her head, I kicked some debris out of the way and reached for my phone to call 911.

Poor Amy had already done a real number on herself. The floor was littered with junk—splintered wood and hunks of broken concrete—all of it smeared with her blood. But it was the potential for neurological damage that had me the most worried.

Apparently, though, Amy's brain was still working just fine. And the whole seizure thing? A great big fake, I realized—when in a single, fluid motion, not only did she sit up...but draw the gun from Jacob's holster and level it at his head.

CHAPTER 32

For a guy looking down the barrel of his own gun, Jacob was incredibly calm. I know him well enough to know that unshakeable exterior is all a big act, though, and inside, he must be totally freaking out.

I almost felt guilty for being selfishly relieved that the seizure had been a fake.

Desperately, I scanned for something I could use to my advantage. We were in a laundry room, with old clothes hanging everywhere. Actually, no, not clothes...costumes. And they looked like they'd been there a while. Cobwebs hung from the nun getup and the white nurse's outfit was patchy with mildew.

Unless I wanted to dress up like a harem girl, nothing within my reach would do me any good. If only I'd been the one Amy had disarmed, this whole thing wouldn't be happening. Now I had nothing at my disposal but a sidearm with no bullets and my dubious powers of persuasion.

I said, "Put the gun down, Amy,"

"We're not here to hurt you," Jacob added.

"Why should I believe you?" she demanded.

Jacob's hands were in the air, though he should be able to

disarm her with a well-placed grab. But at such close range, it was too risky—really hard to miss someone three feet away, even if you'd never shot anything more lethal than a cap gun. Instead of lunging, Jacob tried to defuse the situation in his most reasonable tone. "Haven't we helped you before?"

Evidently, that was not the thing to say. Amy's face twisted in rage and her bloody hands tightened on Jacob's weapon, trembling. "Helped me? No one has ever helped me! Everyone around here thinks they're better than me."

I couldn't speak for the whole town. But more likely than not, her neighbors were just freaked out about socializing with someone who handled dead bodies for a living.

"People can be insensitive," Jacob said soothingly. "But it's more about their own insecurities than you."

Amy jerked her head from side to side. She was shaking hard now, likely more from adrenaline than cold. "I see it. I know. If you're from the right family, you can do whatever you want and nobody will lift a finger to stop you."

I said, "Did the sheriff's kid hurt you?"

"Don't play dumb," Amy snapped. "You know who I mean."

"Is it George?" Jacob ventured.

"George?" Amy barked a bitter laugh. "That stupid brat is no better off than I am."

Okay, so...not George. "Listen," I said, "I promise you, whoever it is, whatever's going on, we can help."

With shaking hands, she pointed the bloody gun right between Jacob's eyes.

After all we'd been through together, how could she possibly doubt that we were on her side? It made no sense—unless you took into account that the majority of our interactions had been with her ka, not her body.

As calmly as Jacob, I said, "Let's talk this out, all right? No one needs to get shot here. I'll slide my gun over to you just to prove I mean what I say."

There. At least the damn sidearm might be good for something.

Gingerly, I plucked the gun from my holster, set it on the concrete floor and nudged it toward her with my foot. Meanwhile, Jacob's eyes tracked his own weapon, and I knew he was about to make the grab.

I also knew that one quick squeeze would put a hole in him—one he was unlikely to recover from.

My eyes were on Amy's quaking trigger finger. The hand was dark and sticky with drying blood and the nails were torn.

If the seizure was fake, why the blood? Especially the torn nails—those didn't add up.

I zeroed in on her fingers. That's when I saw the cause of all the shaking. Not adrenaline. Not fatigue. But the ghostly fingertip of her ka sliding in and out of alignment.

Well, shit. It wasn't Amy in her totality that was leveling a gun at us, it was just her body. And bodies are notoriously hard to reason with.

Thrumming with adrenaline, I was grounded in the physical. Having a gun pointed at your husband's head will do that. But whatever was going on here wasn't just happening on the physical plane. I opened up the floodgates and sucked down white light for all I was worth. My head throbbed hard and my right eye twitched, and the room went hazy-white to my vision as my crown chakra lit up bright.

I wasn't the one who needed the light, though. It was Amy, an untrained medium whose ka was struggling to seat itself in its body.

"Listen, it's okay," I said easily, "it'll all be okay." But I was channeling that bullshit from who-knows-where, saying any random thing to get me in range without even thinking about it. It was almost like watching my body wolf down a melting ice cream cone, except I was still riding around inside myself, fueled by panic, desperate to keep my man in one piece.

I eased up a half step, vibrating with white light—knowing that if the energy jumped to Jacob, this would all be over. Because my only hope of straightening out Amy was to put her ka back in the driver's seat.

I pitched my voice deceptively soft, looking Amy's body in the eye while addressing Jacob, and said, "Don't move."

And when both of them froze, I touched Amy on the shoulder and shoved white light into her for all I was worth.

White light doesn't jump from one medium to another in a big show of fireworks like it does when Jacob and I accidentally cross streams—but it can sure as hell flow. Blinding pain jabbed the tender spot behind my eyeball as crown chakra mojo channeled from the ethers to Amy, using my body as a conduit. Her ka lit up bright. Incandescent.

But instead of seating itself firmly in her body, it stumbled out the other side.

"Make your body drop the gun!" I snapped.

"I can't! There's someone else inside!"

And whoever it was now had full control of the body.

Hands no longer shaking, it swung the gun's barrel toward me. "Touch me again and it'll be the last thing you do."

I put my hands in the air. "Why don't we start by you telling us your name?"

"As if you care."

"Try me," I said.

"It's the name of the girl you were too shy to talk to. Your best friend's wife. Hell, even your mother. For twenty bucks, I'm whoever you say I am."

Imperiously, Amy's ka announced, "She needs to cross over."

"Oh, really?" I said in exasperation. It was not the time or place for an argument, but the conversation ended up serving some purpose after all. It made Amy's body (and whoever was possessing it) try to figure out who the hell I was talking to.

And when her aim drifted, Jacob made his move.

With a shriek, she pulled the trigger and shot, just missing Jacob's head. But a Beretta has a nasty kick, and before the body could recover, he twisted the gun from her grasp and wrenched her hand behind her back.

Amy's ka was horrified. "Watch it—you're hurting me!"

I kicked Jacob's gun out of the way. "Careful," I told him. "Amy might not feel it now, but it's bound to smart later."

He shook his ringing head. "Is this Amy or not?"

"It's...complicated."

Without a gun to wave in our faces, whoever was driving the body changed tactics. "Of course I'm Amy. Your Amy. However you want her to be."

I felt depleted. Hollow. And since the very last thing I needed was for that spirit to jump into me, I said, "Don't let go, Jacob. The body's possessed."

Jacob blanched...but he hung on tight.

This wasn't his first rodeo.

All this time, I'd been so sure it was habit demons running the show. I didn't know what was worse—mindless etheric ticks, or a confused ghost who was strong enough to displace a body's rightful owner and strip off her clothes.

Ghosts who don't know they're dead were Amy's specialty,

so in no uncertain terms, she said, "This woman is in pain. She shouldn't be here. You need to help her start the next leg of her journey."

Normally, our M.O. would be to find the veil, have Jacob drag the spirit over, and let me shove it through. But normally I'd be filled with white light. If I started dicking around with the veil in my current condition, chances were the pain behind my eyeball would no longer be a problem. I'd stroke out and embark on a one-way trip to the afterlife myself.

The spirit was strong—really strong. We'd need to convince her to cross over herself.

"Here's the thing," I told the spirit. "You're dead."

"That's the best you can do?" Amy said incredulously.

The expression on Amy's body—powered by the spirit—went shrewd. "Fine, if that's your kink—but if you want me to take a cold bath first, I charge double." She struggled against Jacob's grip. "But quit with the rough stuff or I'm out."

"She thinks she's turning a trick," Jacob said to me. "This isn't a date," he told her patiently, even as she whapped him with a bruised shoulder. "We're not customers. Miss, you need to take a breath, think about just how long you've been in this basement, and focus on what we're trying to tell you. This isn't your world anymore. You need to move on."

Amy said, "How can she trust him while he's grabbing her like that?"

"Letting go is not an option," I said.

Amy's body elbowed Jacob in the ribs, but he held on tight. With a huff, she said, "Move on? I've lived in Beauchamp all my life." She turned and spat on the floor. "It takes money to start over. Where else am I supposed to go?"

"Somewhere better," I said. "Way better. No more tricks. No

more judgment. But you need to let yourself take that first step."

There was a flash of hope in the eyes of Amy's body...but it was brittle. And brief.

"The place don't matter. People are the same everywhere. And in the end, going from one town to another won't make a damn bit of difference."

Amy said, "She doesn't get that you're talking about the afterlife. She's probably an atheist—they're almost as bad as the ones worrying about hell."

"The input from the peanut gallery is not helping," I muttered.

"But all you're doing is convincing her to stay!"

Jacob struggled with the body. "I can't find the veil and keep her in at the same time."

So basically it was a standoff, with Jacob and me both straining to stay focused on the etheric. The ghost, in its natural element, would eventually wear us both down. My white light was all tapped out, and I was too fried to summon more.

But Amy's ka was lit up bright.

I turned to her, patted my chest, and said, "If Jacob lets go of your body to find the veil, will you get in here and make sure the spirit can't jump into me?"

Jacob looked up sharply. "Vic, no!"

Amy, sick of watching us bungle this whole thing, was eager to dive in and get it all over with.

She moved toward me like an old friend coming in for an awkward hug. I wasn't trying to repel her, but I found myself resisting the takeover anyway. It was pure reflex. Like clenching your ass when you see someone else get reamed.

But I was tapped out, while Amy was bursting with light. And almost as if the energy recognized me as the conduit it had just flowed through, it settled back in with a rightness that allowed me to lower the drawbridge and let Amy in.

Possession is never pretty. There's a certain awkwardness to handing over the controls and letting a new spirit take over. If the GhosTV left me feeling like my shoes were too big, possession felt like someone else sticking their foot inside mine. Most of the time, mediums blank out when someone else slips into their skin suit. But once in a while, if we keep calm and stop fighting the wrongness of it all, we just tag along for the ride.

I'd done it before, when I let Dr. Morganstern step in and neutralize Roger Burke.

And I did it now.

Using my lungs, Amy drew a deep breath, then took stock of the situation. "Wow, you're really tall."

Jacob looked at me in alarm. I tried to tell him I was still there—I was still me...kind of—but Amy was currently the one using the mouth. She told Jacob, "Everything's under control. Let my body go so we can help this poor woman. She's suffered long enough."

I might not be able to say anything to Jacob, but I could still speak to Amy. "He needs to find the veil."

"Find the veil," she said, with a gentle authority that sounded weird coming out of my mouth.

Jacob worked his jaw a few times, wanting to argue, I could tell. But he was just as eager to put an end to the ghostly game of musical chairs as the rest of us. Reluctantly, he let go of the body and took a step back.

As he did, a webwork of red energy powered on, creeping up from his collar and down past his cuffs. I could see it with my spirit eyes, the act of Jacob grounding himself, drawing base chakra energy up through the earth. He didn't look like he did it purposely. More like it just happened when he strained to use a talent that didn't register to his physical senses.

Though that wasn't entirely true.

"He needs to close his eyes," I told Amy.

She casually kicked my Glock out of her body's reach. "Close your eyes," she told Jacob with my voice. "I've got this."

Jacob grumbled, low in his throat, but in for a penny, in for a pound.

Amy wasn't kidding, though, she did have this. Years of crossing over spirits had given her lots of practice. She told the being in her physical shell, "I've lived here all my life, too. We both know what it's like. So do you really think this is all there is? We've been given a life and a consciousness. Why—to simply exist? Or is there something more going on? Not just existence. Purpose."

While Amy spoke to whatever was driving her body—with my voice—Jacob held out his hands and focused. What would normally look like nothing more than a furrowed brow was now a network of red energy. He might be struggling to interpret what it all meant. But I had zero doubt his extrasensory input was working just fine.

"There." He opened his eyes and nodded to a cinderblock wall behind Amy's body. With a sweep of his hand, he brushed a faded waitress getup aside....

And revealed a blood-smeared door.

CHAPTER 33

The door was imposing, to say the least. A fat padlock on the steel frame sent a chill down my spine. Hopefully Jacob wasn't harboring any impulse to try and kick this one down. Any attempt would only land him in the emergency room.

With my mouth, Amy observed, "This isn't supposed to keep anyone out, is it?"

Bitterly, her body replied, "No. He was keeping me in."

"If that's the case," I told Amy, "there might be a key."

The basement swung around me as Amy scanned it with my physical eyes. They landed on a high shelf. "That must be what she was looking for. But because my body couldn't quite reach it and we had nothing to stand on, we only managed to knock it further back, and that's when she panicked and started clawing at the door." She ambled forward, reached up, and snatched a rusted coffee can off the shelf. "I can see where the height comes in handy."

About freaking time something went our way.

Jacob held out one hand for the key with the other pressed to the door. "Hurry," he said. "The veil isn't stable."

I'm not sure how he knew, and probably he wasn't either, but

I believed him. And if the veil decided to collapse before the spirit went through, someone here might end up permanently displaced. Maybe everyone but Jacob.

If I ever caught him feeling sorry for himself for not having a showier psychic talent—if he ever again uttered the words, Just a Stiff—I'd need to remind him of this moment...if I ever managed to fumble my way through it.

Amy's ka swerved my body past Jacob and locked our eyes on the solitary figure seated in the center of the dingy little room, strapped to an old office chair with duct tape—a mossy figure with empty eye sockets and its mouth dropped open in a perpetual silent scream.

The body had been there so long, the stench of decomp was long gone, but a weird funk still hung thick in the air. The basement was damp. What had once been human tissue had transformed into something else entirely.

I might not know as much about dead bodies as Amy Grace, but in my time, I'd seen my fair share. The most macabre stages of death happen within the first few months. The bloat. The slippage. The teeming insect life. This woman had clearly been dead for years...but those years had not been kind. A black stain spread beneath the chair. What was left of her skin hung off her bones like filthy rags. Some sort of mold or mildew, a grayish-brown fuzz, covered the right side of her body. And what I'd initially taken for an overabundance of teeth turned out to be tiny, pale mushrooms sprouting in the gaping cavity of her mouth.

But the worst part was the costume she'd been wearing—a polyester monstrosity of a Japanese schoolgirl outfit—totally untouched by the ravages of time. The cropped shirt with its peter pan collar was still white, despite the fact that it hung off such grisly remains. The pleats in the red plaid miniskirt were still sharp. The knee socks were the only thing that hadn't come through unscathed. They must've soaked up all the decomp as it ran down the victim's legs. Once white, now brown and fossilized, they lay bunched around skeletal ankles.

Jacob spared only a glance for the body, then closed his eyes again and threw open his arms in search of the veil. There were plenty of cobwebs dangling from the floorboards overhead to throw him off, but the psychic atmosphere was so palpable, he brushed the physical distraction away without a second thought.

Amy's body was the last one through the door—but it was the first one to rush the corpse. "Stop her!" I said—and my physical mouth made a weird little groan as my spirit fought against Amy's ka. No doubt there was plenty of evidence to lock up whoever'd done this. But I've learned the hard way not to give a jury any reason to do something stupid.

But Amy's body stopped short of barreling into the evidence as the possessing spirit kept going, sailing right out of the body as it launched itself toward the corpse.

Why anyone would want to be in that horror show of a cadaver was beyond me. I suppose we can't help but be attached to our own bodies, however sorry they might be.

Amy's body had gone down on its knees, but it didn't pass out this time—and it didn't seem too distressed about being on autopilot. It didn't bat an eyelash over the decomposed body, either...but it was none too thrilled with its current state of undress. "Where's my top?" it demanded. "Dammit, it's my favorite shirt!"

"You'd better get in there and hold down the fort," I told Amy's ka.

"But then I won't be able to help the spirit."

I hadn't considered that. But the spirit in question was currently flailing around inside a corpse while Amy's body yelled, "What did you people do to me? I'm bleeding!"

I told Amy, "Your body needs to calm down. I know you don't usually remember what happens when you project, but right now, you're full of psychic mojo. White light. And if you focus hard enough, maybe you can bridge the gap and take the knowledge with you. Even if it's only for a few seconds—you need to try."

"Sounds like the stuff of enlightenment," she said, intrigued—with my mouth. "But what about the deceased?"

"I've done this before—Jacob and I both have. It's our job. Let us do it."

Amy said, "I've never met anyone else with the same calling," and I realized it was her ka's voice I heard now, not mine, as she stepped out of my body. "I do hope I remember. And if not, maybe once this is all over, you can try to remind me."

As Amy slid back into her body, I told Jacob, "I'm back. Hold the veil."

He had questions, I could tell. But he also trusted me to assess the situation—and to be his eyes. He closed his eyes and reached out, focusing hard. I couldn't see his red energy anymore like I could when I was double-booked in my own body, but I could sense it. "You got this," I told him, as Amy, reunited, gained her feet.

She stood, puzzled, as if waking from a dream. A really freaking weird one, no doubt.

Urgently, I said, "Remember why you're here, Amy. Remember your calling."

She'd very nearly been distracted by the mess she'd made of her own hands, and the corpse, and the fact that she was standing there in her underwear with two strange men. But her ka must've managed to carry some of its knowledge along when it slid back home, because when she said, "I wasn't dreaming?" I saw a flicker of recognition.

"Not even close. But our spirits aren't sorted out just yet." I gestured at the decaying schoolgirl. "This woman's been stuck here way too long. Help us cross her over."

"Hurry," Jacob said urgently. "The veil keeps shifting around."

Likely because the ghost was so unstable. It flickered in and out of sight atop its rotting remains, struggling to free the body from the duct tape. I took a cautious step forward, no idea where or when I'd dropped my salt, sucking down white light like my life depended on it. "Miss," I said earnestly to the spirit, "we're here to help."

"I been screaming for days and no one came. I yelled until my voice gave out. How did you hear me?"

Amy Grace, bloody-handed and underwear-clad, crouched down to look into the skeletal eye sockets. "All that matters is that someone finally did." Hold on...Amy could hear the ghost too? Even with a physical body in the way?

Good. I needed all the help I could get.

"What's your name?" Amy asked.

Unlike Jacob and me, she got a straight answer. "Rosa."

Tell Rosa I'm sorry. Jacob met my eyes and I shuddered, while Amy asked, "Who did this to you?"

"It don't matter—he's above the law."

"No one is above the law," I told Rosa. "Even Harris Tucker."

"What are you talking about? Officer Tucker was the only one who didn't treat me like trash."

Officer Tucker? Either Rosa was really good at keeping their relationship on the down low (and at this point, what reason would she have?) or the two of them weren't even on a first-name basis.

Her ghostly features solidified over the horrid terrarium of a skull as she steeled in her resolve and said, "Officer Tucker couldn't stop him. No one could. You get away with anything around here when your name is Beauchamp."

And then the whole story spilled out.

Apparently, while the eldest Beauchamp brother was being excluded from self-aggrandizing statuary, he was busy getting up to no good.

It was thirty years ago, give or take. Roy passed on at the ripe old age of eighty-two and Marlon set about his quest to put his inheritance to work. Up until this point, Leland, the "slow" one, had lived most of his life in a group home. But slow is in the eye of the beholder. Once both the family's patriarch and their loyal family doctor were dead, there was nothing keeping middle-aged Leland from venturing out on his own and sowing his wild oats. Who'd stop him, his younger brother? Apparently Marlon was too busy floundering through his shitty real estate deals to worry about what the brother he hardly knew was up to.

Especially since Leland had his own money: a trust fund. Nothing big. But forty bucks'll buy you a pound of flesh around here nowadays, and back then it was even less. Newly emancipated Leland was in his glory.

He wouldn't have been the only guy in town availing himself of the so-called "lot lizards." Pretty soon, though, he was the darkest one.

"It started with him telling me to leave on my apron. I was a waitress, y'know? And he made me pretend I was getting off my shift and wasn't taking no money for it. Plenty of 'em like to pretend. Maybe it's easier that way. But then one day he showed up with a nurse outfit, a cheap thing from Halloween, and had me wear that. Made no difference to me. Long as I got paid. The costumes got weirder and weirder, though. And once that wasn't enough to get him off anymore, he started getting rough."

He wasn't the only customer to get physical. Though he was the only one to lock her up in the basement of one of Marlon Beauchamp's lousy real estate deals. Rosa dreaded his daily visits and prayed for them to stop.

Little did she realize that once they did, she'd scream herself raw as dehydration slowly leached her life away.

"And he's probably still out there doing whatever the hell he wants—but he's a Beauchamp, and no one can stop him."

"Actually," Amy said, "he's dead."

Rosa's ghost looked up sharply. Her features flickered and blurred over the mossy skull. "Men like that are too mean to die."

"No, Leland Beauchamp is dead, all right. Spent his last years mumbling to himself in the corner of a dingy state institution once his brother put him away again to get control of his trust fund."

"And Leland just left me here to rot?" Rosa demanded.

"I'm not sure he had the capacity to understand what was going on...after the psychosurgery his brother pushed for—essentially a modern-day lobotomy. If it's any consolation, Leland Beauchamp ended up just as much a prisoner as you."

Rosa frowned at Amy. "You're just saying whatever you can to change my mind."

"Not at all. I saw the scar myself. I was fresh out of mortuary school at the time—and it made one hell of an impression."

Rosa wavered. "He's really...dead?"

"I superglued his eyes shut myself. Don't worry, Rosa, he can't touch you anymore. And men like him might have power in this world, but I firmly believe you won't cross paths with Leland Beauchamp on the next leg of your journey. He's too mired in his own perversity to find the path."

Amy spoke with the unflappable confidence of someone who had everything under control. Someone who could handle a dead body without flinching. Who felt it was her sacred duty to make sure the souls of the dead ended up right where they were supposed to be. And even if she couldn't be a hundred percent certain this wasn't all a dream, she threw herself into the role for all she was worth.

"The veil," Jacob said, hands splayed wide. "It's getting stronger."

I pointed to the empty gap in the air framed by Jacob's hands. There might have been a distortion there, but I was too fried to say for sure. If Jacob said it was there, though, that was good enough for me. "There's your chance, Rosa. Your way out of Beauchamp. Can't you feel the pull?"

The ghostly features overlaid on the mossy corpse twisted in confusion. At least until Amy Grace backed me up by saying, "It's finally time. Be free."

The presence of a ghost isn't always as obvious as you might think. If it weren't for Rosa's body, I might have done a quick check of the storage room and figured it was empty. When her spirit rushed toward the veil, there was no sudden change in temperature or telltale flex of the ethers. But as the veil whispered shut behind her, a calm silence stole over the space. Jacob with his eyes shut, Amy in her underwear, me with cobwebs in my hair and the body taped to the office chair.

Finally, I could indulge in something like relief. At least until Jacob said, "We need to call this in."

He wasn't wrong—the discovery of a dead body changed everything.

CHAPTER 34

If it were just Jacob and me down in that mildewy basement, we could have easily fudged the timeline. A few more hours wouldn't make much difference to Rosa, since she was now safely on the other side and the perp was in no danger of getting away. But Amy Grace was confused enough as it was, trying to wrap her head around the lengthy conversation she'd just held with a ghost.

Plus, I'd promised her ka I would help her remember.

Amy's clothes were long gone, and although it was shaping up to be a warm day, I could hardly parade her out of the house in her utilitarian beige bra and panties. I took off my suit coat and draped it over her shoulders, and she hugged it against herself gratefully. "I don't know what happened here," she informed me. "But I'm not crazy. Just so you know."

"Definitely not." I took her by the elbow and steered her through the bloody door, past the tattered costumes, and up the stairs. White light no longer flowed between us, and I had no desire to channel that current again. My head was throbbing and the waterlogged fatigue of staying up all night had settled in my chest, and I didn't care to see if I could push myself even farther.

Once we were safely aboveground, I told her, "Someone's gonna take a statement from you, though...and you should give some consideration as to what you say. Because once you announce that you can talk to dead people, there's no taking it back."

Amy looked up sharply, searching my face. I'm generally not one for extended eye contact, but I looked right back, willing her to remember the connection we shared. "The FPMP isn't any funeral protocol group. It's the Federal Psychic Monitoring Program. And I'm going to give you a choice that no one ever gave me. You can go public—be tested and trained. Or you can stay off the government's radar and go back to your old life."

She wasn't quite convinced. "You think I'm psychic? That can't be right. They tested for that the last time I renewed my mortician's license and my scores were perfectly average."

"Psychic mediums are notoriously tough to spot." I should know. I had yet to discover a definitive way of assessing potential candidates unless we happened to blunder into a ghost together. "You're strong, Amy. With some training, you'd only get better. But you told me you had a calling here, and I'm not about to take that away from you."

I dredged up a stray granola bar for her and sat her down on a windowsill to collect herself and consider her next move. Meanwhile, Jacob came up from the basement looking grim. He took me aside and said, "Pete and Dr. K will be here anytime now. What about the GhosTV?"

"It can't fall into the wrong hands," I told him. "You go deal with it. I'll stay."

He'd been so gung-ho about making the thing disappear, it surprised me when instead of charging out the door to go tear out the key components, he hesitated.

"What is it?" I asked.

Jacob shook his head wearily. "What you said before—that we shouldn't be so quick to do something that can't be undone—you were right."

Normally a gloatable admission if ever there was one. But.... "What about National?"

"They can't know about it. That hasn't changed. But without the GhosTV, Rosa's spirit would still be trapped on this side of the veil."

"There's two sides to every coin. I'll bet the TV made Beauchamp a prime breeding ground for those habit demons—the ones the striptease artists were trying so hard to shake off."

"Actually, no...I don't think they were behind the incidents. It was Rosa all along. Not stripping, exactly. More like desperate to tear off that costume and be free. Thanks to the tuner, she could finally reach out and lead us to her body."

The tuner which somehow suddenly turned on, two years after we saw the last of Jennifer Chance.

Maybe I didn't want Jacob going back to that crappy little bungalow without backup after all.

He sighed. "Vic, I've been holed away in Internal Affairs for so long now, I've forgotten what it was like to see something so dehumanizing—so wrong. Or maybe I didn't forget. Maybe I just blocked it all out. Here, now, after everything we've done, I have to wonder if maybe things aren't just random, and we came across the GhosTV for a reason. That we have a purpose."

"A calling," I said, echoing Amy's words.

"Exactly."

If ever there was a case to hit Jacob square in the feels, it was this one. Not only had he encountered way too many atrocities in the sex crimes unit, but he possessed an overinflated sense of justice—paired with the certainty that only he was capable of setting things right.

I checked my phone. It was later than I'd thought. "The console is too big to move. Amy's got access to a hearse—but it's broad daylight now, and someone's bound to ask questions. And we can't leave it where it is. Sooner or later the party kids will realize the back door's open, and all bets are off. So, what's the plan?"

"We can't leave it here. We can't let it end up with National." He stroked his beard. "I'd vouch for Pete. How well do you know Dr. K?"

Well enough to know I didn't trust him any farther than I could throw him. I don't always listen to my gut. But where Dr. K was concerned, I sensed a certain forced jocularity behind the stilted Russian accent.

The only time I'd ever seen him with his guard down was when F-Pimp National barged into his lab and confiscated his equipment and his research, obliterating years of work in the blink of an eye.

"I can't exactly say we're close," I admitted. "Though if you're getting at what I think you're getting at, there's no love lost between him and National. I don't trust the guy unconditionally, but in this case, the enemy of our enemy is...the best we can do."

Jacob nodded. "I'd rather handle this alone—the fewer people involved the better. But if anyone can help us bury this GhosTV, it's them."

Good thing we were on the same page. By the time the paramedics came for Amy and we called in Rosa's body, Garcia and Dr. K were barely fifteen minutes out.

I'll say one thing about being on Big Brother's payroll: when you need to bump something up the food chain because the local law enforcement is totally inept, they waste no time sending in the cavalry. FBI was summoned—they'd be there in a few hours—and state troopers were filtering in to secure the scene by the time our ride pulled up.

I've often felt just a teensy bit paranoid for rattling keys, crushing ice, or turning up a porno with a super obnoxious soundtrack to camouflage whatever needed saying. But all my caution was rewarded when I held up my notepad with the words, Need to talk in private to Dr. K—and he took the pad from me and jotted beneath it in funny cursive, Wait.

Whereas I tend to travel with a pack of gum, a pocket flashlight and a baggie of salt, the scientist's arsenal was a little more... involved. A series of obscure hand signals passed between him and Garcia, who pulled out a handheld electronic device I couldn't readily identify. He hit a few buttons, lit a few lights, and said, "Go ahead."

Even the head of Surveillance telling me I was off the radar didn't leave me feeling entirely secure. But it was as good a guarantee as I could hope to get, so I pitched my voice low, bent my head to Dr. K's, and said, "We found the last GhosTV."

CHAPTER 35

"You did the right thing," Dr. K told me...for probably the eighth or tenth time. I must've had an especially shitty look on my face. Lack of sleep wreaks havoc on my filters.

As much as it was just a lame platitude, I supposed it was better than what Garcia had said when he got a load of the safe house. "You're lucky there's not a smart camera on the doorbell—those things run less than a hundred bucks. Your faces would be all over a bunch of redundant servers by now. Not to mention the phone of whoever owns this place."

No doubt someone at HQ could have that information for us in two seconds flat. But while we'd reported all the pertinent details of Rosa's murder scene without much creative license, we'd kept the GhosTV firmly under wraps.

As soon as we could, the four of us stole off to the suicide house. Kudryasvstev descended on the GhosTV, photographing the guts from every conceivable angle, while Garcia scanned the rest of the property to triple-check for surveillance. Jacob joined him, and the two of them chatted with an easiness that went beyond trusted coworkers. At some point over the past year, Garcia and Jacob had become friends...as evidenced by the fact that they occasionally ran together. Not just because someone was chasing them, either.

Obviously, I want Jacob to have friends. I just wish they didn't work for the FPMP. Even worse, their little bromance left me standing there awkwardly beside Dr. K without any buffer. I was wondering how much or how little I could get away with saying to him when he decided to break the ice. "Certain someones might think they confiscated all my research. But they didn't get it all." He tapped his temple. "Some crucial parts are still up here."

"Lucky for you they didn't hook you up to some electrodes and force them out."

He grinned at me, flashing the gap between his front teeth. "Fortunately, the machine capable of doing that has yet to be invented."

Which wasn't to say it was impossible.

Dr. K stood and dusted off his pant legs. "So. Is the tuner in working condition?"

"And then some."

"If I were to turn it on...?"

I squeezed the back of my neck wearily. "There's a suicide repeater in the kitchen and the town is stupid with habit demons. But on the bright side, at least the striptease posses-sions should be a thing of the past."

I decided against mentioning that Jacob had popped the queen habit demon while it was crapping out its progeny. As long as the thought-sucking machine was still in its develop-ment phase, I wasn't about to volunteer any information I was better off keeping to myself.

Garcia paused to take in the daisy chain of extension cords. "This is...creative."

In our defense, Jacob said, "We figured we should leave the fuse box alone."

As the two of them headed back to the mechanical room, I heard Garcia say, "Lucky no one stuck a penny in it—this place would be nothing but a smoldering pile of ash."

"Maybe that would be for the best," I said. Aloud, as my utter lack of filters proved even worse than I'd initially thought. Dr. K looked up sharply, and I felt the need to explain. "How did it get here? Why was it playing? What if there's another Dr. Chance flunky lurking around somewhere, just waiting for a chance to shoot me up with Amytal?"

"Ah." Dr. K nodded. "I understand your concern, Agent. But I can put your mind at ease on at least one account. Jennifer Chance, Roger Burke, and Jeffrey Allan Scott were the only ones with knowledge of the tuners. Miss Gutierrez confirmed it long ago. And they have all been accounted for."

While the sí-no wasn't infallible, that knowledge did make me feel somewhat better. I noted that he didn't try to reassure me that Chance and Burke were both dead, since we all knew that a determined enough zealot wouldn't let something as trivial as death get in the way.

"As to how the tuner got here, I can think of one way to find out." Dr. K rubbed his hands together, took a deep breath, and hit the on-switch. "Etheric energy, we theorize, is both a particle and a wave. Particles disperse, but waves have the potential to linger for a very long time. Not just years, but decades. Eventually, they do decay. But with the proper equipment, those decaying waves can be perceived."

"With what, the GhosTV?"

"Not at all—with the talent of a medium. The GhosTV is just an amplifier. And these things you call repeaters are the waves.

Vibrating moments of etheric impact. But the most impressive equipment at our disposal is purely organic."

I was pretty much at my technical saturation point by now. But Dr. K kept on talking.

"Death makes waves. But what if that's not the only thing that leaves traces behind? When this tuner was put in place, it must have been tested. There might be an etheric snapshot of this test," he pointed at my head, "visible only to someone with the proper equipment to see it. So, if we find the right frequency, we can amplify the echo of this moment and see for ourselves."

I knew, in a general sense, how the GhosTV controls worked. I'd used them to help me I.D. the repeaters in Dreyfuss's office. But while my fine-tuning involved holding my breath and consulting a sticky note, Dr. K dove right in, reconnected the plug, and started turning dials. He worked them like a safecracker spinning the combination on a particularly imposing safe. It was part art, part science—and he was the maestro of both.

I'd let my crown chakra energy fall to a low simmer once Rosa crossed over, but when Dr. K worked his magic on the GhosTV, the dingy little living room lit up with a hazy white glow.

"Hold on," I told him, and got my bearings. "I think it's working."

This particular setting was new to me. It felt like I was mainlining white light—through no effort of my own.

Good thing. I was so wiped, I needed all the help I could get.

The TV launched into a commercial for food storage containers while the dog next door started barking. This time, there was no one home to ineffectively tell it to shut up, and the yips fell into a ragged cadence. Frankly, it wouldn't surprise me if the tuner let out some kind of high-pitched sound beyond the range of human hearing. Hopefully Fido wouldn't need to endure the TV too much longer.

I scanned the living room, searching for anything that shouldn't be there. Tracers. Tethers. Hand-sized psychic ticks. Nothing. Though when I looked just right, I thought I saw an afterimage of the TV console only a few feet away from where it sat now.

That information didn't much help, since I already knew it had been right there the first time we broke in. But if I looked just so, maybe the tube would show me a reflection of what was happening when the psychic snapshot occurred. So long as I didn't glitch on whether a reflection was a particle or a wave and overthink the whole thing.

I tuned out the yippy dog next door and focused. In fact, I was watching the echo of the screen with such rapt attention, I nearly jumped out of my skin when someone right behind me said, "Did that Russian guy call you Agent?"

I'd been crouching awkwardly, and I lurched to my feet and whirled around to find a transparent guy watching us with great interest.

White light. I sucked it down faster than the triple-shot espresso I'd pounded between the crime scene and here, suddenly terrified that the suicide would take my body for a spin. It was a lot of light. A lot. The room went hazy, and the ghost solidified. I could still see the mini blinds through him, but just barely, and his own particulars were clear enough now that I'd be able to pick him out of a lineup.

Older guy, late fifties. Scruffy, Caucasian, with the thin, pot-bellied look of someone who got all their nutrition from a beer bottle. But it was his hair that really stopped me in my tracks—the hourglass pattern of his balding. I'd seen it before.

Recently. In the kitchen.

I was talking to Harris Tucker, the suicide repeater.

Or, more accurately, he was talking to me.

A repeater. Talking.

Just when you thought the GhosTV couldn't do anything weirder.

"So?" he prompted. "Are you a Fed, or not?"

Scrambling to make sense of whatever was happening, I stammered, "I, uh...yeah, that's right. Agent Bayne, FPMP."

"Well, you're a day late and a dollar short. My casework made about as much difference as an umbrella in a tornado while I was alive. Don't see how I'm any good to anyone now."

At least I didn't have to inform him that he was dead. "Actually, you might know more than you realize." I gestured at the GhosTV. "We need the details on how this got here."

"Beauchamp is rotting from the inside out and all you care about is this stupid TV?"

"I know about Rosa," I said. That got his attention. "And I know you tried to help her, and couldn't. But if you want someone to hear your side of the story...I'll listen."

Tucker folded his hands behind his back and begin to pace. And when he spoke, it was with the flat, inflectionless drawl of someone with zero hope that anyone would believe him. "It all started with a call to the station, some working girl putting up a big fuss about a john slapping her around. Usually, the girls around here keep to themselves about stuff like that—and we all look the other way. This one was a real mess, though, so I tracked down the complainant and took a statement. But when my boss saw a Beauchamp was the accused, the statement magically disappeared."

Why was I not surprised?

"Would that be Leland Beauchamp?"

Tucker laughed bitterly. "What difference does it make? This happened ages ago. He's long dead now. Just like the girl."

Damn. I'd been hoping the story about the lobotomy scar and the superglue would be enough to put him to rest. "I know how you feel," I said.

He scoffed at me. "Fancy, big-city cop like you?"

No one had ever referred to me as "fancy." Thankfully, I was the only one to hear it, or I'd never live it down. "Twelve years in Homicide—and toward the end, most of my collars walked free."

Grudgingly, Tucker stopped pacing to listen.

"We uncovered your victim earlier today and took it right over Sheriff Carver's head. What happened here is just too big to sweep under the rug anymore. It will all come to light."

Hope flickered in the ghost's eyes, poignant and fragile.

"Rosa is at rest now," I told him.

He hung his head in a mixture of shame and relief. "Rosa," he echoed...and his voice sounded hollow and distant.

That feeling I get when a ghost finally decides to cross over, the satisfaction of fulfilling my calling? It took me a second to realize I couldn't sit back and revel in my accomplishments—not just yet. "Wait! The TV—I need to know how the TV got here!"

Harris Tucker hesitated, flickered, and then solidified. "That thing? It's been here a couple of years, ever since some snow-birds signed a lease on the place."

"A woman and a man? Blonde hair? Thirties?

"That's them. Though they ain't been back since."

"But why would they put it on a timer?" Not that I thought Tucker would be able to tell me, mind you. Just that it made zero sense.

"Oh, that wasn't their doing. It was the landlord—some weaselly bald guy. The snowbirds hadn't been back for a while. He wanted to make the place look occupied so the drug crowd didn't end up using it for one of their parties."

Come to think of it, the combustible fuse box and train of extension cords did smack of Randy Wood's handiwork. No wonder his house-flipping endeavor wasn't working out. Everyone in Beauchamp knew everyone else's business. Randy wouldn't have much luck in the real estate market if he insisted on buying suicide houses.

But speaking of drug parties.... "One more thing," I said. "Ruth Parrish. You know her?"

"Everyone on the force knows Ruth—whether they want to or not. A day didn't go by she wasn't complaining about something. Always sticking her nose where it didn't belong."

"Like...a spy?"

Tucker barked out a laugh. "Ruth Parrish? If she's a spy, then I'm the goddamn President."

He reassured me that between the Library Board and the Garden Club—not to mention her car rental business—Ruth simply wouldn't have had the time to get involved with espionage. While a good spy can pull the wool over anyone's eyes, logistics don't lie, so I supposed my clingy busybody was just an annoyance, not a threat. He also claimed that other than Jacob and me, no one else besides Randy had set foot in the house since Chance rented the place. At least that was some consolation. I didn't need to worry about another accomplice cropping up...or that Chance herself had cheated death yet again to set watch on the last remaining GhosTV.

By the time Harris Tucker faded for good, Jacob and Garcia had joined us in the living room, watching while I did my thing.

Jacob was dusting his fingers against his pant leg—unobtrusively, though I knew it for what it was. The sticky, greasy, dusty, cobwebby residue he felt when the ethers went thick was stuck to him like the fake orange powder in a bag of Cheetos.

Friendly or not, he hadn't announced this new development to Garcia. That was a relief. Back when I was in high school, I learned the hard way—once you carry on about your psychic abilities, there's no retracting your statement.

"Chance and Burke were acting alone," I told everyone. "The timer was set recently—it should correlate with all the striptease incidents. And the guy who set it had no idea this wasn't a normal TV."

Dr. K gazed avidly at the GhosTV and said, "Most importantly of all, it appears that the Etheric Tuner is working."

In fact, the room was still soft-focused and glowy, and my head was buzzing. I slipped past Jacob and down the hall to put a bit of distance between my brain and the broadcast....

And nearly jumped out of my own skin when I stepped into the psychic splash zone of bone and blood and brain.

Tucker's repeater sagged at the kitchen table with half his head gone, only to reappear a split second later, raise a gun to his head, and pull the trigger.

Disorientation rocked me—were there two ghosts? No, this was definitely Tucker. I'd just talked to the guy for five minutes, and there was no mistaking the shape of his bald spot. I'd seen him cross over—I'd felt it. So how was I still looking at his repeater?

Jacob joined me in the kitchen, carefully angling himself in so we didn't brush together and zap each other with mojo. "Are you okay?" he asked softly. "You look a little pale."

"Back up," I told Jacob. "You're standing right in the suicide."

Jacob blanched, then flattened himself against the far wall while I took stock of the situation. The dog next door was still barking its head off. The GhosTV was now blasting a cheesy daytime soap. And Dr. K and Garcia were hastily planning a covert salvage operation.

And two feet away from me, Tucker was killing himself over and over.

"I don't get it," I told Jacob. "Tucker crossed over. I felt him go. So why is he still here?"

"Is he? Or is it just a psychic stain he left behind?"

I took a step closer, and all the nesting dolls within me shifted. Whatever setting Dr. K had tuned in didn't threaten to eject me from my physical shell, but I definitely felt like a body within a body within a body. Clearly, this repeater was not quite a ghost, and there was no resurrecting it. Whichever body carried Tucker's personality—as well as all his guilt—was gone.

I said, "This isn't the whole spirit—just what's left of it, I guess." I swallowed against the dryness in my throat. "But, wow. It's a real doozy."

CHAPTER 36

Garcia cleared his throat from the post he'd taken up in the hall-way where he could provide backup in either the kitchen or the living room—and where he could hear everything we'd just said. "If someone needed to assess a minor psychic event—nothing that would require another team, mind you, just something to take a closer look at—it would buy us a lot of breathing room. And also provide a logical explanation for the B&E."

I rubbed the back of my neck. It felt like someone had been pounding on it with a baseball bat. "The repeater's been here a while. I suppose another day wouldn't kill it."

Technically, the story about finding a repeater in the kitchen wasn't a lie. It just omitted the fact that a GhosTV was playing a few yards away. Still, I had Garcia make the call. I'm not bad at lying. But I don't necessarily enjoy it. Not when I like the person on the receiving end.

Most bosses wouldn't make much of a simple repeater, espe-cially if there wasn't an open case attached to it. Take Con Dreyfuss. He'd blithely planted his desk among three of the nastiest murders I'd had the displeasure of viewing. But Laura wasn't Con. And when we said "ghost," she authorized a cleanup, no questions asked.

Once Garcia got the OK, he hung up with Laura and told me, "You're the lead. Whatever you say goes. But...if it were me, I'd contact the owner, secure the building, buy the TV from him and find somewhere to stash it."

"Do it," I said wearily.

"No problem. In the meantime, why don't you guys go get some rest? The bags under your eyes have bags."

Dr. K, meanwhile, was fresh as a daisy, and thrilled beyond belief over beating National to the final GhosTV. But he'd have plenty of time to play with his new toy.

"Turn that thing off before my head splits open," I told him, not bothering to mince words.

"This headache, can you describe the pain? Dull or sharp, localized or general, throbbing or constant? On a scale of one to ten—"

"The same headache I always get. Times a hundred—which is probably verging into stroke territory."

"Don't forget, Agent, I'm familiar with your scans. If you were at risk for stroke, we would have noticed. But we did note increased blood flow to your forebrain region after you've been working with repeaters."

The words "increased blood flow" were clearly not meant to scare me. But given that I was two feet away from a deluge of ghostly blood splatter, they were no real comfort.

"Take some aspirin with caffeine," Dr. K said easily. "It works wonders for that particular type of headache. In fact, at that truck stop by the highway, they had some right on the counter. And the donuts weren't bad, either."

If he'd just so happened to have some in his pocket, obviously, I would have refused. I might be in bed with the enemy of my enemy...but that didn't mean I was dumb enough to swallow any medication that was in his possession.

But I'd seen that type of aspirin at the counter myself. And unless Dr. K had been playing the long game in a really big way, I suspected they were legit.

Jacob and I left the investigation in Garcia's capable hands. As uncomfortable as I might be with him spending time with my husband, I was relieved that Jacob knew the guy well enough to vouch for him.

As I headed for the passenger door, Jacob smiled to himself. "What?" I asked.

"Just relieved to know that all of you is present and accounted for."

Could he really know for sure? The sun would be high by the time we finally rolled into bed, so my big, dumb body would have no reason to argue about leaving the lights on.

Lucky for me, I'm so inured to caffeine that I'd have no qualms about swallowing a dose and going straight to bed. But when we rolled up to the Filling Station to grab the meds, I spotted a woman in a tacky pink outfit with sparkly matching flip-flops. She was chatting with an old man directly in front of the doors...and she didn't look like she was about to wrap it up anytime soon.

I sank down in my seat and hoped Ruth Parrish hadn't seen us. She might not be a spy, but that didn't mean I wanted to put myself back on her radar. "Forget it," I told Jacob. "Let's just go back to our room and pass out."

"Don't give up so fast. I saw another door around back. I'll go in through the restaurant and be back out before you know it."

I was not nearly so optimistic, and had visions of Ruth chasing her rental car around the building and pawing at my window while Jacob scored the aspirin. But the pain in my head had settled into a pervasive, throbbing, localized ache—at least an eight on Dr. K's handy pain scale—and the thought of blood flow being responsible just made it all the worse.

Jacob maneuvered the car out of Ruth's line of sight, blocking her with a conveniently parked eighteen-wheeler. As he coasted around to the back of the truck stop, I pondered whether the habit demon we'd cleared out had been the chicken or the egg. Had something nonphysical been the cause of Leland Beauchamp's perverted impulses—leading to a murder, a coverup, a suicide, and a vacant property that was the perfect place for Jennifer Chance to set up a GhosTV? Or had the GhosTV called the nasty thing from the other side of the veil and encouraged it to start shitting out babies in the truck stop office?

Unless the things started talking, I don't suppose I'd ever know. The important thing was, they were gone—

"Stop the car!" I called out.

Jacob stomped the brake. My seatbelt snapped back, knocking the breath from my lungs, but I hardly noticed.

Because the entire back of the Filling Station was teeming with habit demons.

The creatures covered the siding in an undulating mass—just like the water bugs in the apartment's dripping basement, but big, nasty and etheric. From our current distance, they looked like actual insects. But then I considered the scale of the objects around them: the door. The ashtray. And, ironically enough, the bug zapper above it. And I knew these etheric "bugs" were easily as big as the gargantuan cinnamon rolls in the donut case.

Jacob scuffed his palms against his knees. "Whatever it is—I feel it."

"I'd have to revoke your nonexistent TK license if you didn't. But given how fried you were after dealing with the queen bee inside, there's no way we can handle this cleanup in one go."

Jacob's eyes were closed, brow furrowed, as he held his hands out toward the windshield. "We can't just ignore them."

"That's not what I'm saying. But Rome wasn't built in a day, and exterminating this place in one shot simply ain't gonna happen. First we sleep. Then we start the cleanup."

Jacob cut his eyes to me, and a weary smile tugged at the corner of his mouth. "If you say so. You're the lead."

Between the habit demon infestation blocking one door and Ruth Parrish blocking the other, we opted to retreat to the motel. Turned out, they stocked single-serve doses of the aspirin in question among all the other overpriced amenities at the front desk—but since the FPMP was buying, I grabbed two...plus a bunch of energy drinks and a box of chocolate chip cookies.

Safely in our room, as I deposited our booty on the desk, I caught Jacob eyeing the pile. "This isn't like the ice cream," I assured him. "I felt dehydrated, plus my blood sugar is crashed right through the floor."

"You were awfully decisive, back there at the Filling Station," he said. Half-jokingly. Maybe.

I yanked off my tie and dropped it on the chair. "I'm me, Jacob."

I'd said it so forcefully, I managed to make him doubt me even more.

"Okay, mister." I crossed the room in a couple of strides and grabbed both his hands, squeezing them in mine. "Listen to me. I'm the guy who throws out the leftovers you claim you're planning on eating...but never get around to. I'm the one who can never find the spot on the shower dial that's not too hot or too cold. I'm the doofus standing there in the grocery store talking to myself about the cereal." I gave his hands an extra squeeze. "I'm the guy you married."

"You're really you," he said.

"I'm really me."

He narrowed his eyes shrewdly. "Prove it."

I dropped his hands and reached for his face instead, cupping his jaw tenderly. I traced a thumb over the curve of one perfect cheekbone and said, "Back at the GhosTV house, I said some things. Or...my body did." I cleared my throat awkwardly. "Things you, uh, do to me. That I like."

His dark eyes twinkled in a barely suppressed smile as I struggled through what I had to say. It was excruciating to keep talking. But somehow, I managed. "It wasn't wrong. The body. Obviously, you turn me on. You must realize that. Some things just go without saying."

Jacob turned his head and brushed his lips against my palm. A tingle raced down my arm that had nothing to do with red energy or white light. "Maybe so. But it's nice to hear the words."

If he was fishing for a reprise of me spelling out just how much I loved him shoving my legs open and plowing me like a hundred acres of Iowa corn, he was fresh outta luck.

"The weird thing was, even though it was my body putting the moves on you, it felt like I was seeing you with a stranger. I was actually jealous. Of my own damn body."

Jacob's gaze darkened. His nostrils flared.

When we kissed, it was a harsh thing. Graceless. Not because I was rattling around in a body two sizes too big, but from the sheer eagerness to feel his tongue sliding along mine. He pulled me up against him, grabbing so hard it hurt, but in the best possible way.

I clung to him, riding his thigh, and my breath huffed against his lower lip. This was the sort of communication he was used to. A grind of my hips. A staggered breath. Bold declarations of passion? Maybe not compared to the explicit stuff my body said. But they amounted to the same thing—you'd just need to know how to read me.

And Jacob did.

His hands ranged down my sides, raking my ribs, kneading my thighs…and cupping my stiffening cock. It strained for his grasp, though my underwear was trapping it against my hip. But not for long.

Clothes came off. My body would have strewn my suit across the room, but I took half a second to fold the pants and drape the jacket over the armchair. Flinging stuff around with reckless abandon might feel good in the moment. But I'd rather not spend the next few days looking like a bum.

Jacob's suit joined mine, though true to form, he allowed his socks and underwear to fall where they may. He steered me toward the bed where the coverlet was polyester and the sheets smelled faintly of bleach. Not our bed, in other words. That might not have been as illicit as a stolen blowjob in a house we'd just broken into, but it had its own seedy charm.

We sprawled sideways on the bed. Kissing. Touching. Struggling against the urge to succumb to utter exhaustion. At least, I was. Jacob, however, had a naughty gleam in his eye as he reached into his toiletry bag and drew out a travel-sized bottle of Florida Water disguised as aftershave.

My exhausted brain tried, and failed, to determine what creative uses he was planning. "Even if my ass was haunted, I could think of better ways to handle it. That's bound to sting."

"This is from my bag, not yours. And you aren't the only one who knows how to refill a bottle." Though he did give it a quick sniff just to make sure.

When he spread my legs to position himself between them, my body thrummed with anticipation.

Actually, no. Not just my body.

All of me.

So, did I wax eloquent about the cut of Jacob's muscles shifting while he bore his weight on one hand and greased my hole with the other? Or the blunt prod of his cockhead nudging into my ass? Or the feathery touch of his chest hair as he sank in deep enough to press us both together from hip to shoulder?

Nah.

I muttered, "Fuck, yeah," and let him fill in the details. Anything more would just make him wonder if I was still me, and besides, the very act of what we were doing spoke for itself. Letting someone else inside your body is the ultimate act of trust. Giving up control isn't something I take lightly. Not after what I'd gone through at Camp Hell.

As much as it might've irked me that Jacob couldn't tell whether or not he was talking to the real me, I couldn't blame him for being confused. We really do contain multitudes—and not just our subtle bodies. The very trigger that shaped my whole contrary personality, the need to be in control, was also the big kink I shared with him. Giving up that control, letting him use my body, cram it full of dick, make it writhe and spurt and shudder...that's what really got me off.

He shoved himself in deep, filling me over, and over, and over. Eyes open. Watching my face to see if he was hitting all the right spots. Watching me.

He got off on getting me off. And I got off watching him do

it. The whole thing spiraled and whipped us both into a frenzy. Cause and effect blurred. He was close. I felt my own peak beckon from the sight of him starting the climb. Him, me. Our bodies, our minds. Our spirits. Our souls.

Everything was connected.

And when I finally did arch my back off that strange mattress and spill my load onto my belly, the only thing that mattered was the release. Even if there'd be nowhere left to go but down, plummeting back to earth just as soon as it began...even then, that brief, shining moment was worth it. Stripped of control. Raw. Centered. And pure.

Jacob rolled off me, panting, and stared at the ceiling as he caught his breath. It was a prime moment to nod off, if ever there was one. But he surprised me by indulging in a little pillow talk instead. "So, back there when we were kissing and your subtle body shifted out...you watched?"

"Thanks for pointing that out. Just living through it wasn't awkward enough."

But Jacob seemed to get a kick out of it. Then again, the psychic weirdness that culled my social circle had always been his biggest turn-on.

"I wish I could've seen you watching. I'll bet I would've thought it was hot."

Hardly. Seeing the world like I do is no picnic, but even so, I didn't bother to contradict him. Even knowing I was alive, no doubt getting a glimpse of my disembodied spirit would've been more hinky than kinky. Jacob might think he'd be into it, but most people conceive of their bodies and their spirits as one inseparable entity.

Then again, you never know, since Jacob never ceased to amaze me.

CHAPTER 37

Between the old murder investigation and the habit demon infestation, our quick weekend assignment stretched into a week and a half—during which, Garcia headed out of town with some large, mysterious cardboard boxes in the back of the SUV, and returned empty-handed just a few hours later. I didn't ask Dr. K how he'd finagled the final GhosTV from Randy Wood, why he'd disassembled the cabinet, where he'd stashed it, and whether he thought it would still work—and he didn't offer any explanations.

That was for the best. The less I could claim to know about the thing, the better.

Laura, meanwhile, offered to send Carl out to help me so Jacob could get back to his regular duties. I suspect she thought she'd be doing us a favor. Little did she realize that while Jacob stood shoulder to shoulder with me while I was throwing salt, he wasn't just acting as my Stiff—he was doing all the heavy lifting.

It was tough at first, with his normal five senses doing their best to override what his base chakra was telling him...and tying his tie around his eyes would only attract undue attention.

But the backside of Beauchamp's major truck stop was a good training ground, with plenty of disgusting targets to practice on—and over the course of our cleanup, he got better at squinching his eyes shut when no one could see to check in with his psychic impressions.

Regular people can't really tell when you're tapping your sixth sense. That's bad when you find yourself shipped off to the nuthouse. But in Jacob's case, we were better off with no one else being any the wiser.

It didn't hurt that we had some relative privacy. I'd hate to say it was a good thing half the employees of the Filling Station had been pushing amphetamines...but it did make a plausible excuse to cordon off the back with police tape. It had only taken the DEA a few hours to pinpoint exactly who was selling, so I couldn't fathom what people thought Jacob and I were looking for now, though they didn't bother us while we did it.

Sunset was tickling at the sky on our tenth day in Beauchamp with the sun beating down on the back of our necks and the smell of diesel making my head throb. Jacob stood, hands on hips, glaring at the spot on the cinderblock wall that was the source of all our problems. Not technically the wall itself, of course. But the uncomfortable patch where the veil was worn thin, like the knee of an old pair of jeans that's hanging together by a few strategic threads.

Jacob huffed out an aggravated sigh. "When we crossed over Rosa, the veil closed behind her. Same as it did for the Fire Ghost. Same as it did for Jackie." Hell, same as it did for Dr. Kamal. "But this—" he gestured at the wall in frustration.

The veil was something I could pinpoint if I really focused. Sometimes I could even see it as a field of distortion. But it was a slippery perception, and when I shifted my focus away, it was always possible I wouldn't be able to find it again.

No such luck with Jacob.

He felt the spot, viscerally, like a canker sore he couldn't stop prodding with his tongue.

"The people in this town are vulnerable," he said. "What are they supposed to do once we leave and more parasites come crawling through that hole?"

I was sure we could pick up that suicide house for a song and spend all our foreseeable weekends cleaning up Beauchamp... though I wasn't about to suggest it. "Listen, Jacob. We've been at this all day. We're hot and sweaty, and probably dehydrated." And the slushy machine in the building we were currently staring at had a pina colada flavor spinning around inside that was weirdly addictive. Not that I thought there were habit demons tugging at my taste buds. At least—I hoped not.

I knew Jacob was preoccupied when he didn't tell me to grab him a sugar free sports drink with electrolytes instead. I considered getting him one anyhow...but he'd been working so hard, if anyone deserved a big sugary treat, it was him.

The mini mart employees regarded me with a certain level of dread now, since it had been my arrival that heralded the arrest of several of their colleagues. But since then, they'd become inured to me poking through the convenience foods several times a day, and the FPMP's money spent just like everyone else's. I pulled a cherry slushy for Jacob (although it was hard not to stare at his mouth when his lips were really red) and the pina colada for me. Considered donuts. Realized the sweet-on-sweet probably wouldn't work and wondered if salty beef jerky might be better. Then decided I'd better forgo the snack food if I could hope to call it a night anytime before we were fully consumed by mosquitoes.

As I strode through the door with a big slushy in each hand, I spotted a couple of state police chatting at one side of the lot. The troopers were nothing like the bozos at the Fifth who muttered "Spook Squad" whenever I showed up at a scene, either because they didn't have any experience working with a psychic medium, so they'd never developed the prejudice...or because they weren't quite aware of what I was, aside from being the Fed who'd uncovered both a drug ring and a murder. Frankly, I was relieved they'd taken such an interest in Beauchamp. With competent police in town—cops who didn't give a damn whose son was at the volume knob—the obnoxiously loud parties that had marred Beauchamp's peace and quiet were shut down fast.

Still...that didn't mean I had any desire to stop and chat.

I angled off in the opposite direction with my slushies— looking pretty natural, if I did say so myself—then nearly face-planted in a drainage ditch at the far side of the mini mart. We'd been through the property with a fine-toothed comb, of course, but like any normal people, we'd settled into the route that involved less climbing and fewer ditches. You don't appreciate how steep these things can be until you have to traverse them with a quart of frigid sugar water in each hand. In thin plastic cups. That have gone sweaty...and very, very slippery.

I skidded down the muddy embankment, kicking up a swarm of gnats. I couldn't wave them away from my face, not without ending up wearing one of the slushies (and I couldn't have said at that point which one was pale yellow and which one bright, staining red). All I could do was squinch my eyes shut, hold my breath, and hope nothing flew into my ear and subsequently laid eggs in my brain.

And as all this happened, I must have tapped the white light. Not that I thought a white balloon would do me any good.

More habit than anything. A knee-jerk reaction to a squirt of adrenaline.

As good as being grounded had felt, that was Jacob's native energy. Not mine. While he led with his intuition and trusted his gut instincts, I was all up in my head, overthinking every last idea. My crown chakra was a real pain in the ass—but I couldn't deny that it had gotten me this far in life relatively unscathed. This weedy ditch was just the type of spot, off the beaten track, to run into a repeater. And as the creeping sense of wrongness tickled at the edges of my awareness, I doubled down on my white light pull and threw my medium talent open wide.

The world is full of death. I expected something to light up to my mind's eye. It might not be a busy intersection teeming with dead pedestrians, but I might still find an O.D. with a needle in his arm. A farmer keeling over in his fields. A hunter taking an accidental bullet to the face.

Instead, I only found a perfectly mundane drainage pipe that let out a distant glug.

White light might not be persistent—it takes effort to keep it topped up—but it doesn't shut off like a reading lamp the second I let go. I couldn't take a few of those "deep, cleansing" breaths my yoga teacher's always going on about, either. Not unless I wanted the gnats to lay eggs in my lungs. And so I grit my teeth, gripped my slushies tight, and—

Something squeezed from the end of the drain. It was clear (ish), more a suggestion of a fat shape than something with actual physical substance. But as white light pounded open the crucial blood vessels in my brain and my crown chakra demonstrated just how wide it could go, the suggestion coalesced into a form.

Specifically, the form of a crawling, bloated sack of a habit demon...spitting distance from my leg.

"Jacob," I called out—and it seemed like my voice was buried under the white noise of an idling diesel engine and the wind sighing over the distant fields. "Jacob," I called again as I dropped the slushy in my right hand and reached for my phone. I fumbled the phone, cold-handed. At least I managed to bat it away from the slushy puddle as it tumbled to the ground...though I couldn't help but notice how in rapidly approaching darkness, it looked more like spilled blood.

I considered lobbing my remaining slushy at the thing when I heard footfalls crunching through the weedy grass. For such a big guy, Jacob moves fast—and before I knew it, he was poised at the edge of the ditch. "What is it?"

"Habit demon." I pointed. "A big one."

When Jacob powers up, I can't see what he's doing, not without a GhosTV playing the talent channel nearby. But like I've come to sense when he's about to start humming along (badly) to a nineties indie rock song, I think I can tell when he's getting grounded.

And I wasn't the only one who'd noticed. The habit demon that had been moseying along toward the gas station reversed and started double-timing it back to the drainage pipe. "Dammit," I snapped, grabbing a stick and swinging it—completely ineffectively—through the bloated parasite. That action hadn't been totally in vain, though, as it reassured Jacob that he wasn't the only one "sensing" something there.

Jacob dove toward it. "Not with your bare hands," I said. But Jacob, being Jacob, didn't even give my warning a heartbeat of consideration before completely discarding it. Over the past several days, he'd wrangled all the other habit demons toward the veil with the psychic equivalent of a force field, holding a margin of distance between his physical body and the etheric parasites. It helped that the veil exuded a pull of its own. But the veil was too far away to do us any good now, and Jacob wasn't about to let this straggler get away. He grabbed the thing like a squishy etheric football, yanked it from its trajectory, and hauled ass out of the ditch and around the back of the building while I was still skidding around in spilled cherry slushy.

As much as I tease Jacob about his recreational running, I can't argue with the fact that the skill does come in handy. By the time I rounded the back of the building, Jacob was already at the cinderblock wall, mashing the habit demon through.

My visual was for shit, but despite the fact that I was full of white light energy, my gut could still sense that it wasn't the wall Jacob had shoved the creature into, but the veil. From somewhere deep inside, I felt the ethers ripple. And when Jacob turned back toward me, dark eyes shining with pride, I knew Beauchamp's habit demon infestation had been well and truly handled...and the veil had sealed itself shut.

CHAPTER 38

Chicago is my home, and I could count the times on one hand I'd been away for more than a week. When I got back, things felt different in a subtle way that was slightly disconcerting. Like I imagine it would feel if I were forced out of my body, only to find that when I tried to click back into place, I didn't quite fit. Traffic sounded louder. The sun-baked pavement felt hotter. And the pervasive undertone of ripening dumpster was particularly pungent.

I doubted the city had changed much in my absence, so it must have been me. Anyhow, I got used to it again soon enough—like new shoes that feel weird when you first put them on, but by the end of the day, you hardly know they're there.

Jacob was chafing against his own new shoes, judging by the look of existential crisis I'd spot on his face when he didn't think I was paying any attention. I didn't envy him having to figure stuff out in his mid-forties that I'd dealt with at twenty-one. But at least he had me to help him muddle through, so he wouldn't need to do it all alone.

And neither would Amy Grace.

The FPMP Midwestern Office might be willing to let an

undocumented empath go their merry way, but they took mediums very seriously. Especially ones with a history of possession. Dr. K had interviewed every striptease artist in Beauchamp and deemed the majority of them to be cases of susceptible subconscious imitation. They weren't, of course. We suspected they were very low-level psychs—medium one, at best—with no other history of seeing or hearing anything out of the ordinary. Outside the range of a GhosTV, their subtle bodies would stay seated. So unless they dabbled in psyactives, they were unlikely to find themselves the victim of another hijack.

Amy was another story, though.

I would've liked to let her go back to business as usual, shepherding the dead while her body admired the refrigerator magnets, blithely rearranged the mortuary, or just indulged in a well-deserved nap. Unfortunately, it was too dangerous. She was a high-level medium—maybe not as high as Darla and me. Not now. Though with some training, she might give us a run for our money.

When Laura suggested I be the one to handle Amy's "onboarding," I reluctantly agreed. Recruiting a new Psych wasn't something I took lightly. Once you're on F-Pimp's radar, you're there for the long haul. But I worried that if we didn't shore up Amy's defenses, someone really pushy might die— someone like Ruth Parrish—and make off with Amy's shoes, leaving her ka wandering around barefoot forever.

I knew how important it was to get her some training…but I also didn't want to influence her decision on what that would look like. Although I was only well acquainted with one of her subtle bodies, it did make up a pretty big part of her total personality. And I had the feeling that it wouldn't go for someone telling it what to do.

I was enjoying some well-deserved comp time with Jacob when she finally got back to me. (If you consider shopping enjoyable, anyhow. But it beat sitting there at my desk, fighting the urge to knock Carl's pencil holder out of alignment just to see how long it would take him to notice.)

There's a cluster of mom-and-pop shops down on Montrose where the signage declares there's no public restroom—in English, Spanish, Korean, and Polish. The deli on the corner sells cold cuts so fresh you can practically hear 'em squeal. I was browsing a dizzying array of imported cheeses when Amy returned my call.

I wasn't much for pleasantries, and thankfully, neither was she. "Just to make sure I understand this right," she said, "your organization is offering paid training and an ongoing stipend?"

"They've got pretty deep pockets when it comes to their talent pool."

She considered the offer, which no doubt seemed too good to be true. I wouldn't blame her for walking away, especially since I'd made no effort to encourage her. There were other forms of protection, after all. Ones that didn't involve the government nosing around in your business.

But when Amy finally broke the awkward silence, instead of telling me to go take a hike, what she said was, "If we arrange for an intern from mortuary school, I suppose my dad can get by without me for a few weeks—especially if George will take some extra hours."

"He's still there?" I asked. Smooth.

"Where else would he find work? It's not as if he ever had many prospects. Funnily enough, though, he's been in a pretty good mood ever since the whole Leland Beauchamp scandal broke. Most people would be horrified to find out their father was such a monster. I guess George already knew."

Either it felt pretty fantastic to be vindicated...or we'd done a good job clearing out those habit demons and given him a chance to clean up his act.

According to Amy, George was instrumental in tying the murder to Leland with physical evidence so the testimony of a medium wasn't the main thing holding the case together. In fact, he'd been positively eager to provide DNA for comparison. It was a rare chance to spit on the grave of a shitty father...and make it stick.

His biggest payback, though, was the referendum the city council recently passed. Thanks to the scandal, not only was the goofy statue in the park retired, but Beauchamp, Iowa was changing its name back to Hicksville. A real pain in the ass, when you consider all the checks, business cards, and return address stamps that would need updating. But the town's residents were no longer so keen on keeping the Beauchamp legacy alive.

Once Amy's plans were squared away, I joined Jacob by the pickles. These were not just your ordinary brined cucumbers. They floated in oak barrels so weathered they looked like they'd come over on the Mayflower. Pickles lurked there just beneath the surface, heavy and mysterious, and maybe even a bit intimidating. But judging by the look on Jacob's face, it wasn't the sodium content he was worrying over.

"Amy is resilient," I said. "She'll be fine."

"Maybe. Or maybe she never makes the connection with her subtle body, and can't integrate her etheric senses with her conscious mind."

Clearly, we weren't talking about Amy. I dropped my voice so that the old Polish ladies gossiping by the sandwich counter couldn't hear and said, "After all those habit demons you dealt with, you're still doubting yourself?"

Jacob's brow furrowed. "It's just so frustrating. Back at the truck stop, we fell into a rhythm, a routine, and I felt like I had a handle on my talent. But now that we're back home, everything feels exactly like it always has, and what happened in Beauchamp seems more and more like a dream. One that's fading fast."

We could always tour some accident-prone intersections at sundown...but repeaters had never really been Jacob's specialty. "Maybe it's for the best that there's nothing for you to practice on around here. As far as I'm concerned, we're all better off if those psychic parasites stick to their own side of the veil."

As Jacob made a grudging sound of agreement, I forged off to see if there was any of that pepper-crusted turkey breast I like, and narrowly avoided a head-on collision with Bob Zigler's wife, Nancy. She was as perky and well put-together as always. As inexplicably pleased to see me, too.

"Victor Bayne! It's been a while, hasn't it? Looking good— you've got a little tan going there. Vacation?"

Just the consequence of scrubbing those habit demons from the back of the truck stop all week. "Not exactly. I'm just grateful I didn't burn too much."

"If you're looking for some amazing pastrami, you've come to the right place."

"Is that what you're getting?"

"Actually, no." She gestured toward the deli case with the paper-wrapped bundle in her hand. "Don't laugh, but I can't resist their olive loaf."

Behind the glass, the cold cut in question was arrayed in all its dubious glory—right between the liverwurst and the head cheese. "That's not funny. It's horrifying."

"My kids would most definitely agree. When they were little, I used to chase them around the house with it."

I almost said, And now you're stuck paying for the therapy, but luckily, I caught myself in time. This is why I don't banter with people. It's too easy to tread on a topic that's way too sensitive to joke about.

Nancy didn't notice my lack of response—she was too busy smiling to herself, thinking back to a simpler time when her kids were still young and her husband hadn't yet considered a career in the PsyCop program. Her smile went wistful, but only for a heartbeat. Then she turned up the wattage again and said, "Who can blame me? Between the olives and the pimentos, those slices look like they're full of little faces."

Yeah. Good thing I'd opted to forego the banter.

"Bob?" she called over my shoulder. "Bob—look who's here!"

Not only did she catch Zig's attention, but Jacob's, too. Our husbands both came over to dutifully say hello. Jacob smoothly... Zigler looking like he'd just seen a ghost.

While Zig was perfectly capable of all the normal social graces that tend to escape me, there was a hollowed-out look to him that chilled me despite the summer sun baking my right arm through the deli window. Whereas I was currently a pinkish tan, Zigler looked gray, from his hair to his skin to his drooping mustache. He'd lost a few pounds, something he'd struggled with the whole time we'd worked together. But he didn't look trim and sharp. More like his stocky solidity was draining away.

Normally, I might just come right out and tell him he looked like crap warmed over. But not in front of Nancy, who'd always been so relentlessly nice.

We chatted about nothing—a recounting of the olive loaf

story, a debate about whether sauerkraut should contain caraway seeds, a comparison of pumpernickel versus marble rye—and the Ziglers hefted their neatly wrapped olive loaf and went on their way. But as they reached the door, Zig paused as if he'd just remembered something he'd meant to tell us, sent Nancy on ahead to the car, and trudged back up the aisle toward Jacob and me.

"So...Iowa," he said awkwardly. "Everything turn out OK?"

Good thing he hadn't been there when we recovered Rosa's skeletal remains. That situation had Zigler-PTSD written all over it. I glanced at Jacob, who was waiting for me to answer, so I settled on, "Yeah—we managed to figure it all out."

"Good." Zig shifted his weight and sighed. "Anyways. Back when you called, I didn't mean to take a tone. It's just...I've been on these meds that didn't agree with me. And being off of 'em agrees with me even less. Go figure."

Meds was a pretty vague word—deliberately so—but I know my pharmaceuticals. Anti-anxiety drugs can be tough to taper off. Uh, so I've heard. Was my pallor that bad when I was weaning off pills? I was hardly a bronze god now—so I wouldn't doubt it.

Jacob had shifted a half step away from us as if to offer Zig and me the semblance of privacy. I thought he was just staring pointedly at the smoked ham. But then I caught his reflection in the deli case and realized his eyes were shut.

The back of my neck prickled—not with the actual sense of some etheric creepy-crawly, but the mere thought of it spreading over to me like an intrepid case of head lice. But Jacob was already on it. And when he clapped Zigler on the shoulder and said, "The important thing is, it all worked out in the end," he did it with such sincerity, Zig hardly seemed to notice the excessive amount of force he'd been whacked with.

"Take care of yourself," I said, as my ex-partner turned and trudged back out into the punishing summer sunshine...and then I sidestepped as Jacob shook invisible habit demon guts off his hand.

Without comment, we both turned back to the deli case, absorbing what just happened. I always maintain that when it comes to anything that shouldn't be on this side of the veil, I'd rather know about it than not-know. Unfortunately, I'd started our excursion excited to avail myself of a decadent selection of cured meats, but now my appetite was gone.

Just as well. Because that olive loaf looked unsettlingly like the sliced cadavers back at the museum. The former owners of those bodies might be long dead. And yet, with the final GhosTV now somewhere in their proximity, who's to say they wouldn't swing by to see what had become of the altruistic act of donating their bodies to science?

"You okay?" I asked Jacob.

When he turned to look at me, pride shone in his eyes, and I knew he was better than okay. He was pleased with himself. And since that was Jacob's default state of being, there was no doubt he'd eventually get the hang of being something more than "just a Stiff."

Chicago's a big city. Worrying about every death, every body, every era, would only make me crazy. All I could really do was take one day—and one ghost—at a time.

A pretty tall order.

Though it seemed a hell of a lot less daunting with Jacob by my side.

ABOUT THE AUTHOR

Jordan Castillo Price has always had a fascination with abandoned houses. With a realtor's help, she once toured a disintegrating mansion filled with rat carcasses on the West Side of Chicago. She also crept through some spongy-floored houses filled with raccoon poop in rural Wisconsin...one of which still had electricity, even though it had been vacant for twenty years.

She can always be bribed with ice cream.

ABOUT THIS STORY

As much as I use insectile descriptions to try and evoke horror, I don't think I'm particularly freaked out by bugs. The other day I was thinking about the first time I'd been bitten by an Asian Lady Beetle (which I frankly can't tell apart from the normal, non-biting ladybug of my childhood.) I remember I felt so betrayed when one of them bit me on the arm!

I'm not fond of centipedes (found one in the bed the other day—ugh) and I do avoid things that bite and sting.

But infestations are inherently creepy.

The amphetamine habit demons are based partly on a tapeworm...sadly, I have personal experience with these, too. My late kitty Frank came from the Humane Society with additional pets living in his butthole. I was unaware of them until I spotted something small and off-white on the couch and picked it up to see what it was. And it moved.

Ew.

This was the inspiration for the queen habit demon in the gas station manager's office.

But the living wall of habit demons was based on something I encountered in Iowa—boxelder bugs. They're considered to be nuisance bugs. They don't bite, don't go after your food, don't do much of anything at all, and they really don't bother me. But I was at a campground in the shower building and came outside, vulnerable and damp, and found the entire side of the building was literally covered with these bugs. They were just sunning themselves and wanted nothing to do with me...but the huge undulating mass of them was pretty creepy!

Speaking of creepy, I've always thought it would be damn near impossible to tell if someone else was possessed. Imagine how much worse it was for poor Jacob when he was supposed to discern if Vic was:

a. possessed

b. grounded

c. just a body

d. hungry

I think he did a pretty good job at figuring it out, though! Good thing for Vic that he happens to be Jacob's favorite subject.